D0193430

VICTORIA
DAHL

GOOD
GiRLs
Don't

HQN™

Recycling programs
for this product may
not exist in your area.

ISBN-13: 978-0-373-77595-8

GOOD GIRLS DON'T

This edition published by arrangement with Harlequin Books S.A.

For questions and comments about the quality of this book please contact us at Customer_eCare@Harlequin.ca.

www.HQNBooks.com

Printed in U.S.A.

This book is for Anne and RaeAnne,
because I couldn't have written it without them.

Acknowledgments

There are a great number of people who contribute to the well-being of this author during the course of a book. My family, of course, who makes sacrifices for the sake of romance every day. Thanks for loving me no matter what. My agent, Amy, who's always on my side. And my editor, Tara, who performs gracefully under huge amounts of pressure, along with the whole team at Harlequin. Thank you.

As always, Jennifer Echols was there for me as a true friend, a cheerleader, and a stern taskmaster. She is a constant in my life, and I couldn't do this without her.

I also want to thank the wonderful women of the Peeners, who provide advice, support, and filthy jokes, as needed.

RaeAnne Thayne and Nicole Jordan are the greatest brainstorming partners in the world, and without them, this series would still be ten lines scribbled in a notebook. Thank you.

Of course, the whole basis of this book is balanced upon the wonderful inspiration of microbreweries everywhere. You taught me how to like beer, and I love you.

Most importantly, thank you to my readers. You are my inspiration and you make it all worthwhile.

And one last special thank you to all my wonderful new friends on Twitter. You kept me company while I wrote this book, although you failed spectacularly at keeping me on track.

GOOD GiRLs Don't

CHAPTER ONE

TESSA DONOVAN STARED across the parking lot of Donovan Brothers Brewery, mesmerized by the flashes and swirls of blue and red across the gray brick of the building. She couldn't help but stare. The police lights were so at odds with the birdsong and pale sunlight of the early-morning hour.

Her brother Jamie stood between the two cop cars parked at haphazard angles near the back door. He wore a dazed expression, probably because he'd never met an early morning willingly.

She stalked across the parking lot and grabbed her brother by the collar of his rumpled T-shirt.

"Hey!" he protested.

Tessa pulled him closer, tugging him down until they were nose to nose. "James Francis Donovan," she whispered, "what have you done?"

"What are you talking about?" Jamie asked, sounding just outraged enough that Tessa almost believed him for a second. But only for a second.

She twisted his collar tighter. "Spill it."

"Come on, Tessa." He yanked away from her grip and waved an angry hand at the police cars. "You're not accusing me of having something to do with the robbery, I hope? I set the alarm, I locked the doors. This is not my fault."

Tessa ran a suspicious eye down her brother's body. He looked like he always did. Tall and handsome and laid-back. His jeans were worn out by a thousand washings, his T-shirt faded to cloudy gray. His light brown hair was sleep-tousled, but that was nothing new. Unfortunately, neither was the guilty shift of his eyes when she looked into them.

"Damn it, Jamie."

"Tessa—"

"I know the robbery wasn't your fault, but you said you were the one who found the door open. So what the hell were you doing here at seven in the morning? And why'd you call me instead of Eric?"

Eric was their older sibling, and though they all owned equal shares of the brewery, Eric had always taken the lead. He was the logical person to call to report that the brewery had been robbed. But Jamie had called her instead. Not good. Not good at all.

Jamie ran a hand through his hair and stared up at the pale blue sky. "It's bad, Tessa."

Her heart fell to somewhere below street level. "What's bad? *What?*"

"Monica Kendall came by last night."

"No. Oh, no, no, no." Monica Kendall was the vice president of High West Air and the key to the distribution deal that Eric had been working on for months. "Jamie, please tell me you didn't. Even you wouldn't be that stupid."

"Even *I* wouldn't? Nice thing to say to your brother."

"Jamie!" she screeched. God, she wished the cops would turn the lights off on the patrol cars. The colors were digging into her eye sockets.

Jamie finally gave up his outraged stance. His shoulders slumped. His head fell. "I don't know what happened," he murmured. "She said she wanted a tour of the brewery. Of course, she sampled a few of the beers and then…"

"And then?"

"She needed a ride home."

Tessa's sunken heart flopped weakly. She knew exactly what he meant. Women loved Jamie, and at twenty-nine, he was in the prime of loving women right back. "No," she muttered again. "This isn't happening."

"I took her home," he said. "I had to."

"You could've called a cab!"

"Tessa… Christ, I just thought I'd get her home and take a cab back and… I didn't mean to—"

"You didn't *mean* to? Good God, you are such a dog! Try thinking with your brain sometime, Jamie. Just on special occasions if that's all you can handle."

His eyes flashed green hurt, and Tessa immediately felt terrible. He'd been lobbying for more responsibility at the brewery lately, trying to step up to the plate, but Eric had resisted. If he found out about this…

"Okay," Tessa said, taking a deep breath to calm herself. "Okay, as long as her dad doesn't find out. Monica won't say anything, right? Why would she?"

The blank regret on his face told a different story, but before she could get it out of him, the back door of the brewery opened and one of the officers came out. "A detective is on his way over. He'll want to walk through with you when he arrives, Mr. Donovan."

"Thanks," Jamie muttered.

Tessa craned her neck to try to see through the cracked door. "You're sure the tanks are okay?"

Jamie nodded. "Everything looks fine except for a couple of missing computers and one keg."

The break-in should have been the most upsetting event of the day. On any other day, she'd be crying and wringing her hands over the violation. But if Eric found out what Jamie had done with Monica Kendall, it would ruin her brothers' relationship, and her brothers…they were all she had. She had to fix this, somehow.

"Please, Jamie," she said as the officer paced toward his car. "Tell me there's no more bad news."

He sighed as if he'd been holding his breath. "It was stupid. You're right. Really fucking stupid. But it seemed like it would be no big deal this morning. It was fine. Only I didn't realize… When we pulled up to her place last night, I thought it was just a house up in the foothills. But it wasn't. She lives in the guesthouse. Her dad's guesthouse."

For a moment, the world actually turned around Tessa's head. The sky and the clouds and the dark green pine trees—they rotated in a slow, sick spin. Tessa closed her eyes and prayed.

"When she was pulling out of her garage, her dad jogged right past. He saw me."

"Oh, God." This was the perfect storm of bad news. Their brother had been working Roland Kendall for months, trying to convince him that Donovan Brothers beer would be the perfect microbrew to serve on the fleet of the brand-new High West Airline. Eric had worked stubbornly toward this moment, intent on getting the brand into new hands, new customers. A few weeks before, he'd finally arranged a private meeting with Roland and his daughter, Monica. They'd made their final pricing offer. The deal had almost been done, the contracts sent over.

And now…disaster in the form of Jamie Donovan. "I'm going to kill you," she said flatly. "This one woman. Just this *one* woman you had to avoid touching."

"That's not fair," he snapped. "You two always talk like I'm with a new woman every night. I haven't dated in months!"

Tessa crossed her arms and paced away from him, trying to think. "Are you sure he saw you?"

"He saw me. Though I suppose it's possible he didn't recognize me."

"Okay. We can handle this," Tessa said, thinking fast. "First of all, don't say anything to Eric."

Jamie shook his head. "I need to tell him."

"Are you insane?" she snapped. "Eric is going to be furious. With both of us! I took your side on this, damn it. I told him to let you help with the negotiations. You are *not* telling Eric."

"He's going to find out. And I'm not interested in hiding from him like a kid avoiding punishment. This is my company, too. If I screwed up, I'll face it."

"This isn't just about you, Jamie. We're a family, and I don't want this to be the wedge that finally drives us apart. So keep your mouth shut until I find out what Roland Kendall is going to do."

He threw his hands up in frustration, but Tessa ignored him. Sometimes the best defense was a good offense, and Tessa was on the attack today.

"Here's what you're going to do," she said in a rush. "I'm going to leave. You call Eric as if he's the first one you called. If he asks, you went home with a woman and she dropped you off this morning, but do *not* mention Monica Kendall. I'll come back in twenty minutes or so and act like I've never been here."

"God, you've gotten devious," he muttered.

He had no idea.

"I'll call Roland Kendall later and see if I can read him. You keep your mouth shut."

"Tessa," he started, but she stalked away from him, heading down the street toward her house.

She knew she should be worried about the robbery, but that seemed far and away the least of her problems. Even losing the deal with High West wouldn't exactly be a family tragedy…except that it would be.

Eric was becoming more and more withdrawn into his role as head of the family. Tessa could understand that. He'd filled the shoes of their father since their parents had died in a car accident. Eric had only been twenty-four when he'd become responsible for two kids and a business. So Tessa could understand why, thirteen years later, he might have trouble stepping back from that. But he had to.

If Eric needed to relax a little, Jamie needed to add some stress to his world. He couldn't keep living like a carefree bartender for the rest of his life. Hell, he didn't even want to. He wanted to step up and act like a full-fledged partner. Minus, apparently, any restraint when it came to women. But plenty of successful men had that problem. There was no reason Jamie shouldn't join their ranks.

Tessa spotted another patrol car approaching, followed by a suspiciously nondescript sedan. She ducked her head, trying to escape the crime scene undetected. Her house, the house they'd all grown up in, was only three blocks away. She'd change from her yoga pants to jeans and brush her hair as if she'd been up for an hour before receiving Jamie's call. Speaking of…

She hit redial on her cell phone. "Did you call Eric yet?"

"He's on his way," Jamie muttered, then reminded her, "I don't like this."

"I know. But we have to make this right."

"He's our brother, Tessa, not our dad. I don't answer to him."

"No, but you owe him. We both do."

While Jamie's sigh was still echoing through the phone, Tessa hung up on him and rushed up her front walk. She'd done all she could for now. She couldn't call Roland Kendall for several hours at least. If he hadn't placed Jamie's face yet, her phone call might trigger the connection. She'd have to be patient, and plan this deception with ruthless care.

It shouldn't be that hard. She'd been managing her brothers' relationship since the day her parents had died. She played referee, defused fights and forced them to spend time together over Sunday dinners and holiday feasts. They were the only family she had left and she wasn't going to lose that, certainly not over a business deal.

"I can handle this," she insisted to herself as she turned onto her street and rushed toward home. "It'll be okay."

So why did she feel so sick inside?

DETECTIVE LUKE ASHER whipped the latex gloves off and tossed them into the alley Dumpster before turning to shake hands with Eric Donovan. "Eric, it's good to see you again, though not under these circumstances."

"Well, Jamie was just telling me that not much was taken. In fact, I was surprised to see you here."

"I'm sure you won't be out more than your insurance deductible on the computer equipment. But we're more concerned with the information *on* the computers. Social Security numbers, credit card information. There's been a rash of these types of break-ins at local businesses. Patrol called me when they realized the alarm had been circumvented somehow. That makes it less likely to be a casual robbery."

Eric's eyes slid toward his brother. "Are you sure the alarm was circumvented? Maybe it was never set."

Luke was sure he'd never seen someone snap from relaxed to furious as quickly as Jamie pulled it off. "I told you I set the damn alarm, Eric."

"I know you think you did," Eric said.

Jamie's mouth twisted and his hands balled to fists. "Screw you."

Hoping to restore peace, Luke raised his hands. "There's no doubt about this. Jamie definitely set the alarm. The alarm company shows it was armed at 9:30 p.m. and turned off at 1:00 a.m."

Jamie shot a look of pure fire at his brother, but he didn't seem satisfied with the vindication. His tension held tight when he paced over to a patrol car, his arms crossed as if he wanted to keep his hands still. Strange. Luke had known Jamie for ten years, and his demeanor had always registered on a scale that started with sleepy and topped out at laid-back.

Luke cleared his throat. "Do you know what payroll information was kept on the computers?"

Jamie glanced over his shoulder. "Tessa will know more. She takes care of all that stuff. She should be here any—"

"We outsource payroll," Eric interrupted. "So the information is limited. And I don't think there's any credit card information on the PCs these days. Hopefully the damage will be minimal."

"Good," Luke said. "We're almost finished in there. We're just dusting for a few prints and then we'll get out of your way. I hope this'll be nothing more than an inconvenience for you. They hit a temp agency a couple of weeks ago. That place had thousands of Social Security numbers on file."

"Yikes."

"Yeah. If you'll excuse me, I'm just going to take a look around out here." Luke walked to the back of the building, hoping to note anything out of place, but the exterior seemed fine. Wooden pallets were stacked in neat columns. A ten-foot-long carbon dioxide tank sat next to the building on clean concrete, untouched by weeds or debris. The same applied to the big stainless-steel grain silo.

He knew from the layout inside that the padlocked corrugated door rolled up to reveal the bottling area and a small loading dock. If he'd been thinking of the brewery as a bar, he would've changed his mind back here. Not one bar in the world had a back lot this clean.

When he didn't find even a hint of something suspicious, Luke circled the front of the building. Sunlight deteriorated beer, Jamie had explained earlier, so the few windows in the place were high up and always locked.

Luke was just rejoining Jamie and Eric when he noticed a woman approaching across the parking lot. Her blond ponytail bounced as she rushed closer. Luke found his eyes dipping down, taking note of the tight jeans and gorgeous thighs. Aside from a killer body, she looked perfectly innocent, pink-cheeked and bright-eyed.

"Hey, guys," she said breathlessly. "What's going on? Do you know anything more?"

Eric reached for the woman to give her a hug, so Luke used his detective skills to determine that this was the sister. They didn't pay him the big bucks for nothing. Also, she looked a lot like Jamie Donovan, though smaller and way prettier.

She shot Jamie a tense look. Jamie's gaze fell to the ground, his mouth tightening. Whatever passed between them seemed set aside when she looked at Luke and smiled. "Hi," she said, offering a hand. "I'm Tessa Donovan."

"Detective Asher," he said. When he took her hand, he felt the fine bones of her fingers and smelled a faint flowery scent that made him clear his throat in defense. His life was way too complicated to leave room for noticing how a pretty woman smelled.

Luckily, she followed Eric Donovan through the door to see the damage. Luke was left alone with Jamie. "So how've you been, man?" he asked. They'd been a year apart at the University of Colorado, but they'd attended a lot of the same parties. Emphasis on *a lot.* "Jamie?" Luke prompted.

"What? Oh, sorry. Yeah, everything's good, aside from this. How are you doing? I hear—" Jamie seemed to catch himself at the last moment, clueing Luke into the fact that Boulder might have a population of one hundred thousand souls, but it was still a small town. The rumors about Luke hadn't stayed confined to the police department.

"Everything's good," Luke said, answering the unfinished question.

"Oh, great!" Jamie slapped him on the shoulder,

but when Luke's partner emerged from the brewery, tucking a notebook into the pocket of her jacket, Jamie's eyes went right to her belly. It was getting hard to miss.

"Did you meet Detective Parker?" Luke asked as if things hadn't turned awkward. "Jamie this is Simone Parker. Simone, this is Jamie Donovan. We went to the U together."

"Pleased to meet you," she said, her voice sweet and soft as ever. People were always surprised by her femininity, despite that her flawless brown skin and dark, wide-set eyes left men a bit starry-eyed. They thought female police detectives had to be tough and hard-nosed. But Simone was simply the sharpest cop he'd ever met, and she'd made the rank of detective by outsmarting everyone around her.

Simone excused herself while Luke handed Jamie a business card. "All right. Call me if you think of anything else. I'll be in touch."

"Great. Hey, she's beautiful, man."

Luke paused in the act of turning away and winced at the implication. He wanted to clarify that Simone was his partner and *not* his girlfriend, but that would lead to questions he didn't want to answer. Couldn't answer. So he forced himself to finish the step he'd been about to take, and he headed for the car he shared with Simone.

Up until a few months ago, it had been an easy place to occupy. Now her pregnant belly took up all the space in the damn car and pushed out the breathable air. Despite his years as a detective, Luke couldn't figure out what the hell had gone wrong. And Simone wasn't talking to anyone.

CHAPTER TWO

TESSA KEPT HER EYE on the clock as she prepped the barroom for the evening rush. It was four forty-five and Roland Kendall hadn't returned her call.

She hadn't meant to leave him a message at all. After carefully calculating the absolutely perfect time to contact him: after lunch when the morning was far from his mind, but before five, just in case he was heading out for drinks before hitting his box at the Rockies game. She didn't have his cell phone number and she couldn't think of a good reason to ask Eric for it.

So she'd called Kendall's office at two-thirty, and when his secretary had said he wasn't available, Tessa had hung up. But when she'd called again at three, the secretary had pointedly asked, "May I take a message, Ms. Donovan?" Damn caller ID.

Now Tessa was stuck waiting for a return phone call. She hated waiting. Thank goodness she was working the bar this afternoon. Her office had become a suffocating box and her new computer wouldn't arrive until tomorrow. But the bar work was soothing, especially at this quiet hour. They didn't serve lunch, so their only customers were the regulars who wandered in from the sandwich shops across the street. Though there were often brewery tours during the week, none were scheduled today, so Tessa was free to sweep and wipe down tables and chairs, and even give a nice spring cleaning to the laminated beer menus. All without once taking her mind off the clock. Five o'clock loomed on the horizon and there was still no word from Roland Kendall.

Jamie wasn't there to bitch at, so Tessa called up the Twitter application on her phone and began typing. She was the only one interested in social media as a marketing tool, so she was in charge of their Twitter account, but Jamie…Jamie was the face of the company. And the voice.

She smiled as she finished up her message from Jamie Donovan.

My sister won an argument & made me admit I was an idiot. Drop in tonight & tell me you lost an argument too & get half off your 1st pint.

There. She felt a little better, but as if warning against relief, Eric's voice drifted in from the back room as he placed another furious call to their alarm company. Actually, if his voice was any indication, they were now the brewery's *former* alarm company. Any lightness she'd felt was immediately swept away.

She was straining so hard to listen to Eric's conversation that she jumped like a startled cat when the front door opened. Before she could summon up a smile of invitation, she recognized Jamie's sun-rimmed silhouette.

"Jamie!" She rushed forward so she could whisper her question. "Did you call Monica?"

"No." He looked even more miserable than Tessa felt.

"Why not? I left you a message. I can't get ahold of her father and—"

"Because it was a meaningless night, Tessa. For both of us. If I call her today, she might think I'm interested in something serious and that is not going to help the situation."

Tessa reconsidered. "Oh. You may be right. If she decides she wants to see you again, that'd be disastrous."

"Exactly. As it stands, we left on neutral terms."

"Wow, you've got a whole language for this."

"Shut up," he snapped. "I'm not some kind of man-slut."

"Okay, I'm sorry. That was below the belt. So to speak." When he only scowled harder, Tessa stood on her tiptoes to kiss his cheek. "Don't be mad."

"Whatever. Did you talk to Roland Kendall?"

Tessa shook her head as Jamie took the rag from her hand and began polishing the bar. It looked just fine, but it was never quite shiny enough for Jamie, as far as she could tell. "I left him a message, but I haven't heard back."

"He knows it was me, Tessa. We've got to tell Eric before he hears it from Kendall."

"Not yet. If there's even the slightest chance Kendall

didn't recognize you, then we are *not* telling Eric. Do you know what he'd do to you?"

"He'd never trust me with anything but the bar and act like I was born with half a brain? Yeah, I'm familiar with his opinion of me."

Tessa kept her mouth shut as she stacked glasses. Strangely enough, even though the place was called Donovan Brothers, Tessa seemed the only one at ease with her role at the brewery. Eric held on to the brewery with both hands, loath to let his siblings take on new responsibilities, and Jamie struggled against his brother's iron grip. Tessa was trying to help Jamie without upsetting Eric, but good Lord, Jamie seemed to trip over his own feet every time.

Tessa headed for the back to slice lemons for the hefeweizen, but when she walked through the double doors, she was nearly trampled by their brewmaster, Wallace Hood.

He didn't glance in her direction as he stalked past, rushing from the office area back to his glassed-in paradise of beer tanks and tubing. Eric stepped out of his office.

"What's wrong with Wallace?" Tessa asked.

"He's convinced his tanks were violated. I've told him that nothing in there was touched."

Tessa watched as Wallace ran a gentle hand over one of the steel behemoths, his brow furrowed in furious worry. She understood that. If circumstances were different, she'd want to clutch her computers in her arms, too. But they were long gone, and she had bigger worries to hug to her chest.

One of those worries shook his head and sighed. "The alarm company should be out in an hour to check the wiring and box, but our contract is up next month. I'm not renewing."

Just as she'd suspected. Eric was not the forgiving sort. The reminder made her avoid his eyes as she turned and headed for the kitchen area. The brewery didn't serve food beyond peanuts and pretzels, but they did host occasional catered events, so the kitchen was fully outfitted. Still, it had none of the homey friendliness of the front room, so Tessa never lingered. Plus, she really had to get out of here. The sight of Eric only reinforced her sense of urgency. She cut the lemons into wedges with the ease of someone who'd done it thousands of times. Prepping the bar had been her first job when she'd turned twenty-one.

Wallace's voice was muted by the floor-to-ceiling glass, but every time she looked up, his jaw was moving in furious conversation with his equipment. His lips were probably moving, too, but she couldn't see them past his full, dark beard. She had no idea how old he was. Somewhere between thirty-one and forty-nine was her best guess. He was six-five, he had the body of a professional linebacker and he wore mountain-man-style plaid shirts every day. Despite the fact that he'd worked at the brewery for ten years, the only other thing she knew about Wallace Hood was that his alternative lifestyle did not match his appearance in the least. In fact, his personal life was so complex that she'd never quite figured it out. He was neither gay nor straight, but refused to classify himself as bisexual. He was both intensely private and mysteriously social. Men and women moved through his life as if he'd installed a revolving door in his bedroom.

Usually, watching him in his giant glassed-in room was like watching an interesting movie, but today his silent diatribe only increased her tension. The whole damn building was bubbling with stress, so she piled her two dozen sliced lemons into a plastic container and hurried toward the front room.

Jamie took the bowl from her and popped the top to be sure the lemons were good. He was strangely perfectionist about some things, so she'd learned not to take offense and merely washed her hands and tipped her head toward the empty seating area. "It's been slow. The warm weather has kept everyone outside, but I expect you'll get a lot of thirsty people in soon. I'm running a special for half off the first pint tonight, so if anyone mentions Twitter, that's the offer."

"Got it."

"The signage for the new golden wheat is almost ready. Eric tapped it this morning."

Tessa was drawing him a sample of the new brew when the front door opened. At first, all she saw past the sunlight was a jacket and a tie. Then she recognized the man wearing them. Detective Asher, he'd said. "Hi, Detective!" she called.

"Good afternoon, Miss Donovan," he said with a smile that disappeared as quickly as it flashed over his face.

"Just Tessa," she replied, feeling her smile widen. He was cute. Really cute, in a jaded, hard-jawed way.

Like he'd stepped out of some noir detective novel, muttering about having seen too much life already.

"Then call me Luke."

"Luke Asher…" She frowned and cocked her head, taking in his brown eyes and nearly black hair. She looked him up and down suspiciously. His eyebrows rose. "You've been to my house," she said.

"Pardon me?"

"You were friends with Jamie in college."

"Oh, right." His brown eyes crinkled. "I stopped by with him a couple of times. I'm sorry. I don't remember meeting you."

Jamie snorted. "I doubt I introduced you to my teenage sister."

"Ah," he said, and Tessa thought she saw his eyes flicker down.

She let her gaze wander, too. Yeah, she remembered him now. He'd been a slim guy who'd waited quietly for Jamie the couple of times that her brother had stopped home to grab something from his room on his way out for fun. Tessa had watched him from the dining room table as she'd done homework. He'd been cute then, but now…

Luke Asher seemed to have grown into his lanky frame. He was still about six-two, but now his body looked powerfully lean. His skin was tan, and creases around his eyes made it look like he often squinted thoughtfully into the distance while puzzling out an investigation.

He was talking to Jamie about an old classmate

when he glanced over and saw her staring. One eyebrow quirked in question.

"Oh, um… Do you have any news about the investigation?"

"Nothing yet. We've only found one print we can't identify, but there are still a few employees we haven't printed yet. I'm sure it belongs to one of your people. None of the robberies have turned up any useful prints."

"You're sure it's connected?" Jamie asked.

"I'm not ruling anything out yet, but that's what my gut says."

Oooh, gut instincts and fingerprints. And she could just make out the edge of his shoulder holster when he put his hands in his pockets.

Despite all her worries, Tessa felt a sudden and startling jolt of attraction.

Jamie interrupted her ogling. "Did you get anything from the security cameras?"

"Nothing," Luke said. "Your cameras are focused on the parking lot and loading dock. I'd recommend two more cameras pointing at the doors."

"Yeah. Got it. I'll let Eric know."

Luke Asher's eyes slid to her, and the hair on her arms stood on end. "Did you speak to your payroll company yet?"

"I did. It's all good news. The program on the PC is encrypted, and data protection is part of our plan. They've already started contacting the employees, even the old ones. They've also alerted the credit agencies. So far it looks good. As for the credit card information, that's uploaded live with every transaction. Nothing stored in the computers."

"Great," Luke said. "They might not bother trying to crack the encryption. It'll probably be easier to just break into another place. And even if they crack the program, the credit alerts should help. Keep your fingers crossed."

"Oh, I will," she said, sneaking another peek at his gun.

Jamie cleared his throat, and Tessa shot him a look of wide-eyed innocence. It had never failed her before. "I'll go update Eric," she said cheerfully, leaving the flirting for later when her brothers weren't around and things weren't so chaotic.

Hopefully this would all blow over soon, and then she'd give Detective Luke Asher a friendly citizen's call.

"WHAT THE HELL do you think you're doing?"

Luke blinked in surprise at the anger in Jamie's voice. "Excuse me?"

"I know you, man, and I saw the look you were giving my sister."

"I wasn't looking at your sister at all." He didn't flush at the utter falsehood, because he knew he wasn't going to date Tessa Donovan. It had only been a bit of harmless admiration. Her T-shirt had been tight in all the right places.

"I know how you are with women," Jamie growled.

"I'm not any way with women, Jamie. Whatever I got up to in college, I left in college."

Jamie set down his rag and crossed his arms. His eyes narrowed. "I'm not just talking about college."

"What the fuck is that supposed to mean?" Luke snapped, earning a glare from Jamie.

"I've got no problem with you, Luke, but I heard about your divorce. You're not the kind of guy I want dating my younger sister."

Luke's shoulders snapped so quickly into solid tension that pain shot down his spine. "You don't know what the hell you're talking about."

"I may never have met your ex-wife, but she has lots of friends still in Boulder. People come to a bar to talk, and I've heard enough to warn you to steer clear of Tessa."

They glared at each other for a long moment. "Plus," Jamie added, "there's the little issue of your—" Voices from the back room alerted them that the other Donovans were about to join them.

Luke cracked his neck. "She's not my type. Let's just leave it at that, all right?"

"Good enough," Jamie muttered.

Luke wanted to defend himself. Hell, he wanted to go on the offensive and punch his old friend in the face, but he was too busy reeling, so he just turned and left.

He'd been aware that people must have talked about his divorce, but he and his wife had been living in L.A. at the time. He'd hoped the worst parts of it had been lost in translation. But clearly some of the details had crossed state lines.

Not that it mattered. Tessa Donovan's smile was

wide and pretty, but the girl was as fresh and new as a wildflower. And Luke… Luke felt bruised and broken already at thirty-one. No, Jamie didn't have to worry about his sister. Luke wasn't going anywhere near her.

CHAPTER THREE

TESSA HAD PLANNED to sneak into Eric's office and search for Roland Kendall's mobile number, but Eric kept hanging around. The only number she'd been able to nab was Detective Asher's. Taking that as a sign, she slipped his card into her pocket just as Eric came back in.

"How are you holding up?" he asked.

"I'm fine!" she answered too loudly. "Why wouldn't I be fine?"

Eric gave his head a puzzled shake as he collapsed into his chair. "It's not every day that we're robbed."

"Right. Yes. The robbery. I'm just glad it wasn't worse, I guess."

Eric ran both hands over his face. "Well, I'm exhausted, even though I haven't gotten a damn thing done today." He squinted at her past his fingers. "You look like crap yourself. Why don't you head home?"

Leave it to a brother to boost a girl's spirit. She had a brief fear that Luke Asher had only checked her out because he'd been worried about her health. But surely her breasts looked okay despite the pale worry on her skin.

"Go," Eric said.

"What about you?"

"I'm going to stay to help Jamie close down tonight."

"Eric, it wasn't his fault."

"I didn't say it was." The flat tone of his voice belied the words.

She felt Jamie's presence at her back before he spoke. "You didn't have to say it," he growled. "We all know exactly what you're thinking."

Eric sat back in his chair and crossed his arms.

"I know you think I'm an eternal screwup, Eric, but there's no question I set the alarm. Even you can't argue with that."

"No, but somebody turned it off."

"And?"

"And you're the one who hires the extra bartenders around here. We both know their qualifications rarely extend beyond 'guys you once partied with.'"

"Fuck you, Eric. That's not true. I hire guys who are good with the customers."

"And not so good with showing up on time or coming in when they're supposed to work."

Tessa held up her hands to try to stop the violent tension spinning through the room. "Guys, just—"

"You're a real asshole," Jamie snapped. "Besides us, the only people who have the alarm code are Wallace and the guys who've closed down the front room, and they've all worked here for at least three years. Some of the temp help I've brought in might not have been ideal, but they only ever work fill-in."

Eric shrugged, his mouth still tight with disdain.

"I'd like to see you try to run the front," Jamie said. "It requires personality. Ever heard of it?"

"Stop!" Tessa ordered. "Just stop. Everybody's tense. So—" Before she could finish, Jamie walked out. Tessa almost stopped him. Her instinct was to calm things down. Make them both apologize. But she didn't have the energy, not with all that hung over their heads. So instead of picking up the threads of her family and trying to weave them back together as she always did, Tessa let them hang there and walked away.

She was tired, as Eric had so kindly pointed out. Tired of playing the peacekeeper. Tired of trying to fix things. But it didn't matter if she was tired. She couldn't imagine how exhausted Eric must have been those first few years, when he'd taken on two teenagers and the brewery. He'd done his part to keep the family together; Tessa could do her part, too.

But she was starting to worry that she didn't know how to fix this mess. Jamie might not have screwed up the alarm, but he'd done something far worse. The chances that the High West deal would go through... she knew they were low. Really low. But she couldn't give up hope. Not yet.

She waved a listless goodbye to Jamie just as the first group of office workers walked into the bar, relief hanging around them like a cloud. Their workday was over. It was almost over for Tessa, too. Almost.

She pulled the ponytail holder from her hair and shook out as much tension as she could. The drive to the High West office would take nearly an hour with the traffic. Roland Kendall almost certainly wouldn't be there, but she had to try.

And in the meantime… Tessa fluffed her hair and cranked up the stereo.

She meant to think of nothing. Driving soothed her. Something about the road and the music and the hum of the engine. It was the only place she could just *be* and not think. But today it didn't work. Today the music made her think of Luke Asher.

He'd been a quiet kid, but now he looked mysterious. Almost dangerous. Dark and strong. As if she could lean on him and he'd banish her problems with one cold look.

Maybe it was just the hint of forbidden fruit. Her older brothers had rarely brought friends around when she was a kid. When they had, as Jamie had said, there'd been no introductions made. It was an unwritten rule that male friends were not allowed to simply hang around the house as if they lived there. But that hadn't stopped Tessa from watching their brief visits with close attention.

Yeah. Forbidden fruit. And big strong shoulders. The kind of man who'd take care of all her problems, or at least make her forget them.

But at that moment, the fantasy was so far-fetched that Tessa switched off the music and set aside thoughts of Detective Asher. He might be able to solve the mystery of the robbery, but there was nothing he could do about the tangled mess Jamie had created. If anyone was going to do the rescuing today, it'd be her.

So she squared her shoulders and rode off into the

sunset, clutching the steering wheel as if it were a weapon. Tessa to the rescue, one more time.

LUKE SUSPECTED ONE of the university students was behind the robberies. Not because he hated college kids—he only marginally disliked them—but because a college kid would fit the profile. Smart, tech-savvy, daring and in need of quick money. That also described the kids who'd dropped out of school and never managed to quite leave town. And there were a lot of those. Then, of course, there were the educated meth heads. Plenty of those around, too. In other words, without fingerprints or a hot lead, this case would be solved by running down every tiny detail, even the ones that seemed inconsequential.

Luke ran the surveillance video one more time, just for the hell of it. It offered little detail. At around 1:15 a.m., a shadow crossed the video of the loading dock. A few minutes later, it crossed again. This repeated a few more times, and that was it. No body, no height, no description. Just an approximate time of the robbery, and he'd already had that.

He backed up the digital feed a little farther, then farther still, looking for movement, just in case someone had cased the back door earlier in the evening.

But the only person who appeared was a woman with a blond ponytail and a happy smile. Tessa Donovan.

Luke very purposefully didn't pause the video and look at her. Instead, he shut it down entirely just to avoid the temptation. She was cute, and that was that.

There were thousands of cute women in this city. Granted, most of them were way too young for him, but then so was Tessa. Oh, she was past college age, but her eyes were still clear and bright and happy. She made Luke feel ancient.

"I'm heading home," Simone said, gathering up her purse and briefcase. She wasn't quite waddling yet, but she was definitely moving with more care. Luke shut his computer down and grabbed his own stack of work. "Here," he said, reaching across his desk to grab for her heavy case. "Let me get that." But she was still quick enough to jerk the briefcase out of his reach before he could touch it.

"I've got it," she muttered, irritated by his offer of help. Lately, she always was, and that pissed Luke off. They were partners, damn it. They were friends, or they once had been.

"It's seven," he said as he followed her toward the front door. He watched her back as she shrugged. "You've been here since eight. You shouldn't be working these kinds of hours."

She slammed the door open with both hands, the briefcase banging against the glass. "You're working them."

"Simone. Don't be stupid."

Her shoulders snapped straight and she stopped so quickly that he had to grab her arm to keep from knocking her over.

"What," she ground out, "is that supposed to mean?"

"I don't know, but I'm going to guess from your reaction that you feel stupid about something."

"Luke—" She cut herself off at that one word, but he could read fury and sadness and resentment, all tied up in that one syllable.

She walked on, heading straight for her car, but he followed, waiting until she opened her door and ditched her bags. Before she could slip into the driver's seat and escape, he put a hand across the door. "Please talk to me."

"I don't want to."

"I know that, damn it. It's pretty obvious. Why?"

"It's none of your business."

He felt a sharp stab of pain and a sudden anger. He tried his best to tamp it down, but some of it leaked past his hold. "It is my business, because the whole town thinks I knocked you up."

"So tell them that you didn't."

"And then what? They're going to want to know who did, and I can't answer that question. What the hell are they going to think about you, then?"

"I don't care." Her face was as blank as any hardened criminal's under interrogation. She'd always been good at that, but Luke used to be the one she'd actually talk to.

"What the hell is wrong with you?" he growled.

She met his gaze with a cool stare, and when he tossed up his hands and backed away, Simone simply got in her car and shut him out. He felt the dull, hard thud of the door all the way through his body.

If he had knocked her up, he could understand this, but he and Simone had never had sex.

Luke retreated to his own car, then sat there with the

windows down, trying to breathe his way to calmness. After a few minutes, he made his hands unclench from the steering wheel, and he laid his head back. The sun was setting and the breeze was cool enough to soothe his temper. He heard the subtle whir of a pack of bikes sliding past the parking lot. Then the click of dog claws against the cement. His gut still burned, but the rest of him was calm when his phone rang. By the time he raised it to his ear, Luke had convinced himself it was Simone calling to apologize.

"Asher," he said neutrally.

"Hi, this is Tessa Donovan."

His head snapped up so quickly that the world blurred around him.

"Am I bothering you?" she asked.

Tessa Donovan? "No, it's fine," he managed to say.

"You're not in the middle of a big murder investigation or something?"

Luke smiled. "No, we don't get a lot of those around here. Luckily there are enough lesser crimes to keep me busy."

"Luckily!" She laughed, and the sound was richer than he'd expected, not the least bit like a giggle at all.

"So what can I help you with?" he asked.

"Well, I don't seem to have a dinner companion. Could you help with that?"

"Um." Not the smoothest answer, but Luke's brain was having trouble making the transition. "Pardon me?"

"Dinner? I'm driving up from Denver right now, but I'm almost home. I could be changed and ready in forty-five minutes."

"For dinner."

"Yes. Unless it's against the rules. I don't want to get you put on desk duty because I'm a material witness."

Luke found himself grinning at his dashboard. "You didn't witness anything. And you watch too much TV."

"Wow, you figured that out quick. You really are a detective."

Shit. She was cute as hell. "I promised your brother I'd stay away from you."

"Really? Well, that's interesting. Which brother?"

"Jamie."

"He told you to stay away from me?"

"He did."

"Why?" she asked.

Luke wasn't stupid enough to offer up his divorce at this point, not even the truthful version of it. *Especially* not the truthful version. "Why? Because I'm a man. And you're his little sister."

She chuckled again, and this time it was a soft, sensual sound. "Well, what my brother doesn't know won't hurt him."

Yikes. Luke's brain stuttered, preventing him from coming up with a witty response. Or any response at all. Dinner was tempting enough, but when she said something naughty like that...

Luke glanced over at the empty space where

Simone's car had been parked. He thought about going home to his empty condo and having yet another cold sandwich for dinner. He'd promised Jamie he'd stay away from Tessa, but this wasn't medieval England. Tessa was right. What Jamie didn't know wouldn't hurt him.

"Should I pick you up?" he asked.

His question met silence, but he was sure he could actually hear her smiling.

"Absolutely," she said before rattling off her address.

When Luke hung up, anticipation was streaking along his nerves like fireworks. Hadn't he just been telling himself that she wasn't his type? Then again, what was his type? Jaded and dumped like him? What a tragedy that would be.

Still, Tessa Donovan was a complication he didn't need. Too sweet to be a quick hookup. Too innocent to date a guy who'd already been married and divorced. This was going nowhere. But he needed some kind of distraction for a few hours, and he was damn glad the distraction was going to be her.

CHAPTER FOUR

TESSA PUT HER HANDS on her hips and made a slow turn, watching herself in the bathroom mirror. The shirt was perfect. Vivid blue and draped just right so that it looked entirely modest even though the neckline scooped low. She leaned slightly down to be sure she was showing just the right amount of cleavage—a lot. Perfect. Luke Asher had only seen her in Levis and T-shirts. Hopefully he'd like skinny jeans and high heels even better. She knew her ponytail made her look like she went to the U, so Tessa had quickly blown out her hair and left it down. She added some red lipstick to top off the look, then gave her reflection a nod.

Jamie was working the bar tonight, and Eric was closing up with him, so she didn't have to worry she'd run into one of them. And that was a good thing. She had enough to worry about.

As she'd expected, Roland Kendall hadn't been at his office. She'd had no idea what she was going to say to him, anyway; she just needed to know which cover-up to enact. Was it a matter of swearing Jamie to secrecy and hoping that Monica Kendall never told a soul? Or was it DEFCON level 5, wherein she pulled off the miracle of calming down an angry father while simultaneously convincing him to go through with the deal and forget he ever saw a thing?

It would be difficult, but she was sure she could pull it off. Hadn't she convinced the principal not to call Eric that time she'd been caught skipping class to go river rafting? Hadn't she gotten Jamie off a year-long academic probation without even a hint to Eric that anything was going on? If she could handle the public education system, surely she could handle one sixty-year-old businessman. His daughter was a grown woman, after all. Maybe Roland Kendall wasn't even upset.

It was a foolish and stupid hope, and that's exactly why she'd called Luke Asher. She couldn't just sit around and do nothing. She'd go crazy. Five minutes into her drive home from Denver, she'd been close to hyperventilating. Luke had been the only thought strong enough to distract her.

And she hadn't been able to shake the appeal of his quiet strength. He was a man who needed nothing from her. No emotional tiptoeing. No complicated negotiations. No pretense of sweet temper and sisterly innocence. Whatever Luke was interested in, it was something he might *want* from her, but not something he expected.

Ignoring the brief thought of how pissed her brothers would be if they knew about the men she'd dated, Tessa gave herself one last review before she switched off the light and walked out of her room. Her heels snapped against the old wood floors of the house. The floors needed refinishing, but every time she considered it, she decided it could wait another year. This was the house they'd all grown up in. It was the house where her parents had raised them. Every scar on the oak was a story, and she didn't want to let those stories go.

She wanted everything to stay the same.

Entering the living room just in time to hear the hum of a car pulling up to the front curb, she bit back a smile, then waited for the knock on the door before walking toward it. She hadn't listened to all of Eric's advice about boys—in fact, she'd ignored most of it—but she had found him to be right about some things. Men liked the thrill of the chase…almost as much as women did. So Tessa tried to encourage a good give and take. She might ask a man out, but she wouldn't rush breathless and smiling to the door. She might let him get to third base on the first date, but then she might not answer his calls for a week. It kept things interesting, and that was just the way she liked it.

Though when she opened the door it was damn hard not to grin in nervous excitement. Luke looked like he had stories to tell and things to teach her. His black hair had the slightest unruly wave to it. His brown eyes were dark as chocolate, but hard with sadness. His body was hard, too, and lean. He'd changed out of his work clothes, and now wore black slacks and a pale blue shirt. His eyes traveled down her body so quickly that Tessa would've missed the glance if she hadn't been watching for it. He was good.

"You look great," he said.

"Thank you."

"Where would you like to eat?"

"Why don't you surprise me?" she suggested as she locked the door behind her. "Take me to one of your favorites."

She could feel him watching her, but when she turned around, she didn't catch even a flicker of his eyes. Yeah, he was good. Some sort of cop skill, maybe.

And a gentleman. When she walked down the porch steps, Luke put his hand under her elbow, and he didn't even accidentally brush her breast with his fingers. Still, a sizzle crept up her arm where his skin touched hers. The pads of his fingers were slightly rough and made him seem that much more intriguing.

He opened the car door and when she slipped in it smelled like leather and…perfume?

"Did you just finish another date?"

He glanced at her out of the corner of his eye as he got into the car. "Excuse me?"

"It smells like perfume in here."

"That's from my partner. Maybe her soap or something."

"Oh, your partner is a woman? The pregnant woman?"

"Yes."

"Is that weird? Having a female partner?"

He cleared his throat. "It's not weird, no. She brings stuff to the table that I don't have."

Tessa smiled. "I'd hope so."

"I meant, you know…perspective. Questions I wouldn't think to ask. Plus, some witnesses or victims are more comfortable dealing with her. It works great."

"Aw, that's sweet."

Frowning as if she'd insulted him, he pulled out onto the narrow street. "I'm not sweet."

Boys. Tessa leaned toward him and lowered her voice to a whisper. "It's okay, Luke. Despite what you've heard, men can be sweet and hot at the same time."

"I see," he said. "Good to know."

She couldn't quite tell if he was blushing, but he was staring hard out the windshield, very carefully not looking at her. Tessa waved at a neighbor who jogged past and felt very glad she'd called Luke. He had a bad-boy aura she found appealing, and yet he was a polite police detective who had no problem working with women. In other words, the guy was smoking hot. She might have to break her third-base rule for him. Though it'd always been more of a gentle suggestion than a hard-and-fast rule. A girl had to keep her options open.

Luke finally spoke. "I was surprised by your call."

Not a question, but an opening. Tessa made a sound that was equally noncommittal.

"Jamie seemed clear that you wouldn't be interested in a guy like me."

"Oh, I think what he was making clear was that he wouldn't *want* me to show interest in a guy like you. And why is that?"

"Why is what?"

"Why did he feel compelled to warn you off, aside from you being a man? Are you dangerous?" Oooh, just saying it aloud formed a hot weight low in her belly. Clearly he was dangerous enough to turn her on and make her forget her problems.

"No. He thought I was checking you out."

"And were you?"

Luke pulled up to a stoplight, and this time he turned the full force of his dark gaze on her. His mouth quirked up into a half smile. "I think I'd better plead the fifth."

"Isn't that an admission of guilt, Detective?"

"Legally, it's a neutral position."

"Oh, but it's morally damning, isn't it?"

"Morally?" His deep brown eyes sparkled and the weight in Tessa's belly melted all over her insides. "Oh, yeah," he said softly. "Morally, it's a big problem."

Tessa made a point not to giggle like a schoolgirl, but it was a close call. No wonder Jamie didn't want her dating Luke. They'd gone to college together, and her brother had likely seen girls drop their panties at the first hint of Luke's smile. His features were a little harsh. His jaw a little too cruel looking, but the sparkle in his eyes transformed him into a charming rogue. Tessa was glad her tight jeans would keep her panties firmly in place…for a few hours.

She waited till she was sure her voice wouldn't squeak before she spoke again. "So what will you do when she has the baby?"

Luke seemed to choke on his breath. "What?"

"Your partner? What will you do when she's on maternity leave?"

"I'll work by myself," he said brusquely. "That's all."

"Is it a sensitive subject?"

"No."

No. And that was it. Interesting. Maybe he was worried she wouldn't come back. Or maybe he thought she shouldn't. Either way, he changed the subject. "Any more news on your employee files?"

"Honestly, it looks pretty good. Thanks to the security systems at the human resources firm I pushed last year."

"You sound triumphant."

"Eric doesn't like change," Tessa said, glancing out the window as if lightning might strike at such an understatement.

"Interesting. That's a classic oldest-sibling issue, I think."

"Oh, he's got issues," she started, then she noticed that Luke was slowing to turn into the parking lot of one of Tessa's favorite restaurants. The little Mexican café had a patio that was shaded by mature aspens and provided the perfect place to sip the best margaritas in town. "Good choice," she said approvingly.

"Sounds like this was a test."

"One of many," she answered with a smile that was all challenge.

Luke raised an eyebrow and turned off the car. When he got out and circled around, Tessa waited.

He opened her door, and when she stood, she was only inches from him.

He tipped his chin down so that their faces drew even closer. "I wasn't sure I was your type," he said softly, draping his arm over the open door. "I thought you'd made a mistake asking me out to dinner."

"Oh? Have you changed your mind?"

This time, he didn't bother to hide the way his eyes dipped down her body. "You look different tonight. Less like..."

"Your friend's little sister?"

The sexy quirk of his mouth widened into that wicked smile. "Yeah."

"Good. Because I already have two brothers, Luke. I don't need another man around asking me to be a good girl."

Luke's eyes dilated, his lips parted, but he stepped back so quickly that her hair shifted forward in the breeze he created.

"I'm glad I don't remember you as a kid," he said.

"Yeah," she said with a big smile. "Me, too."

Oh, it was going to be fun playing this game with him. Lots of fun. And good Lord, if she didn't need fun, who did?

APPARENTLY TESSA DONOVAN didn't want to be a good girl. Not anymore. And not with him.

Luke couldn't get the thought out of his head as they shared dinner and drinks and exchanged stories about their lives. Luke had been raised by a single mom in various apartments in Denver, and Tessa had grown up here in Boulder in the same big house she lived in now. He couldn't quite imagine that kind of continuity. He'd never lived in an actual house his whole life. He and his wife had owned a condo a half mile from the beach in L.A., but he wasn't about to bring that up.

Still, he seemed to remember that not everything had been wine and roses for the Donovan family. "Your parents passed away when you were young, right?" Another thing he couldn't imagine.

"I was fourteen."

"What happened?"

"They were driving in the mountains at night. There was a rock slide, and they drove head-on into a boulder. It was quick, at least."

"I'm so sorry."

"It was a long time ago, and we had one another. That's one reason my brothers are so protective. Eric, especially. He had to take over raising us."

"That's pretty amazing." And so damn touching that it resurrected Luke's guilt about going out with Tessa, adding another awful layer to it. She was an orphan. Great. Sure, she looked sexy as hell tonight in her heels and tight jeans and that damn shirt that flashed an intriguing amount of cleavage whenever she leaned forward. But that wasn't the real Tessa. The real Tessa was a sweet orphan girl in a T-shirt and a ponytail who deserved to find a little stability in her life. She'd had it rough enough without a man like Luke around.

She leaned forward, and the mounds of her breasts made another brief appearance. Jesus, her skin looked soft and sweet.

"So," she said, "you lived in Denver and then you came here for school and never left?"

Yikes. He really didn't want to talk about his life in California. But avoiding the question would only draw more curiosity. "My first job as a police officer was in L.A."

"Wow, was that scary?"

"Scary?" He was distracted by her mouth. It made a little O of surprise and she leaned farther forward. Her mouth…her cleavage… Luke found himself thinking some very dirty things about Tessa Donovan.

"Scary!" She gestured and her breasts pushed up. He swallowed. Hard. "Big-city scary."

"I was shot, if that's what you mean."

"Shot?"

Uh-oh. He'd gone too far. Tessa jerked back in her chair and the view disappeared. And now he was just sitting there with a lap full of regretful lust. He never talked about being shot. Her cleavage was a damned menace.

"Oh, my God! Where were you shot?"

"In the shoulder. It wasn't a big deal."

"How did it happen?"

"A bullet came through a wall. I was in the wrong place at the wrong time. That's all."

"Oooh, you're so stoic and manly about it."

Luke felt his scowl tip up into a smile. He reached for his margarita. "Oh, yeah? You like that?"

"I sure do. Come on. Don't tell me that story hasn't gotten you laid a few times."

Lime juice burned like hell when it went down your

windpipe, and that was knowledge Luke could've happily lived without. As he coughed, Tessa lifted her own margarita and winked. "You probably practice that sexy damaged-cop thing in the mirror."

"Excuse me?" he choked out.

She waved her fingers toward his chest as she took a delicate sip. "I've got you all figured out, Detective Luke Asher."

"Have I already suggested that you watch too many cop shows?"

She shrugged. "Maybe I do. I hope you're not refusing to play along."

At that moment, Luke was pretty sure he'd play whatever games she wanted. She thought he was *sexy.* And damaged. Maybe if he told her how screwed up his life was she'd get off on it. Then again, maybe this was a sign that she was naive and sheltered and he should really back off. After all, he'd seen enough screwed-up cops to know there was nothing appealing about them.

But the bill came, and Tessa asked, "Are you ready?" and Luke found himself saying yes. Yes, he was ready. But ready for what? Even as he stood and pulled out her chair and followed her out of the restaurant, his brain was telling him to end this here. She was too young, too sweet, too related to protective men. He did not need more complication in his life. Then she took his arm, and her hip bumped his. A breeze blew her hair toward him, sweeping it along his shoulder, and the scent of her shampoo drifted through him. She smelled...delicious. Like a treat that would be really, truly bad for you. Luke found himself thinking of kissing her neck and dragging his mouth down the neckline of that shirt. He thought of pulling it down farther and devouring her.

Christ, he wanted to strip her naked and have her for days.

He opened her car door, and Tessa winked as she got in, as if she knew what he was thinking. But surely not. She was flirting, not giving him the green light to jump her. She probably had no idea of the kinds of filthy things men fantasized about.

Luke shook his head to try to clear it. A girl like Tessa Donovan wasn't looking to fall into bed after one date. Which was good news. Because he clearly had no willpower where she was involved.

By the time Luke settled into the driver's seat and started the car, he'd talked himself down to a reasonable state. Her cleavage wasn't in view. Her hip wasn't touching his. Luke's libido was under his control again. And then she touched his thigh. Just laid her hand on his thigh as if she had the right to do that. Holy shit, this girl had no idea what she was doing to him. There was an incredibly short distance between the nerves of his thigh and the nerves of his cock.

"That was fun," she said, sliding her hand up an inch higher before she slid it right back to her side of the car. The air in the hot car felt cold against his thigh now that her hand had deserted him.

He inhaled very slowly. "Yeah, that was fun," he said with a casual smile.

Her gaze dipped to his mouth, and she smiled, as

well. "Would you like to—?" A high-pitched tune interrupted her words with cruel timing. Tessa cringed and reached for her purse.

Would you like to what? Scowling, Luke put the car in gear and pulled out as Tessa glanced down at the phone. She bit out something that soundly strangely like, "Oh, balls."

"Did you just say 'balls'?" Luke asked.

She turned a look on him that seemed to accuse him of complete insanity. Shaking her head, she put a finger to her mouth to shush him. Embarrassment fell over him in a scalding wash. He'd just said *balls* to this girl.

"Hey, Jamie," she said into the phone, and Luke felt another rush of heat. He'd promised Jamie he'd stay away from Tessa; now Luke was holding his breath in the seat beside her.

"She called?" Tessa asked, turning her head to face the window. "Okay. Do you think I should call her back…? Well, someone has to talk to her. She didn't say anything in the message?"

Luke unashamedly listened in, but he couldn't hear Jamie's side of the conversation. He'd gotten a weird vibe from these two at the robbery call, not to mention this afternoon. There was a tension between them that they were pretending didn't exist.

Tessa made a couple of affirmative noises before telling her brother she'd call him later. She was quiet when she hung up, any hint of flirtation gone from her body language. Luke tried to let it go, but he was a cop at heart.

"Is everything okay?"

"Oh, yeah!" she said too brightly. "Just brewery stuff."

"Are you sure?"

"Of course. Are cops always so suspicious?"

Yeah, she was lying through her charming teeth. "You don't have to tell me, Tessa, but it was obvious to me that you and Jamie were hiding something at the brewery this morning. Does it have anything to do with the robbery?"

"What?" she breathed, her voice weak with shock. "No, of course not." Now there was honesty in her eyes.

"I didn't really think so or I would have pushed it at the scene. So do you want to talk about it?"

She wasn't flirting with him anymore, but somehow Luke found that he liked her even more now. Her eyes were soft with worry, and he could see pale gold flames streaking through her green irises. Her mouth was still pink and beautiful, and her teeth pressed into her lower lip as she considered his offer. Her teeth. Her lip. The tiny indentation she made with the pressure. The hint of moisture that glistened against the pink…

A car horn blasted the air, and Luke looked up in utter shock. He was stopped at a four-way stop sign, and there were two cars behind him. *Real smooth, Asher.*

But Tessa didn't seem to notice, thank God. She was too busy frowning down at her hands. "It's not my story to tell. Suffice to say that I know something I don't want Eric to find out about. It's family stuff."

"I understand." Oh, boy, did he.

"It's no big deal," she insisted. But clearly it was. She stayed quiet for the rest of the drive, staring out at the gingerbread houses of the street. It was strange to think of her living in one of these big old houses by herself. Yet somehow it fit her perfectly. He could picture her wearing one of those frilly aprons while she baked cookies and—

"Oh, shit!" she yelped, ruining the pretty picture he'd painted. "Eric is here." Instead of caressing his thigh again, her hand slammed into his chest. "Stop!"

He followed her wide-eyed stare to the sight of her place three houses down. A pale gray SUV sat at the curb, glowing under the streetlight.

"I'm sorry. He comes by pretty often. He's probably looking for dinner."

"Oh, I—"

"Don't drive up! Just let me out here."

"Tessa…this is a little weird."

"I know. I'm sorry! But I had a good time." She reached for the handle before stopping abruptly and turning back to him. "A really good time." The girl was quick as a damned thief, and before Luke knew what she was up to, her fingers touched his jaw, and then her lips touched his mouth. Without giving him even a second to respond, Tessa was out the door and waving as she hurried up the narrow sidewalk. But Luke was sure she'd transferred that tiny hint of moisture from her lip to his. He certainly convinced himself that he could taste her. And sure enough, the sweet taste stayed with him for hours.

CHAPTER FIVE

THE NEXT MORNING, Tessa smiled and waved at Eric as he walked past her office door. As soon as he disappeared from view, she leaned over her desk, nudged the door shut with an outstretched hand and picked up the phone. "Answer," she ordered Jamie as the phone rang, but it went to voice mail after one ring. Granted, it was only 9:00 a.m. and she wouldn't normally call him this early, but he hadn't returned her call last night. She didn't bother leaving a message. She'd already left three. Jamie was probably passed out in some girl's bed while his phone beeped helplessly from the pocket of his jeans.

She cursed him for his ability to so easily forget his problems, even as she fondly considered how she'd tried to forget her problems last night. Damn Eric for interfering. Her brothers were seriously cutting into her private life. But at least Eric had suspected nothing more than a girls' night out when she'd strolled in the night before.

Before she could pick up the receiver again, the phone rang and Tessa snatched it up. "Hello?" she said desperately.

"Hey, Tessa! It's Wendy. I got your message about the break-in."

She liked the temp waitress a lot, but Tessa still slumped in her chair at the sound of her voice. "Oh, good. I know you haven't worked in a few months, but your information was still on the computer."

"I already called the credit agencies to check in. Like you said, an alert has been placed on my name and Social, so I think it's all good."

At the sound of male voices, Tessa craned her neck to see through the glass window in her door. Eric was talking to Wallace in the hallway.

"You need anything else?" Wendy asked.

"Oh, are you still planning to fill in for us in the barroom this summer?"

"Absolutely. It's just that this course load is killing me this semester."

"No big deal. You're welcome back anytime, Wendy."

She hung up just as Wallace started gesturing in angry jerks. Not an unusual scenario. The man was a genius, and like most geniuses, he was temperamental. Deciding that Eric would be occupied for a few minutes, Tessa dug out Roland Kendall's number and tried his office one more time.

"This is Tessa Donovan again. Is Mr. Kendall available?"

"I gave him your message yesterday, Ms. Donovan. I'm sure he'll be in touch soon."

Tessa stuck her tongue out at the receptionist's voice, then nearly bit it off when the office door snapped open. Tessa threw the phone into its cradle before she realized it was Jamie.

"Oh, Jamie. Thank God. Why didn't you call me back? If you want me to talk to Monica, then—"

"Did you go out with Luke Asher last night?" Jamie demanded.

"Um… What?"

"Eric said you were out with someone last night and you wouldn't say who. Was it Luke?"

"That's none of your business."

"It was him, wasn't it? I saw how you two were looking at each other."

"Jamie, seriously. I'm twenty-seven. Cut it out."

"No, *I'm* serious, Tessa. Stay away from Luke Asher. He's bad news."

Utterly confused, Tessa leaned to the side to look past Jamie to the hallway beyond. "Am I being Punk'd? I thought that show was canceled a long time ago."

"Damn it!" he shouted. Tessa jumped an inch out of her chair when his fist thumped her desk.

"Sheesh. Calm down."

"I won't calm down. He's not someone you should be hanging out with, much less dating."

"Oh, really? Who is? A priest? Luke's a friend of yours. If he's good enough for you to hang around with, why not me?"

"Because I'm not a woman."

Tessa rolled her eyes. Her brothers didn't like her hanging out with any male over twelve and under eighty. "We just went out for dinner. We didn't participate in a Roman orgy, I swear."

Jamie's face flamed red immediately. "Tessa!"

Sometimes she felt she was living in the middle of a Jane Austen novel. "I like him, all right? Just leave it alone."

He crossed his arms. "I like him, too. He's a great guy. How else would he have gotten so much action in college?"

"Oh, really? As much as you?"

He raised an eyebrow in silent acknowledgment.

Tessa cleared her throat. "That was in college."

"Sure it was. And his current nickname is Magnet."

"Magnet?"

"Yes," he bit out. "As in Babe Magnet. I heard one of the other cops call him that when he wasn't listening."

Tessa tried not to smile. She could understand the reputation. The man had a lethal attraction.

"And," Jamie continued, pointing his finger at her, "have you not noticed the fact that his partner is currently pregnant up to her damned ears?"

"So?"

"So, the kid is his, Tessa. Jesus. *Pay attention*."

She felt all the air leave her body in a whoosh, and it took all of her little-sister outrage with it. "What?"

"He knocked up his partner, and now he's letting her swing in the breeze."

"How do you know that?"

Jamie spread his arms out in her small office. "I'm a bartender, Tessa. I hear things."

"So…" Tessa's mind flailed. That was why he'd

been so awkward when he'd talked about his partner. "So maybe she's the one who wants him to keep his distance."

"I don't give a damn what the reason is. His life is all fucked-up, and you don't need any part of that."

"Like my life is so *un*-fucked-up right now?"

"Watch your language," he muttered.

Tessa closed her eyes and tried to call up the patience of a nineteenth-century noblewoman.

"And," Jamie continued in a lower tone, "it's my life that's messed up, not yours. By the way, what the hell did you post on Twitter last night?"

"Nothing. It's not important. Just…" She made a frantic gesture for him to close the door. Jamie shook his head, so she slapped his arm as hard as she could. He glared at her, but closed the door.

"Give me Monica's number," she hissed.

"No."

"Are you going to call her back?"

"I don't know."

"Come on! I can't get in touch with her dad and we need to find out if he knows!"

"He looked right at me, Tessa. He knows. We need to stop screwing around and tell Eric before he finds out from Kendall."

"No! We can't! Just let me… I'll go down to Kendall's office right now, okay?"

"No, I'm going to tell Eric. This is one disaster you can't cover up. I don't even want you to."

As he turned toward the door, Tessa leaped up and grabbed his shirt.

"Hey!"

"Please don't. Please!"

Jamie seemed alarmed to find her sprawled over her desk. Her pack of paper clips slipped to the floor with a crash. "Tessa, calm down."

"Tell me you won't tell him and I'll calm down."

"You're being ridiculous."

"I'm not." She felt tears spring to her eyes, and she hadn't even summoned them to soften him up. Jamie's shoulders fell, and when she knew he wasn't going to dart for the door, she let go of his shirt and climbed off her desk. "He's going to be so mad, Jamie."

"I know that."

"He'll never let you take on more of the business."

"Maybe I don't deserve to take on more."

She knew that wasn't true. He didn't have any responsibility, so he didn't act responsibly. But Eric didn't see the logic in that reasoning. He wanted Jamie to prove himself first, and every year the tension grew between the two men. Something had to give. And Tessa was afraid her family would be the thing to break.

"You said you'd give me a chance," she pleaded.

"I didn't say that. I just stopped arguing with you."

"Please, Jamie." His jaw tightened in stubbornness. She grabbed his hand and wrapped both of hers around it. "Pleeease?"

She knew the moment she had him. She always did. And not a second too soon. Her office door snapped open again, and Eric stuck his head in.

"What's going on?"

"Nothing!" she answered.

Jamie held her gaze, and for a moment, the serious line of his mouth worried her. She gave her head one tiny shake and squeezed his hand one last time before letting him go.

Eric clearly didn't buy that they were just having a cozy brother/sister talk. "Guys," he said flatly.

Jamie took a deep breath and Tessa closed her eyes. *Please.*

"The person Tessa was with last night? It was Luke."

Oh, great. She opened her eyes and narrowed them at Jamie. Surely he could've thought of a save that didn't throw her under the bus.

"Luke Asher?" Eric's voice sang like a blade drawn from a scabbard. "I hope you're kidding."

Tessa was done with this. If Luke really had gotten his partner pregnant, then Tessa wasn't going to see him again. And if he hadn't…then it was still none of their business. "Forget it, both of you. It was one meal, and it's over, okay?"

"Promise?" Jamie asked.

Tessa scowled at him. "I'm not a kid anymore." But she crossed her fingers just in case that still counted. Both her brothers glared at her. They looked nothing alike, aside from their height. Eric was dark-haired and pale-eyed. Jamie looked like a golden-haired mess next to him. But they both wore identical expressions of stern disapproval, and she could picture the exact same frown on her father's face. They loved her. They wanted what was best for her. Just as she wanted the best for them.

She snatched up her purse. "Okay, boys. I've got to go. I'll be back in a couple of hours."

Their expressions turned even darker. "Why?" Eric asked.

"Because I have a doctor's appointment."

"What's wrong?" he demanded.

"Um, it's a girlie thing. You know…" She leaned forward and cupped her hand over her mouth. "The gynecologist."

"Oh." Eric stepped back so quickly that his shoulder hit the doorjamb. His face turned red. "It's just a checkup, though, right? You're not, um, engaged in anything that…"

"No," she answered with mock seriousness. "I'm not 'engaged in anything.'"

Sometimes she wondered who had raised whom in this family.

Now that she had both her brothers backing out of her office in horror, Tessa was free to go. She bit back a self-satisfied smile as she kissed Eric on the cheek. "I'll be back in a couple of hours."

But once she hit the door, she raced to her car. She was wearing jeans and a brewery T-shirt, and she didn't want to see Roland Kendall that way, so she had to stop at home before she drove to Denver. No matter what it took, she was going to get an answer from that man today.

SHE'D DONE IT again.

Instead of telling Luke face-to-face, Simone had left a message on his voice mail that she had a doctor's appointment. His *office* voice mail. She hadn't called his cell phone, because she knew for a fact that Luke wanted to go with her. He wasn't the father of her baby, but he was her best friend, or had been at one time.

So why didn't she want him there? Was it possible that someone else was going to the appointments with her?

The message had said she'd be in at twelve, which probably meant her appointment was around eleven. He glanced at the clock. He could drive by in a half hour or so, see if her car was in the doctor's parking lot. If only he knew who her doctor was...

Luke stretched and faked a yawn, taking the opportunity to glance around the office. Most of the detectives were on the phone. The rest were gathered near the coffee machine, gabbing about something. His sergeant was nowhere to be seen.

Rising to circle around to Simone's desk, Luke told himself not to look guilty. There was nothing weird about him sorting through her stuff. They worked the same cases. They shared the same space. Still, he felt a flush climb up the back of his neck as he tugged open the top drawer and pushed some papers around. It didn't take much. The corner of a business card appeared. He pulled it free of the pile and immediately spied a stylized logo of a woman holding a baby. Bingo.

Luke tucked the card into his pocket and circled back to his desk just as his cell phone rang. "Asher."

"Hey, it's Jamie Donovan. Do you have a minute to swing by the brewery?"

Perfect. Now he had an excuse to leave. "I'll be there in a few."

He slipped on his coat and grabbed his keys to head out. The doctor's office was on the way to the brewery, so he drove by just in case. Simone's car wasn't there, but it was early yet. Luke had the sinking feeling that he was stepping over a line here, and he was still trying to shake off the guilt when he walked into the brewery. The front room was empty, but before he could head to the back, Jamie came through the swinging doors.

"Hey, Jamie. What's up?"

"Stay the hell away from my sister, Luke."

Amazingly, Luke had been so caught up in the drama with Simone that he'd forgotten about the problem of Tessa Donovan. He just stood there with a dumbfounded look on his face.

"You promised to leave her alone."

"She asked me to dinner."

"So you should've said no."

"I did. But…" He cleared his throat. "Then I said yes."

"Whatever. It doesn't matter. She's no longer interested. I told her about your partner."

Any guilt Luke had been feeling snapped into cold fury. "What about my partner? You don't know a damn thing about it."

"I know she's pregnant. And you're the father. And I know you're trying to date my sister. That's all I need to know."

"You're wrong," he managed to push past clenched teeth.

"About what?" Jamie snapped.

He refused to say more. It wasn't right to talk about Simone this way. She never said a word about it to anyone. She'd always been a private person, and he couldn't disrespect her that way.

Jamie shrugged. "Whether you're the father or not, it's hardly the only issue."

"Oh, yeah? What else puts her out of my league?"

Jamie shifted, running a hand through his hair and looking everywhere but at Luke.

"What?" Luke snapped, expecting to hear more about the divorce.

Jamie finally met his gaze. "Tessa is a virgin."

"Uh… What?"

"You heard me."

Luke wondered if the stress of the past few years had finally broken him. "You're not serious."

Jamie's frown turned to a scowl. "You're damn right I'm serious."

"But…that's… How do you know?"

"She's told me as much herself."

"She *told* you?" Luke asked weakly. Something that felt suspiciously like horror was rolling through him in waves. Tessa was a *virgin?* Good God. She hadn't said a word. Except that part about being a good girl. Had that been a hint? "Wow," he breathed.

"So when I say you're not good enough for her, I mean you're not fucking good enough for her, all right?"

Luke rolled his shoulders. "Look. I don't like to talk about Simone, but what you've heard isn't true. I'm not that guy. And I'm not looking to jump your sister's bones. It was just dinner. We had a good time."

"Well, make it the last time, all right?"

"What if I don't want to?"

Jamie crossed his arms and dropped his eyes to the floor. "This is my sister."

"Fair enough. But—"

"There is nothing about you that's good enough for her. You're damaged. Your job is dangerous. Your partner is pregnant. And even aside from your reputation, there are the stone-cold facts of your divorce. You can't argue those away."

Luke's heart paused.

"She had cancer, man. How could you have walked out like that?"

Luke's vision went dark at the edges, and he considered warning Jamie that he shouldn't say that sort of thing to a man with a gun strapped to his body. Because in that moment, Luke wanted to kill someone. He really, really did.

"We're friends, Luke, but—"

Luke cut him off with a hard laugh. "That friendship was a long time ago, obviously."

"I'm sorry. It's none of my business, and I wouldn't make it my business, but I don't want you anywhere near Tessa, got it?"

"Fuck off," Luke said. He slammed through the front door of the brewery, blood rushing so hard in his ears he almost walked right into a car that pulled up. Two business types got out of the car, each of them eyeing him warily. Luke just stalked around them and got into his own car. Even two states away, he couldn't get away from it. Luke had been married and divorced in California, which was one of the reasons he'd moved back here. Yeah, word got around the department, but he hadn't expected it to get back to everyone. He should have known better. Eve wasn't from Boulder, but she'd gone to school here. People talked. They always did. Hell, the police wouldn't solve any cases if people weren't so inclined to spread rumors.

God, what a disaster.

His rage leveled off to frustration, a constant, scalding burn beneath his skin. Everything about his divorce was frustrating. Not that that shocked him. His marriage had been frustrating, too, but he'd loved her like crazy.

"Shit," he spat out. At least the anger had smoked out his guilt about spying on Simone. He didn't feel even a twinge as he started the car and headed back toward the doctor's office. But he was still reeling under a healthy dose of *Holy crap, Tessa Donovan is an untouched innocent* as he wove his car through streets filled with packs of hunched-over bikers. Frankly, the various emotions careering through his body left him feeling vaguely ill.

When he arrived at the doctor's office, there was Simone's car, right up by the door in one of the spaces marked with a stork. Maybe she was alone, then. Luke rolled down his window and settled in to wait.

The cool spring sunshine did nothing to temper his mood. He stared unmoved at the pale green leaves of the aspen grove at the edge of the parking lot. A wall of gray clouds gathered at the horizon, and Luke chose to focus on those instead. By two o'clock, the town would be beset by thunder and lightning, a fairly common occurrence on spring days. What a relief that would be. The sun and chirping birds and flip-flops were just too much to take.

So he watched the clouds gather beyond the building and let his eyes slide to the entry each time the door opened. A half hour later, the door swung out to reveal Simone, alone. She juggled a stack of pamphlets while digging for keys in her purse.

Luke slid out of his car, and when his door shut, she looked up. For a moment, Simone only looked concerned. "What's wrong?" she asked.

"Nothing. I was just…worried about you."

Her eyes jumped to his car, then back to him, and her face stiffened. "Are you following me?"

"No."

"Really?" she snapped. "Because I don't remember giving you the name and address of my doctor."

"I didn't follow you. I…detected my way here."

"I'm not in the mood for jokes. This is outrageous."

He knew she was pissed. Hell, she was way past pissed if her flaring nostrils and reddening face were any indication. So Luke tried to tamp down his own feelings. "I'm sorry. I don't want you going through this alone."

She pushed past him and hit the unlock key, then threw everything into the passenger seat before rounding on him again. "How did you know I was alone?

Or…" She gestured toward his car. "Was that the point of this? To find out who might be here with me?"

"No. No! It's not about who the father is. I—"

"Really? Because you ask me every damn day. I'm sorry people think it's you. I tell everyone who asks that it's not. You're the one who stopped denying it!"

"I'm trying to protect you."

She threw her hands high. "I don't need your protection!"

"Why not?" he yelled. Before the words had even left his mouth, he scrubbed his eyes with one hand. "I'm sorry. I didn't mean to yell, I just… You've totally shut me out."

Simone's hand touched his arm, and when he looked down, he realized she hadn't touched him in months. Not that she'd ever been overtly affectionate, but she'd never avoided him before.

"I'm sorry, Luke," she said. "I'm sorry for what people are saying. And I'm sorry I can't talk to you. I am." Her fingers curled around his elbow, digging in. "I'm sorry about it all."

Oh, Jesus. He started to reach for her, but she jerked away and dropped into the driver's seat of her car.

"Just leave it alone, all right? I'm fine." She slammed the door, nearly catching Luke's elbow in the process, and he jumped back just as the engine roared to life. Simone roared out of there like a pregnant NASCAR driver, and she left Luke more frustrated than ever.

The door of the office opened behind him, and Luke looked back to be sure it wasn't a big hulking bastard wearing a sign that said I Knocked Up Simone Parker.

But it was just a petite blonde woman in pink scrubs. No such luck.

Thunder cracked in the distance, and Luke looked at his watch, hoping that he'd been standing there for hours and the day was almost done. But no, it wasn't even noon. The whole day stretched before him, and most of it would be spent sitting next to his stubborn-ass partner. And now he didn't even have the small hope that Tessa Donovan might call again.

Shit. The nausea in his stomach had focused itself into one spot, and Luke could already feel the ulcer starting. Yet another one to add to his collection.

CHAPTER SIX

BITCH, TESSA THOUGHT to herself, squeezing her fists tighter. Her knuckles shone white beneath the skin, and her nails bit into her palms, but she squeezed harder. She wanted to get up and pace, but she wouldn't give Roland Kendall's snotty receptionist the pleasure. The woman was already nasty enough, and she'd clearly relished the past four hours of watching Tessa squirm.

Two hours into it, she'd been forced to call in sick to work. She'd explained to Eric that her doctor wanted to run routine blood tests but she needed to go to a lab in Denver. To temper the lie, she said she'd take a vacation day and do some shopping, too.

He'd seemed distracted, and when she'd asked why, Eric said he was having trouble getting in touch with Roland Kendall. Tessa had felt as if she'd been flashed into another dimension at that moment. A world made of ice and anxiety.

But she'd talked herself down. Eric always had trouble getting in touch with Kendall because Kendall made a point of being hard to reach.

Nothing had changed except that now he was keeping two Donovans waiting.

Tessa glared at the receptionist's bent head, focusing

hard in the hopes that frustration would act as a magnifying glass and burn a hole into the woman's scalp. But she didn't even twitch. Not until Kendall's office door opened and the man himself came into view.

Tessa sprang to her feet as Kendall walked out with his arm thrown around the shoulders of a man Tessa recognized from the newspaper. The Denver mayor, maybe? No, someone more important. A congressman.

Though she was standing three feet away, Kendall ignored her entirely as he walked his friend out.

For a moment, she considered following them out, then decided that kind of determination might get you arrested when a U.S. congressman was involved. So she held her ground, and a few minutes later, Kendall returned. He spared her a hard look.

"Mr. Kendall," Tessa said brightly as she stepped into his path. "I'm Tessa Donovan."

"I know who you are."

Uh-oh. His voice dripped frost and disdain. He knew. There was no other explanation.

"I hoped we might be able to speak in private for a few minutes."

"Is there really any point to that?"

Oh, God. This was bad. "I hope so, yes."

"I'll save you the time. I—"

"Please?" she asked softly. "Just one minute?" The man finally relented, whatever good that would do her.

He stalked into his office with Tessa on his heels. She closed the door behind her.

"Sit," he said gruffly, waving toward a chair. She sat, but when he only stood above her, looming and stern, she stood again.

"My brother—" she started.

"Yes," he spat, "your brother."

Tessa cleared her throat and tried to think of some tack that might work. Unfortunately, the path to "please forgive my brother for doing your daughter" was narrow if nonexistent. "His behavior was…unwise."

"Unwise!" Kendall said. "This is a multimillion-dollar business and he couldn't keep his pants on for the time it takes to strike a deal."

"Ah…" Tessa's mouth wanted to say something about Kendall's daughter not being able to keep her pants on, either, but she took a deep breath instead of slapping him in the face with that. "As a young businessperson myself, I've seen how work and social lives can so often intersect—"

"Unwise," he repeated as if Tessa hadn't spoken. "What kind of idiot risks a business deal over sex?"

Your daughter? her mind screamed. But she smothered her anger with a solemn nod. "Mr. Kendall, I'm sorry. It's—"

"Your brother should be the one apologizing."

"Oh, of course. He wants to. That's why I've been calling. Absolutely. To schedule a meeting between you two."

He seemed to buy that hook, line and sinker, probably because he assumed Tessa took care of phone duties around the office. The man was archaic.

"Screw it," he growled. "It doesn't matter. The deal is off."

"No," Tessa breathed. "No. This is business, Mr. Kendall, just like you said. Jamie and Monica are adults who let things get out of hand while they were discussing business—"

"He put his hands on my daughter!" Kendall shouted. "Do you really think I'm going to do business with the man now?"

"You won't have to! Eric and I will take care of everything. If you never want to see Jamie again, I understand. I'll keep him away from your daughter, too. I promise." Okay, she had no idea how she'd keep that promise, but panic bubbled through her like she was a shaken soda can. Every single criticism Eric had ever thrown in Jamie's face was about to turn into solid stone. A giant boulder of scorn and anger and frustration between the two of them. And where would that leave her? Her brothers were all she had.

Kendall paced away from her to stare out the window that overlooked the whole front range from Pike's Peak to Long's Peak. He glared at the mountains as if he could crumble them with his eyes.

Tessa crossed her fingers until she lost all sensation in her hands. *Please, please, please.*

"No," he finally said.

"Mr. Kendall, don't make a final decision now. You're angry. Of course you are. So just give it a couple of days. We're a family business like the Kendall Group is. It gives us our strength, but it makes things complicated, too, doesn't it?"

His eye twitched. Just his left eye, and she took that as a good sign.

"My father started Donovan Brothers twenty-five years ago, and he named it in honor of the brother he lost in Vietnam. Both our parents died when Eric was only twenty-four. Just a kid. He could've sold the brewery. Anyone else would have. But he took over and built it up to what it is today. It's a strong company, but it's strong because of family, just like your companies are. Please. Take a few days. Look at the numbers Eric gave you. This deal would be good for both our families, I promise."

He looked up at the ceiling and took a deep breath. "The answer is still going to be no. But I'm going to New York for a few days, so I'll sit on it until I get back. A week. That's the best I can do."

"Thank you so much, Mr. Kendall. That's all I ask. Just a few days." She rushed forward and grabbed his hand. "Thank you," she said again, shaking his hand too hard.

He finally extricated himself and waved her toward the door, and Tessa walked out surrounded by a bubble of hope. She didn't even sneer at the receptionist as she passed. A few days. A few days of not panicking, and she just might pull off the impossible. If only she could get all the men in her life to cooperate at the exact same time....

LUKE LOOKED OVER the pile of files to see Simone grab her jacket and walk out of the station without a backward glance. Sure, it was quitting time, but she could've at least waved on her way out. Or given him the finger. She was clearly still pissed about him following her. Well, that was fine. He was still pissed about everything else, so his self-righteousness was safe.

Closing the manila folder in front of him, he transferred it to the short stack of files, and grabbed another from the tall stack. He and Simone were going through every commercial break-in from the past two years to see if they could link any of them to the newer robberies. Five hours later, and they hadn't found a damn thing.

He was thankful for the quiet of the glassed-in conference room, but the stark fluorescents were giving him a headache on top of the headache he'd had when he came in. Luke closed his eyes and laid his head against the seat back. The tight muscles of his neck stretched. His spine popped. But his mind still twitched like a dying fish. He'd come back to Boulder to simplify his life. Yet another failure to chalk up on his list.

When his cell rang, he ignored the first few chirps before he stretched and looked down at it. He couldn't have been more surprised by the name on the screen than if it had been Santa Claus.

"What the hell?" he muttered. He hit the call button and put the phone tentatively to his ear.

"Luke?" a sweet voice said.

"Yes."

"It's Tessa. How are you?"

"I'm… Yeah, I've been better. I wasn't expecting you to call."

"Oh. Did Jamie talk to you?"

"Yes," he said, his muscles tightening anew. "He did."

Silence drew between them for a moment, and then he heard Tessa inhale on the other end of the line. "Is it true? About your partner?"

He closed his eyes. "No."

"Does everyone think it's true?"

"Yes."

She sighed and Luke waited for the next question. "Why?" she finally asked.

And Luke found himself telling the truth about it for the first time. "Everyone thinks it's me because Simone and I are close. We were best friends. But we were never lovers."

"So who's the father?"

It was Luke's turn to sigh. "I don't know. It's a long story."

"You sound sad."

Sad. Yeah. That actually made him smile. "I guess that's one word for it."

"Pissed?"

He smiled wider. "Maybe."

"Do you want to talk about it?"

Luke frowned at the pen he was pushing around the table. "I don't think that's—"

"Come on. Just come over. Bring me dinner."

"I…" Okay, this was awkward. Given any other circumstances, he would put up his hands and back slowly away from a hot virgin with two protective older brothers. Why the heck did she have to be the only person who managed to make him smile these days? *Damn it,* he said silently, rubbing a hand over his eyes.

"All right," she said, her voice pulling down in disappointment. "I understand. I guess I'm the definition of complicated."

Her? Good God. "Don't be stupid, Tessa. I'll be there in half an hour. Burgers okay?"

"I assume you mean burgers from the Sink?"

He grinned at the table. "I do."

"Cheeseburger with guac," she said quickly. "No onions. And park behind the house." With that reminder of how idiotic they were both being, Tessa hung up the phone, probably afraid he'd call it off. Because any sane man would.

Yeah. That sounded about right. Any *sane* man.

At least he could claim one small comfort. There was no possible way he was sleeping with Tessa Donovan tonight, so she was probably the safest woman he could have dinner with.

"Even I'm not that stupid," he muttered as he packed up his files and grabbed his keys. "No way."

CHAPTER SEVEN

He wasn't a misogynistic asshole with a pregnant girlfriend. He was just a hot single cop who was bringing her a cheeseburger.

Tessa smiled as she fired up the stereo, damn happy with the way this day was turning out. It might even call for a little Van Morrison. Yeah, it definitely called for Van Morrison. Tessa turned on "Brown Eyed Girl" and danced into the kitchen to finish tidying up.

She'd saved the day—probably—and now she was going to get the man—maybe. What more could a girl ask for? Feeling a lovely bond with all the other women in the world, Tessa typed up tonight's Twitter message and sent it out.

Feeling my Celtic roots tonight, ladies. You know what that means. Come on by & and say sláinte.

Jamie had been wearing his kilt tonight, and their Twitter feed was already buzzing with it.

She was still grinning when a car door shut in the alley behind her house, and Tessa rushed to the back door to open it. But her smile fell when she saw Luke.

He looked exhausted. As if five days had passed since she'd seen him and he hadn't slept a wink since.

"Luke! You look awful!"

His brow crumpled even as his mouth turned up at the corners. "That's a terrible way to greet a man who comes bearing burgers."

"I'm sorry! You just look tired."

"Fair enough. I am."

Tired, but still hot and strong. So she kissed his cheek as she took the bag from his hand and led him into her lair. "Red wine with burgers, do you think?"

He raised an eyebrow.

"I don't want to think about beer tonight," she explained.

"Red wine, it is."

Half a bottle and two burgers later, they were sitting snug on her couch with the music turned down to a whisper so they could talk. "So tell me why you look so beat up today. Big murder case?"

"You're determined to turn me into a TV show, aren't you?"

"Well, for a minute there, you were headed into *Jerry Springer* territory. I'm trying to steer you back toward *CSI*."

"Oh, right. *That*." The tightness around his eyes told Tessa that this was what had been weighing on him.

She raised her eyebrows and waited.

"I don't really talk about it." He paused as if that would be enough, but Tessa didn't let him off the hook. "My partner. It's complicated."

"Complicated as in…you're in love with her and she has a boyfriend?"

"No!" He shook his head. "But you put it in perspective, I suppose. Complicated as in, she's pregnant and she won't talk to me about it."

Tessa felt the exact moment when her heart began to melt. She could actually feel it go warm and squishy inside her. "I'm sorry, Luke."

"She's not married. There's no boyfriend. She's alone."

"Maybe she's okay with that."

His frown turned angry for a moment. "That's the thing. Simone *would* be okay with that. So why the hell isn't she?"

"She won't tell you anything?"

"Nothing. And I…" He raised a hand as if he were going to make a point, but his fingers hovered, half curled, before he dropped his hand to his knee. "I just want to fix it."

Aw. Tessa took his hand and curled her feet beneath her to scoot a little closer. Men were such adorable creatures. He was going crazy because he couldn't fix everything for his partner.

She stroked his fingers until they curled around hers. "How far along is she?"

"Seven months, I think."

"And she wasn't dating anyone last year?"

"No. Not that she told me."

She wove her fingers between his and stroked his thumb with hers. "Is she… Is it possible she, um, went to a clinic and did it herself?"

Luke sighed, and his body relaxed back into the couch as if someone had cut his strings. "It's possible. I've never asked her if… She doesn't date much, so there was talk. Stereotypical bullshit, and it's nobody's business but Simone's."

Tessa squeezed his hand.

"But…I thought she'd tell me."

She cocked her head and studied his face as he stared at some faraway spot. "You're sure you're not in love with her?"

He smiled and his eyes finally found her. "It's not like that between us," he said. "Promise."

"I'm glad," she whispered, and his eyelids dipped. He stared at her mouth. Tessa suffered a nearly irrepressible urge to lean forward. To taste him. To lick at his bottom lip until he devoured her. But she didn't kiss him; she just stroked his thumb, over and over. Luke blinked slowly, and then he pulled her in.

Triumph roared in her blood, but it was premature. Luke's mouth hovered over hers, but their lips didn't touch. Her breath quickened. His hand curved around her neck. For a long moment, Luke rested his forehead against hers.

Just as it occurred to her that he might not kiss her at all, Luke whispered, "Damn," and his lips touched hers.

Tessa's heartbeat jumped to a frightening pace. He kissed her so softly, but she could taste him as his mouth parted, slowly opening her body to him. His tongue touched hers and she gasped into him.

Oh, God, he tasted good. So good. Tessa's body

VICTORIA DAHL 87

went hot in a sudden rush of lust. She spread both her hands on his chest, but Luke didn't deepen the kiss as she'd expected. His hand stayed light against the back of her neck. His tongue still teased her. He seemed content to taste and taste again. But Tessa wanted to drown.

Something about this man inspired a strange mix of urgency and vulnerability that turned her into a bundle of need. Clearly, Luke wasn't laboring under the same burden. His tongue slid over hers with such slow sensuality that she found herself whimpering, hoping he only needed a hint.

But no. It was just his mouth on hers, his fingers against her neck. Then his other hand rose to spread over her shoulder, and shivers shot along her skin.

Screw it. She was all in. Tessa eased closer and straddled his legs.

"Mmph," he said against her mouth. Ignoring his surprise, she pressed her belly to his and took advantage of her new leverage to kiss him deeper.

Luke groaned and his fingers finally tightened against the back of her neck. The roughness of his hands only made her hotter. She was wet already, aroused as all hell, and they'd only kissed. Tessa wrapped her arms around his neck, burying her fingers in his hair so she could press her body more firmly to him. The hand that had been holding her shoulder slid down until his fingers framed her ribs.

Now, finally, his kisses grew rough. Gorgeously rough. His mouth tasted of heat and wine, and the scent of his skin clung so tightly to him that she had to press closer and closer to get enough of it. Her shifting proved that she wasn't the only one aroused. But when she rolled her hips into him, Luke jerked his head back, breaking the kiss.

"Wait," he gasped.

Tessa froze. What the heck?

"We can't…"

"Can't what?" she asked with a frown that felt decidedly grumpy.

"Can't…do any of this."

Tessa scooted back a little so she could meet his gaze. "Do you have a girlfriend? Not your partner, but someone else?"

"No. That's not it. I don't have a girlfriend."

"Good." She started to scoot forward again, but Luke's hands gripped her hips and held her back. He shook his head, his eyes going wider as each second passed. He looked…scared?

"What's wrong?" Tessa pressed.

"Nothing! I just… I should go. That's all."

"You're kidding. You need to leave *right now?* In the middle of this?"

He didn't answer, just watched her as if she might grow tentacles at any moment.

Tessa shrugged. "Just give me a few more minutes." She leaned in and kissed him before he could say no. Her ploy worked for a moment. He moaned when their tongues met and immediately picked up the kiss where they'd left off.

She would've smiled if she could have, but Tessa

didn't want to frighten the man. She had him just where she wanted him: under her and falling fast.

And it felt good. It felt good and that was all she wanted right now.

No, NO, NO, Luke's brain was chanting, but the message broke up before it reached his body. Her mouth was so *hot*. Just pure wet heat. He wanted to get deeper. Deeper inside her fiery body. Good Christ, what would that feel like?

Stop! his brain bellowed. Luke's body jerked at the command, and he managed to pull away. "Stop," he groaned.

This woman was a virgin. He had no intention of taking her virginity, so there was no point going any further. His resistance was more effective this time. Tessa scrambled off his legs and stood in front of him.

"What is *wrong* with you?" she demanded.

So many things. But he wasn't going to add "deflowerer of innocent women" to his list of dubious accomplishments, so he croaked out, "Nothing," and pushed to his feet.

Tessa backed up and crossed her arms. "Well, you *look* like you were having a good time." Her eyes dipped down to aim her gaze at his lap.

He fought the urge to shield himself from her sight. She probably understood what happened down there, anatomically speaking. Her brothers hadn't mentioned anything about a convent education.

"I'm sorry, Tessa," he said, holding up his hands in

surrender. "I shouldn't have come over. I'm honored, but…" He backed away, heading for the door.

"Honored? What the heck are you talking about?"

"Look," he finally said. "I know, okay? I know."

"Know what?"

"About your…" He made a vague gesture toward her middle.

Tessa shot an impatient glance down her body. "This is getting really weird, Luke. Just go."

She'd given him permission to escape, but now he couldn't move. Tessa's sweet face was creased in a frown of confusion. He'd rejected her, and she didn't know why. If she'd really wanted to have sex… Surely that kind of rejection could scar a virgin for life. What if he permanently damaged her blossoming sexuality? His mind spun with horror.

"Go," she said. "I won't jump you when you turn your back on me. Shoo. You're free!"

He should never have come over. This was too much pressure. Luke turned up his palms in a helpless plea. "Maybe we could just watch a movie or something. Get to know each other as friends."

Tessa drew herself straight and gave him a tight smile. "You seem like a really nice guy, Luke. Honestly. But I'm starting to get a weird Madonna-whore-complex vibe from you. And I don't feel like watching a movie. Or pretending to be a saint. So I'll see you around, okay?"

"Madonna-whore complex?"

"It's a psychological term for men who—"

"I know what it is and I don't have it!"

"Oh, come on. You think I'm nice. You're *honored* that I'm sexually interested in you? And then there's the pregnant woman you want to save. The first step is admitting you have a problem."

He'd been cursed. He was sure of it. Cursed to never have a simple, straightforward relationship with a woman. But he was a willing participant, wasn't he? He'd come over here knowing damn well that he shouldn't. Then he'd kissed her because...just because he'd wanted it so badly. And she was way off base about his interest in her. He thought she was nice *and* he wanted to fuck her all at the same time.

Tessa growled and squeezed her eyes shut. "Oh, just go already! You look so cute standing there. It's not fair."

He could not leave like this. There were too many rumors floating around about him as it was. He'd be damned if he'd add sexual deviant to the list. Luke took a steadying breath, and he said it. "You're a virgin."

Her jaw dropped and she took a step back. "What?"

"Not that there's anything wrong with that, but...I can't pretend I don't know. I'm sorry. This is incredibly awkward."

Tessa uncrossed her arms and held her hands up in a calming motion. He recognized it because he'd used it a thousand times in his career. "Okay, I'm not sure what kind of fantasy you're creating here, but I don't want any part of it."

"Fantasy?"

"Yeah, it's a little early in this relationship for role-playing."

"Are you kidding me? I *stopped* you!"

Her eyes slid to one side and then the other, as if she were searching for answers in her living room. "I don't understand. Why would you think I'm a virgin?"

"Because your brother told me!" he snapped.

Tessa inhaled so loudly that even she seemed startled. She slapped a hand over her mouth and stared at him with wide eyes. "You're kidding." The words were muffled by her fingers.

"No. Jamie told me to stay away from you because you're a virgin. I tried, but—"

"I'm not!" she yelped.

"What?"

"A virgin!"

He cocked his head and raised a doubtful eyebrow.

"Oh, come on! If I were, do you think I'd have waited twenty-seven years just to lose it on a couch to a man I barely know?"

"Er…I thought maybe you liked me a lot?" He wasn't sure how he felt about her laughter, but Luke chose to feel relieved.

"Well—" she giggled "—the look on your face when you pushed me off really takes on new meaning."

"Yeah?"

"You looked fucking terrified."

He was so shocked at hearing her say the F word that Luke burst into laughter.

"Need another glass of wine?" she asked.

Jesus, did he ever. But he glanced toward the back

door as if he had a brain in his body and it had finally kicked in. "Thanks, but I think I'd better go."

She said, "Wait!" but he was already moving toward the kitchen.

"I'm sorry, Tessa. But this is just…" He shook his head. "Too much."

"I know," she said as he opened the heavy pine door. "I know it's crazy, but it was my brother. Not me."

He opened the screen door and started to step out.

"Actually," she said sharply, "it was my brother and *you*. I had nothing to do with this. If you leave now, you're just going to give me time to decide *you're* too complicated."

Luke froze, one foot hovering over the threshold. She had no idea. Actually…she did. She knew more about Simone than he'd told anyone.

"Or…" she drawled, "you could stay. And convince me to give you another chance."

Hand braced on the doorjamb, Luke bowed his head and tried to calculate the correct decision. On one hand, his life was too complicated, and hers wasn't very far behind. He didn't need this right now. And she didn't need to be dragged into his mess. On the other hand, he liked her. He liked talking to her. She made him feel better. And she wasn't a virgin.

But no. That was exactly the reason he shouldn't stay.

Luke made the best decision he'd made in years. "I'll call you tomorrow," he said, and he walked out into the night alone.

CHAPTER EIGHT

LUKE EMBRACED the next day with a foul attitude and fierce scowl. He managed to get through the two-hour monthly meeting without biting anyone's head off, but it was a close call. And being civil to Simone was beginning to strain his sanity. When the Denver P.D. called and gave him an excuse to get out of the office, he jumped at it.

"Denver's got seventy-five burglary files for us to go through. You want in?"

Simone didn't look up from her computer screen. "No, you take it."

He left without another word. He needed to get over his frustration with his partner, but today wasn't the day. Today he was horny and pissed at the world, and he was better off working in another city. Not that he wanted time to think. He was sick of his own brooding, so he put on a Nirvana CD and cranked it up. Anyone else's angst was better than his own.

By the time he walked into the Denver P.D. headquarters, he felt marginally better. "Hey, Asher!" one of the guys called out. "Did you come down for some advice from real detectives?" Luke recognized the guy as someone he'd graduated from the academy with and gave him an affectionate one-fingered reply. The other detective didn't let up. "Did someone steal some tofu from a health food store up there?"

Shaking his head, Luke pushed through the doors to the records department and got to work. He wasn't the least bit bothered by the jabs. He'd put in his time in Los Angeles, after all, and he'd take the relatively quiet streets of Boulder any day. He hadn't been shot once since he'd moved back. Or stabbed. Or divorced. Maybe that would be his new mantra.

He downed his cup of clichéd bad coffee and turned his mind to the cases in front of him. Every single one. And three hours later, he'd found something pretty damn interesting.

Tapping his pencil against his forehead, he waited for a call back from his contact in the Denver property crimes division and paged through the files again, just to be sure he'd read them right.

Detective Ben Jackson finally called back.

"So you had a rash of similar robberies starting a year ago?"

"Yep. Nine of them. You noticed that, huh?"

"I did. Computers stolen. Identity crimes followed. And they stopped six months ago?"

"You got it. We could never prove they were related. No fingerprints. No traceable accounts. But of course…"

"Yeah, that's awfully organized."

"That was my take."

Luke tapped harder. "And our break-ins started about a month after these stopped."

"Hell of a coincidence," Ben said.

"Yeah. Why don't you go ahead and solve this case for me, Detective Jackson? Who do you like?"

"I've got nothing. Do your own fucking work, man."

"Interesting," Luke drawled. "What you're saying is, Denver couldn't handle it and you're looking for a little help from Boulder."

"Taunt all you like. It's your problem now. Maybe it was some high school kid who started at the U."

Luke hung up and tapped his forehead a few more times. He eyed the case files, trying to calculate how long it would take him to fill out all the paperwork to get copies sent to Boulder. Maybe he could just memorize them all.

"Crap," he groaned. This was going to be more painful than walking away from Tessa had been last night.

An hour and a half later, he finally broke free of the records department, a stack of printed forms in his hand. The trip had worked, anyway. Right now, he'd give anything to be back in Boulder, in his car next to his secretive and pregnant partner, and *not* having sex with a nonvirgin woman who'd probably never speak to him again.

But since he was only three minutes from his mom's house, he decided to drop in and say hi.

Yet another bad decision.

Her door was open to the spring breeze and Luke could hear women's voices from the kitchen. He knocked on the wooden frame of the screen door. "Mom? It's me."

He hadn't grown up in the little 1920s bungalow, so he didn't feel comfortable walking in. His mom had bought it just five years before. Her first house. He was proud of her.

But when the voices stopped and the two women walked around the corner of the kitchen wall, he stepped back so quickly he nearly fell off the stoop. Yeah, he'd known his mom and his ex-wife were still close, but he hadn't realized how close.

"Luke," his mom said as she opened the door. Her round face was tight with a worried smile. "Eve is visiting from California."

"Yeah, I see that." He didn't have any choice but to step inside. Well, he had the choice of looking like a complete ass and walking away, but he was bigger than that. Or small enough not to want to give Eve the satisfaction.

"Hi, Luke," she said, holding out a hand.

It felt damn strange shaking the hand of a woman he'd shared a bed with, but he shook it, anyway. "You look good," he said. She did. Her hair was long again, and even back to its old auburn color. Her skin was bronzed and healthy instead of gray with illness. She looked…happy. He was startled by the shot of relief that mixed up with his anger.

"You look good, too," she said. "Really."

"Thanks." Luke cleared his throat and tried to catch his mom's eye, but she'd decided to take that moment to straighten the photos that sat on the nearest end table.

"So," Luke ventured awkwardly. "Are you in town for work?"

"Yes, there's a big natural foods convention in town, and I'm working the booth for Good Grains."

"Cool," he said before they descended into an awkward silence. He hadn't seen her since he'd left L.A., and he felt on fire with the strangeness of it.

"Oh, God, come here," she said suddenly, sliding her arms around his waist.

Stunned, Luke put his arms around her shoulders and returned the hug. She smelled the same, and he couldn't stop his vicious frown. It felt so damn weird to hold her. Familiar and totally wrong all at once.

His mom mouthed, *I'm sorry,* from behind Eve's back.

"You really do look great," Eve said, giving him one last squeeze. "Your mom told me you're seeing someone."

"Tessa?" he said in utter confusion, then realized that his mom knew nothing about Tessa. As a matter of fact, her eyes widened noticeably, but Eve just smiled.

"Is that her name?"

"Uh, sure. Anyway, Mom, I just stopped in to say hi. But you're busy and I need to get back."

Eve grabbed his arm. "No, don't leave because of me. I'll go."

"Really, it's no big deal. I've got to go."

His mom twisted her hands together and gave him

a wide smile that wobbled at the edges. "I'll call you!" she said as he stole out the door.

"You'd better," he muttered.

His skin burned from the focus of their eyes on him as he walked away. He got into his car without looking back, even though the compulsion was so strong he had to clench his eyes shut as he slid into the car.

Luke pulled away from the curb. He was heading the wrong way, but that was the least of his worries. "Jesus Fucking Christ," he whispered, shaken to the core, as if someone had just knocked the wind from him.

Eve.

She'd once been his whole life, and their divorce had left him walking through fog for a long time. But now he was realizing he hadn't seen her face for nearly three years and he'd been...fine. And now that he *had* seen her? He was still fine. His time in L.A., his marriage...that felt like another life. Like it didn't have much to do with Luke anymore.

He knew that wasn't really true. After all, his stomach still hadn't risen back to its normal place. But he wasn't the least bit tempted to punch a hole through anything. He wasn't fuming.

In fact, by the time his mom called ten minutes later, he managed to answer with a clipped, "Hello," instead of anything less polite.

"Luke, I'm so sorry. I had no idea you'd come by today."

"So you knew she was coming?"

"I... Yes. You know we still talk."

"I do." It bothered the crap out of him, but he'd accepted it. Eve was the daughter his mom had never had, and she hadn't stopped loving Eve after the divorce. But Luke had been pretty outraged at first. Eve had left him, after all, and he'd thought his mom should've been pissed off and protective. Apparently his mom was a better person than he was.

"She'll only be here one more night."

"She's *staying* at your house?" he barked.

"I'm sorry," she said again.

Luke sighed and rubbed his neck. "Look, I was just surprised. Okay? It's no big deal."

"Good. I'm glad. You looked awfully sick for a moment."

"I'm fine."

"So if you're fine…"

"Yeah?" he asked warily.

"Who's this Tessa you mentioned?"

If he hadn't been on a busy freeway, Luke would've put his forehead to the steering wheel and groaned. Since that wasn't an option, he just shook his head in complete disbelief. "Are you really asking me that right now?"

"Yes, I am. I told Eve you had a girlfriend to make it clear you'd moved on. I had no idea I'd stumbled onto the truth."

"Sorry, but you're off base. No girlfriend."

His mom didn't give up. "So who is she?"

"She's a girl I've gone on one date with, and there's a decided possibility that will be the only one. That's it." He left off the date on Tessa's couch, because he was pretty sure it didn't qualify as anything other than a drawn-out misunderstanding.

"Well, keep me in the loop."

"I don't think so."

She laughed so hard she snorted. "Okay, but I miss you. Drop by again soon."

"I love you, Mom, but no more dropping by. I'll make an appointment next time."

He hung up and glanced at the dashboard. It was only three, but he felt like he'd just put in a sixteen-hour day. With traffic, it'd be after four by the time he got back to the station. Maybe he'd just call it a day and go home to crack open his dusty bottle of Scotch. If a man didn't deserve a night of drinking after a scene like that, when did he?

Never, apparently, because his phone rang a minute later, flashing Simone's name. Luke didn't even bother sighing when he answered the phone. "What's up?"

"Care to interview a robbery suspect?" She sounded downright happy. "Someone got caught with his fingers in the pot."

"Another robbery? At three in the afternoon?"

"Nope. Patrol pulled over some guy on a warrant, and they found a Donovan Brothers keg in the trunk."

"No shit. All right, I'll be there in thirty, and I'll let you know what I found in Denver."

Luke hung up and hit the switch to the lights hidden in the grille of his car. As he wove through traffic, all his weariness vanished in the reflection of flashing lights. Maybe he could salvage something from this day after all.

CHAPTER NINE

THE PUNK WHO SLOUCHED over the scarred table of the interrogation room could've passed for fourteen, but he was a few years past juvenile hall. At first glance, Luke had figured the twenty-two-year-old stick figure in skinny jeans would confess within five minutes. He clearly wasn't cut out for prison, and he'd been picked up on a warrant for failure to show on charges of petty larceny. With evidence from the brewery robbery right there in the trunk of his car, this kid was in trouble. Then again, he also wasn't the brightest bulb in the box. If he hadn't skipped his first hearing, he would've gotten off with time served and probation.

So yeah, the kid was in a bad spot, but he was sticking with his story that he'd found the keg in an alley and picked it up.

"Listen, Tommy," Luke said. "You go by Tommy, right?"

"It's Thomas."

"We're not interested in you, Thomas. I know the break-in wasn't your idea. You were probably brought in at the last minute. So who called you in?"

Thomas rolled his eyes.

"I'm serious, Thomas. You tell us who orchestrated the break-in at the brewery, and we'll help you out."

"I told you," Thomas ground out. "I found the keg in an alley."

"Oh, yeah? And I bet you only picked it up so you could return it for the recycling deposit, right?"

"Come on. Yeah, I wanted the beer, but I didn't steal it."

The kid's hands were clenched into tight fists, making the black dots tatted onto his knuckles stand out.

"All right, Thomas. I have no choice but to get in touch with the D.A., then." He cut his eyes to the door and Simone followed him out.

"Let me try alone," Simone said as soon as the door closed.

Luke shrugged. "If you think it'll make a difference."

"He keeps eyeing my stomach with an odd look."

"An odd look like he's schizophrenic and he thinks the baby's plotting to jump out and get him?"

Her mouth flattened. "Luke."

"All right, as long as you think it's safe."

Simone went back in, and Luke motioned a uniform to the door before he slipped into the room next door to watch Simone on the monitor.

"Where's your friend?" Thomas sneered.

"He's on the phone with the district attorney, discussing your case."

The boy slouched lower, snorting in false arrogance, but just as Simone had said, his eyes slid down to

VICTORIA DAHL

her abdomen and paused. Simone put her hand to her stomach and let it rest there.

Thomas's chin jerked toward her. "My girlfriend's pregnant." Even over the tinny sound of the monitor, Luke could hear past his bravado to the vulnerability beneath.

"How far along is she?" Simone asked.

"Six months."

"Have you felt the baby move yet?"

He cracked a smile. "Yeah."

Simone slipped into a chair, but she kept her hand on the round bulge of her belly. "You look excited," she said. "Proud."

"We're gonna get married as soon as I can find an apartment."

Her smile disappeared. "But not if you're in jail."

"Shit." He kicked the empty chair, and Luke started to rise, but the chair only shifted a few inches. He was frustrated, not threatening.

"We're trying to help you."

"I didn't do it! I swear to God, I had nothing to do with it. Look, I'd turn over anyone's name I could if it'd help me, but I can't. I found it in an alley, just like I said."

"When did you find it?" Simone asked.

"This morning. I told you already. I was driving behind some apartments checking for stuff people had thrown. Furniture and shit, you know? Stuff for the baby."

"What's the address?"

He rolled his eyes. "Crap, I don't know. It was those apartments on Sixteenth, off of Pearl."

Simone raised an eyebrow. "Those apartments have security cameras, Thomas. We'll check them, you know."

"Good! Check them!"

She nodded and got to her feet. "All right. Let me see what Detective Asher is up to."

Luke met her in the hallway.

"He didn't do it," Simone said.

"Yeah, let's get those tapes and see who did. Why don't you ask him if he'll take a ride and show us where he found it. He'll do it for you. And let's get the keg dusted right now."

And just like that, it was easy between them again. Two hours without an awkward moment as they scoured the alley and harassed the manager of the apartment complex and peppered all the residents for any information they might have. In L.A., this case wouldn't have warranted more than five minutes of attention, but here a theft ring got his full focus. It felt good. As if they were actually making a difference instead of just cleaning up after violence.

Simone squinted up at the one camera that was pointed toward their part of the parking lot. "Fifty bucks says the owner's going to ask for a search warrant."

"Shit. I'm not taking that bet. I'd start the process now, but it's six. No judge is going to stay late for a property crime. Tomorrow will have to do."

"You think the angle's good?"

Luke tilted his head to one side and then the other. "I don't know. It'll be close."

"Yeah."

The manager emerged from a metal door and gave them the news they'd expected. The owner was someone in California and he was covering all his bases. He wanted a warrant, so there was nothing else to be done tonight.

It was past seven by the time they got back to the station and typed up their notes. Somehow, as Luke pulled out into traffic, he made the decision to stop by the brewery and give the Donovans an update. It was as good a time as any, since Tessa wasn't likely to be there.

Funny how much relief felt like disappointment.

TESSA WAS ON A ROLL tonight. Every single draw was perfect. The place was busy, but not packed, and everyone was in a fine, mellow mood. She smiled with real happiness as she dropped off three porters to a table of men watching the baseball game on the corner screen.

On her way back to the bar, a woman touched her sleeve to stop her. "Where's that cute guy who usually works here?"

"It's his night off," Tessa said for the twentieth time that evening. It was always the same. She wasn't offended. Jamie was a popular tourist attraction. She'd posted on Twitter that he'd be off tonight, so there were actually fewer disappointed faces than usual.

"Hey, Tessa!" one of her regulars said from the next table. "Why don't *you* ever wear a kilt?"

"You're thinking of a schoolgirl uniform, Fred. It may be plaid, but it's not the same thing, and you'll never talk me into one."

Fred slapped his knee and howled.

Laughing, Tessa cleared the empty pint glasses from Fred's table and shook her head. "You'd better get home. Joyce will toss your dinner in the trash if you're not home soon."

He snapped upright and looked at his watch with a curse. Tessa slipped him his bill without another word, then turned and walked right into Luke Asher.

Luke reached to steady her tray of glasses, but he grabbed too quickly and nearly knocked it from her hand. "Sorry," he said as he put one hand to her shoulder and one to the tray. He frowned. "What are you doing here?"

"Well, I guess that answers the question of whether you came to see me."

Happy with the flicker of discomfort she saw cross his face, Tessa eased past him. She had to level the playing field, after all. The man had walked out on her last night. After that make-out session in his lap, she was more than willing to give Luke another shot, but there was no reason for him to know that.

Hiding her smirk, she slipped behind the bar and stacked the glasses in the tray that was headed for the dishwasher. She wiped off her hands before turning to find Luke standing at the bar. "Did you come here to negotiate with my brother over the price of my maiden-hood?"

"Jesus, Tessa," he muttered. The tips of his ears turned red.

"I'm sorry. I'm sure there are still details to be worked out. I don't want to interfere."

"I get it. You're trying to torture me."

"Is it working?"

He sighed loudly enough that she heard him over the background music and the baseball game. "You're not half-bad at it," he said.

"Thanks. You want a beer?"

Luke narrowed his eyes as if he was trying to dis-cern her motive, and boy, did he have a great suspicious look. It was dark and *penetrating*. Tessa felt the hair rise on her arms. Her nipples tightened. Luke had the whole cop thing down to an erotic art.

"Sure," he finally said. "I'll have a beer."

"You want a menu?"

The creases at the corners of his eyes tightened. "Why don't you choose for me?"

Oh, a challenge. Tessa cocked her head and let her eyes wander down as much of him as she could see. She took a step back, and returned his narrowed look. "Hmm."

His left eyebrow rose like a dare.

"All right," she murmured, and went to draw his beer. When she slid it across the bar toward him, he didn't look impressed, but he raised it to his mouth.

"India Pale Ale," Tessa said. "Looks nice enough, but it's got a bitter kick to it."

He swallowed and set the glass down hard. His eyes didn't yield even a glimmer of humor. "Has a bite despite its innocent appearance? I think you accidentally gave me your glass."

Tessa bit the inside of her cheek to keep from smiling. "No, mine is the amber ale. Smooth, sweet and pretty. The perfect taste for any occasion."

His mouth finally softened, and Luke raised his glass. "I'll drink to that."

Tessa tossed her ponytail and left him to nurse his drink while she collected Fred's bill and gave the other tables another quick look.

"So," she said as she came back around the bar. "What are you doing here?"

"I've got a small update. We picked up a guy who had the keg in the trunk of his car. Right now, we don't think he was one of the people who broke in, but we're following up on some other details." Luke reached into the pocket of his coat. "Do you recognize him?"

She looked closely at the picture of the thin boy who stared sullenly at the camera. "No, I don't recognize him. And he's young enough to stand out around here."

"Are your brothers here?"

"No, it's just me and Wallace."

"That's the brewmaster?"

"Yep. Do you want to ask him? He's usually not here so late, but he has a couple of small batches going. He gets pretty caught up in his experiments." She leaned close to whisper, "Spicy chocolate stout," but she was really just looking for an excuse to catch his scent. Mmm. Man, he turned her on.

Luke cleared his throat before edging back to take another drink of his beer. Either he liked it when she leaned close, or he was desperate to get away from her. But considering that he'd willingly accepted a drink and a seat, Tessa decided to go with the former.

"Come on," she said softly, giving him a secret smile. "Let's go in back."

His eyes widened.

"You can have Wallace look at the photo."

"Oh, right. Sure." He rose and followed her through the swinging doors. The office hallway to the left was dark, but the kitchen was more than bright enough to see Wallace leaning down to whisper into a girl's ear.

"Oh," Tessa said, drawing up short. Luke ended up flush against her back for a second before he stepped away.

Wallace looked up with his standard grouchy scowl. "I'm on my way out," he grumbled. The girl at his side smiled as if she were looking forward to a treat, at which point Tessa realized the girl was actually a delicate young man whose hair was styled into a straight, dark fall down his back.

Nothing unusual for Wallace.

"Do you have one second?" she asked. "Detective Asher has a picture he wants you to look at."

Wallace shrugged and reached for the photo. He stared at it for a good long while as if there were thousands of faces to page through in his memory. That didn't surprise Tessa. The man dated a lot. A *lot*. He tilted the photo back and forth, then shook his head. "Don't know him."

"Thanks," Luke said.

Wallace grunted, put his arm around his date and they walked out the back door without a word.

Luke turned to her with raised eyebrows. "I had no idea Grizzly Adams was gay."

"He's not. Grizzly Adams is enthusiastically bisexual."

"Oh. That's… Okay, let's stop calling him that. It's affecting my childhood memories. I loved that show." He frowned toward the door. "Seriously, he looks like a mountain man."

"I know. And he's grumpy as hell, yet beautiful creatures flock to him like he's the pied piper. It's entertaining, to say the least. I'm not sure what kind of powers he has, but they're potent."

He shook his head. "I think I need to finish my beer now."

"I'll bet. Sorry we couldn't help with the picture, though."

"It was a long shot."

Tessa left him at the bar to finish his beer while she took care of customers, but her neck burned with awareness that he was there. He hadn't left. But she'd be damned if she'd make the first move tonight. Still, it was hard not to watch him. He wasn't anything like Jamie had said. Babe Magnet, he might be, but she'd given him full opportunity to have sex last night and he'd declined. *Declined.* Sheesh.

Half an hour later, there were only two tables left, and Tessa had time to take a seat next to Luke. "You're still here."

"I like watching you work."

"Oh, yeah? Do I wipe down tables with flair?"

He tilted his pint glass and looked into the last flecks of foam. "You smile at people. You're nice to them."

Warmth prickled over her skin with uncomfortable intensity. She was glad she was sitting next to him and not facing him. He'd paid her a simple compliment, but the honest sincerity in his words embarrassed her. "It's my job."

"No, that's not it," he said, and left it at that.

Tessa squirmed. "You're just too used to hanging around criminals."

Luke set his glass down and turned toward her. "When I'm not around you, I know this is a bad idea."

Her heart fluttered. "This?"

"I'm too complicated. You don't need to think about it or figure out if it's true. I'm telling you straight up. My life is way more complicated than you know. I'm not long-term material."

"Oh. I see."

"So you should tell me you don't want to see me again, Tessa."

Despite her words, Tessa couldn't see anything at all. What was he saying? He was warning her off, but he wasn't leaving. He didn't want a long-term relationship, but he'd walked out on the promise of sex last night. "I told you I don't need another big brother protecting me."

He rubbed the back of his neck and sighed. "If I were thinking of protecting you, I would've left half an hour ago."

"But here you are."

"Here I am."

Tessa glanced up at the clock and then looked at the few people who were left. One of them signaled her. "I'll be right back," she said.

Ten minutes of work, and Tessa was left with two messy tables and a wave goodbye to the last of her customers. She cleaned up, drew herself a half-pint of amber ale and tilted her head toward the pool table. "I've got twenty-five minutes before I can lock up. Wanna play a few rounds of nine-ball?"

He met her gaze, not saying a word, as if he were giving her time to change her mind. Then he rose and walked toward the pool table. Smiling, Tessa grabbed some quarters from the till and followed.

Ten minutes later, she was pretty sure he was trying to scrape his pride off the floor. "Damn," Luke grumbled. "Did you major in pool in college?"

"Oh, please. I work in a bar. And I majored in economics."

"Really?"

Tessa shrugged. "With a minor in accounting. The brewery budget is a little small for macroeconomics. What about you?"

"Criminal justice, just to be predictable. Honestly, I

would have gone straight to the police academy, but my mom's a teacher. I didn't want her to disown me."

"I didn't know that! What does she teach?"

"High school English. She has a lot of experience with teenagers, which was a damn good skill set for raising a son on her own."

Tessa prepped the table for another set of annihilation and studied him past her lashes. "Do you get along with her?"

Luke smiled, but then his smile stretched to a laugh. "Yeah. As a matter of fact, I just saw her today."

"Oh? So, what's funny?"

"You know how moms can—" His laughter fell away to reveal shock at his own words. "I'm so sorry. I forgot…"

"Don't be silly. I like hearing about other people's moms. It makes me happy."

Luke shook his head and walked around the table. Her pulse quickened with each step he took. By the time he stopped in front of her, she felt like a bird was trembling in her chest.

He curved his hand to the nape of her neck. "Everything makes you happy, Tessa."

"That's not true," she whispered, but then he was kissing her, slow and deep, and Tessa was too happy to bother with talking.

CHAPTER TEN

SHE PARKED HER CAR in the garage and signaled Luke to park right behind her. She'd invited him over for a glass of wine, but they both knew why he was here.

Or... Tessa frowned as she unlocked the back door. Was there a possibility he didn't know he was here for sex? Because they'd certainly stumbled over a few misunderstandings the night before.

But as she turned on the lights, Luke came in behind her and he unknotted his tie and slipped it off. Maybe he did know why he was here. Then she noticed how tired he looked and wondered if she should just tuck him into bed.

No fricken way. She poured two glasses of wine and waved him toward the couch. Then she slipped off her shoes and settled right down on his lap, her knees straddling his hips.

"Now," she murmured, "where were we when you so rudely interrupted us last night?"

A short half hour later, Tessa was flat on her back on the couch, her jeans unzipped, her arms curled around Luke's neck, and his mouth on hers. The only thing that could make this better would be Luke's hand easing down the front of her pants, and God bless him, he was taking care of that right this moment.

Now that he'd finally made the decision to have her, there was no hesitation. His fingers slid into her panties and touched her, and Tessa moaned into his mouth. She was surrounded by him. His whole body pressed against her side, his tongue worked rhythmically against hers and now his fingers were taking up that same slow rhythm, rubbing her clit. Jesus, she was in heaven. Or purgatory. Her whole body felt close to boiling, after all.

She felt his fingers get slicker as he worked her, lubricating her with her own wetness. Finally, he slid his hand lower, pushing one finger deep into her pussy.

"Oh, God," she gasped, tearing her mouth from his to draw a deep breath. "God, yes." He fucked her slowly with his finger, while the heel of his hand pressed her clit with each thrust.

Tessa tilted her hips up, urging him deeper, faster, but he was unmoved by her obvious begging. He went slow. So slow. Sliding and rubbing and pushing against her. She was dying.

"Luke."

"Mmm." His mouth slid to her neck to suck there. White shivers danced down her spine and coiled around her sex. His teeth scraped her skin and she gasped, rolling her hips. "Oh, yes. Faster."

"I don't think so," he murmured.

"Please."

"No."

Startled, she opened her eyes and looked at the ceiling. No? A man who said no? In *bed?* Before she could puzzle that out, Luke pushed another finger inside her. Tessa cried out at the delicious pressure, but true to his word, he didn't quicken his pace. He stroked her slow and steady until she was so close she dug her fingernails into his arm. Oh, God, everything was so *tight.*

"Please," she whispered again. "Please, please, please." But Luke was heartless. He ignored her begging. He ignored her clawing nails. And his ruthlessness finally paid off. The tension slipped higher and higher, and when it broke inside her, Tessa cried out on a wordless scream. Her hips jerked. Her thighs trembled. And Luke didn't let up until her final, broken whimper.

"Oh, God," she panted. "Luke… That was…"

As her heartbeat slowed, she realized he was breathing nearly as hard as she was. Poor guy. He was probably in a world of hurt. But her limbs were just so *heavy.* Tessa stretched hard, sighing when his fingers slipped free of her.

She never wanted to move again, but this man deserved her very best effort. He'd clearly given his.

His hand slid up to grip her hip as if he were afraid he'd float right off the earth if he didn't hold on. She loved that she was his anchor, if only for this one brief moment.

Fighting the urge to close her eyes and melt into the couch, Tessa ran her fingers down his side. "You still awake?"

"Oh, you're funny," he said gruffly.

"Not sleepy, Detective? Can I call you detective?"

"No."

She scooted on her side to face him, then wound one leg around his thighs to settle herself nicely against him. "Maybe sometimes?" she purred. "Detective?"

His eyes glittered behind his lashes. "Maybe, sometimes," he said. "If you're good."

His wicked smile surprised her. So did the strength of his hands as he lifted her up.

"Have I been good?" she asked in a breathless voice.

Luke helped her to her feet and stood himself, nearly flush against her. "Not yet," he said. He pulled her T-shirt over her head. "But soon. Very soon."

THE BARE SKIN of her back felt like silk beneath his fingertips. Silk or satin or some other unbearably beautiful thing. Something smooth and warm and delicate. Another time, when he wasn't shaking with need, he'd put his lips to every inch of her skin. But tonight he felt too close to breaking, so he only unclasped her bra before he got too clumsy with lust.

He felt like he was in high school again, making out with this impossibly cute girl on her living room sofa, overwhelmed with the thought that he was about to see her naked.

Luke slid off her bra and smoothed a hand over her ribs until he cupped her breast. She sighed just as he knew she would, then made a low purring noise when he rubbed her nipple between his fingers. He would've spent a few minutes on that alone, but Tessa pushed her own jeans down, and how was he supposed to resist that?

Meaning to help ease her jeans off, he lowered himself to the couch, but the sight of her body caught him up like a trap. Her breasts were small and gorgeous. The nipples deep pink and hard with arousal. And as she pushed her jeans farther down, her panties slid off, too, and Luke just sat there like an idiot, his hands on her bare hips as he tried to divide his attention between her breasts and the golden brown hair between her legs. He touched her, and found her still slick from her orgasm, and couldn't resist sliding his fingers into that heat.

"God," she groaned as he put his mouth to her waist and bit gently up to her ribs. "Luke. I need…"

Yeah, he knew what she needed, so he shoved her jeans the rest of the way down and pulled them from her legs. And now his own need had set upon him with all the finesse of a bare-knuckled fist. It was all he could think. *Inside her. Now.* Now.

Luke leaned back on the couch to tear at the button of his pants. Just as he got the button free, she straddled him, settling her ass against his knees. Her legs were spread now, her sex plump and wet, and Luke felt brutal as an animal as she reached for his zipper. Everything in his mind and body had focused on her. Her thighs and sex and her hands reaching in to—

"Christ," he rasped as her fingers wrapped around his shaft. She stroked him as if he needed more stimulation, and Luke saw stars.

"Very nice, Detective," she crooned, her sweet grin

completely at odds with the dirty picture she presented. "Is this all for me?"

Oh, God. It hurt to laugh, but he found himself chuckling and groaning at the same time. Then her fingers traced around the head of his cock, and he was shaking again. He was glad she felt playful, but damned if he could take it a moment longer. Luke slid his hand into his back pocket to wrestle his wallet out. As he pulled a condom from it, Tessa put her knees more firmly to the couch and scooted closer to him. She took the condom from his hand and rolled it on. Her smile was gone now, too, and her breath came faster.

As he watched, she fisted his shaft and positioned herself above him. For a moment, they both stopped, waiting, and then Luke put his hands to her hips and slid her down.

Her pussy squeezed him in pure heat. When it felt too tight, even for him, he raised her up a tiny bit before easing her down again. "Fuck," he whispered, watching his cock penetrate her.

Finally, she was settled against him. He kissed her and she rocked into him, burning out hundreds of synapses in his brain. When her body softened a bit, he began to fuck her.

If he'd still been under any illusion of virginity, this would've destroyed it. Though she let him set the pace, Tessa rode him like she knew exactly what she wanted, rolling her hips and arching her back. She reached up and pulled her hair free of the ponytail, and when she shook it out, Luke had to close his eyes for a moment. He was trying to hold tight to control, and her hair falling down her shoulders as her breasts bounced with her movement… That wasn't something he could handle at the moment.

He concentrated on his thrusts, rising up to meet her hips, feeling the way he fit inside her. He slid his hands up her hips to her waist and ribs and breasts. She sobbed when he pinched her nipples, so Luke pulled her hips tight against him and sat up to put his mouth to her.

"Yes," she urged as his teeth scraped her nipple. He shifted them both closer to the edge of the couch, then began to slowly rock into her as he sucked hard at her breast.

"Oh… That's…" Her words disappeared into a soft groan as she rolled into his thrusts. Both her hands clutched his hair, her nails biting into his scalp. For a moment, Luke was so lost in her lovely whimpers of pleasure that he forgot his own desperate situation. His control slipped, and he cursed as pressure gathered at the base of his cock.

He lifted his mouth from her, gritting his teeth as Tessa worked herself against him, and now her breathy sounds were pure torture. She was the most beautiful thing he'd ever seen. Even as his jaw got tighter and tighter, her face went soft, her eyes closed as she lost herself. He never wanted this to end. Never. But his body strained toward orgasm.

"Fuck," he breathed. She was close. Her sighs were inching higher. Her teeth pressed into her lower lip. Luke curved his arms around her and pushed off the

couch, turning until it was her ass perched on the cushions and he knelt between her legs.

Biting back a scream, Tessa opened her eyes and
stared at him in shock.

"Sorry," he murmured. Instead of burying himself
in her over and over, Luke spread his fingers over her
belly and feathered his thumb across her clit.

"Oh!" she gasped.

He held himself still, deep inside her, as he rubbed
her clit until he felt her thighs tremble against him.

"Oh, God," she cried out. "Fuck me, please."

Jaw jumping with tension, he waited, holding off
until her spine arched, and she begged one last time.

Finally…finally, he gave her what they both wanted
with brutal, deep strokes. Tessa came screaming, her
hips jerking into his thrusts, and just as she began to
quiet, Luke came, his vision going dark as pleasure
crushed him in a pulsing grip.

He collapsed, still gripping her hips. He rested his
forehead against the back of the couch and breathed in
the scent of her shoulder. She smelled good, like soap
and sleep-warmed skin. She rested a hand on the nape
of his neck and petted him in slow strokes. Christ, he
felt like purring.

It'd been a while since he'd had sex, and it had been
a helluva long time since he'd felt anything *close* to
that good.

Tessa weaved her fingers into his hair and pulled
him gently up to kiss his mouth.

"Do you want me to go?" he asked quietly.

Her fingers tightened, and she pulled him back a

little farther so that their eyes met. "Don't be silly," she whispered, and his relief told him just how much he didn't want to leave.

When this was over, it would hurt, and Luke didn't even fucking care.

CHAPTER ELEVEN

TESSA WAS DRIFTING in a lovely, warm, supremely satisfied place when she heard the heavy thud of a car door closing. She opened her eyes, immediately awake, and saw that the other side of the bed was empty.

Damn. She'd been hoping that Luke would wake her up this morning before sneaking out. She'd hoped he'd wake her with some more of that crazy good sex. But he'd needed to get to work, probably. Her hours started later than most people's.

But God, that would've been nice. Plus she wanted to ride him while he was totally naked. Oh, well. Maybe tonight.

Just as she was relaxing into the pillow, smiling at the thought of another hour of sleep, Tessa heard the lock on her front door slide open. In that awful moment, she registered two very important things. One, the sound of the car door had come from the front of the house, and Luke had parked in the alley. Two, her shower was running and she wasn't in it. And then, of course, came the third awful truth: letting her brothers have keys to her house had been a stupid, stupid idea.

Tessa jumped from bed with a curse just as Eric's

voice floated in from the kitchen. "Tessa? You up yet?" The clink of bottles told her he was rifling through her fridge, which gave her a few minutes to do…something. First things first. She needed to cover her naked body, and quick.

Tessa bounded from bed and grabbed the robe she always threw over the chair in the corner. She tied the belt in a frantic knot, then dropped to her knees to scoot Luke's clothes under her bed. One shoe was missing, though, and she wasted a good ten seconds looking for the other.

The fridge door closed.

"Balls," she cursed, just as she spotted his other shoe and threw it into her open closet.

Feet slapping the wood floor, she raced for the door of her bedroom, shutting it behind her as Eric started down the hall. Unfortunately, the sound of the shower still echoed through the wood.

"Hey," Eric said. "Rough night?"

Tessa put a hand to her tangled hair and swallowed hard. "Yeah. I was just getting in the shower. What's up?"

"I feel like we've been passing each other by lately. I thought I'd come over for breakfast."

"You mean you forgot to go to the grocery store again?"

"No," he said, but she noticed he had a piece of leftover fried chicken in his hand. Breakfast, indeed.

"Well, maybe we can catch up over lunch today." Not that she had any intention of meeting him for lunch.

"I'm kind of running late this morning." She gestured toward her door. That turned out to be a mistake.

Eric narrowed his eyes at the door, as if he'd just realized it was closed. And why would a woman who lived alone need to close her bedroom door?

Then the shower turned off. The fall of water hadn't seemed very loud, but the absence of it created a vacuum of sound that rang in her ears.

Tessa's skin went numb, even as her muscles turned to painful knots. Eric was only a foot away from her. She had a front row seat to the emotions that chased across his face. Confusion, alarm, worry and then hard, cold fury. His pale gaze swept down her robe, which she belatedly realized was her summer robe: pale silver and silky and sensual.

"Who is he?" he growled.

"Eric," she said, putting her hands to his chest when he reached toward the door. "I'm not a kid anymore."

"I'll kill him." His voice was so low it scared her.

"Don't be ridiculous," she said.

He reached past her. Tessa grabbed his wrist, but his hand was already turning the knob. As the door swung inward, Luke's voice flowed into the hall with perfect clarity.

"Tessa, I used your towel. I hope that's okay."

She watched helplessly as Eric's eyes went wide. He bared his teeth as if he were a guard dog. Tessa did the only thing she could think of. She pushed him back into the hallway. Hard. "It's none of your business."

"What?" Luke called, but then she felt his presence at her back, and her brother's eyes narrowed to slits.

"Shit," Luke breathed so softly she barely heard it.

"Yeah," she whispered back. Warm humidity snuck past her limbs as steam left the bathroom. She didn't have to look back to know he was wearing a towel and nothing else. She could see it in the furious hatred on Eric's face.

"Eric," she said calmly. "Go. We'll talk about this later."

"You're kidding me, right?" he barked. "I'm not going anywhere!"

"Yes, you are. This is my house and my room, and you have to go now."

Eric ignored her, pointing at Luke as if he could kill him with the tip of his finger. "How the hell could you do this to her?"

"I didn't…" Luke started, but his words faded into a silence that pulled at them like weights.

"Go," she said to her brother as she backed into her bedroom. When he didn't move, she shut the door in his face. And then she locked it.

Eyes wide with horror, Tessa slowly turned to face Luke. He looked much grimmer than she'd hoped to see him this morning. "I'm so sorry," she whispered.

Eric's footsteps moved away from the door and Luke just stared at her until they faded. "Why don't I go talk to him," he finally suggested.

Tessa shook her head frantically. "No way. I'll talk to him. I just…"

"You might want to mention that you weren't…"

She waved him off. "Yeah. I know. I just need to find a way to ease him away from being mad at you."

"Ha!" Luke shook his head. "That's not going to happen. I'm hoping to find a way to get to work without a black eye."

"He won't hit you."

"Uh, he'd be happy to hit me right now, Tessa. Best-case scenario, he knows exactly what we did last night."

"Oh." She felt her cheeks start to burn.

"Yeah, exactly. Worst case, he knows what we did last night and he thinks I bullied you into it. So yeah, he's capable of violence."

She nodded and hurried to her dresser to pull on sweats and a T-shirt. "Okay, wait here. And, you know…" She waved toward his bare chest. "Get dressed."

"Yes, ma'am."

"Your clothes are under the bed. And check the closet, too."

Tessa slipped into the hallway, trying to pat her hair down as she snuck toward the living room. If one brother thought she was a complete innocent, then the other did, too. She'd played her role too well, damn it. Now, how was she going to spin her way out of this one?

She expected to find him brooding on the couch, but instead Eric stood next to the front door with his arms crossed. When she took a few steps closer, she realized why he hadn't taken a seat. The clothes that Luke had pulled off her last night were still strewn across the floor in front of the couch.

Crap.

Her feet slowed until she stopped. They stared at each other.

Eric spoke first. "You don't know anything about this guy."

"I do," she said.

His jaw tightened as his eyes darted to the couch and back to her. "I'm sorry to tell you this after…after you…"

"For God's sake, Eric. I've dated for a long time. College, high school—"

"High school?" he screeched.

"I don't mean that! I just…" She squeezed her eyes shut in frustration. "I just meant I don't need protecting. I'm fine."

Eric hung his head as if the weight of the world were pulling down on him. When he looked up, his eyes held sorrow. "Luke Asher's partner is pregnant with his child."

She was hit with such relief she actually smiled. "No, that's not true. Simone is just his partner. The baby isn't his, Eric."

He narrowed his eyes.

"I'm serious."

"Well, that's hardly the only—"

The door of her bedroom opened, and Eric cut himself off and looked toward the hallway. Tessa turned to see Luke step into the room. "Eric," he said neutrally.

Her brother didn't answer. When she looked at him, he growled, "We'll talk about this later," before he opened the door and left. She watched the door until she heard his car start.

"See?" she finally said. "No black eye."

Luke's arms were suddenly curving around her. "Are you okay?"

She pressed her face to his shirt. "I'm fine. Honest. But I'm not sure Eric's okay. And what about you?"

"Me? Hell, even a brother bent on righteous murder can't ruin my good mood this morning."

Tipping her face up to kiss his neck, Tessa smiled at the smell of her soap and shampoo.

"Crap. I'm late." But even as he said it, his fingers spread and smoothed up and down her back.

"Okay." She pressed one last kiss to the warmth of his neck. "You go."

"I feel like I should hang around. That was a big night, with you becoming a woman and all."

Tessa pushed him away with a growl. "You're worse than my brothers."

"Not true. I adjusted to reality a *lot* better than they will. I think I showed admirable courage in the line of duty."

She raised one eyebrow. "Wow. You might deserve an award."

"Oh, I think I do." He stepped closer, sneaking his arms around her waist.

"Good," she said, pressing herself into his hard

body. "I've got a whole box of them in my closet just for this situation. Well…half a box after last year. It was a good one."

Luke smiled, then grinned, then he threw his head back and laughed. Tessa just stood there smiling like an idiot. He had a gorgeous laugh, deep and booming. She put her ear to his chest to listen to the rumble, and then his heartbeat, and finally his sigh.

"I really do have to go," he whispered against the top of her head. "I've got to catch some bad guys. Or at least do a lot of paperwork."

She kissed his chest. "You watch too much TV."

He laughed again, and kissed her, and Tessa's skin was still tingling when he left. Maybe it was a good thing that her brothers knew about Luke, because Tessa liked him more than she'd liked any of the men they hadn't known about. Maybe way more. She touched her lips where they felt sparkly with heat and smiled against her own fingers.

Or maybe she just watched too much TV.

CHAPTER TWELVE

TESSA OPENED THE BACK door of the brewery as quietly as she could and slipped into the kitchen. It was empty, thank God. She tiptoed across the gray tile and edged her head around the hallway. Eric's door was halfway open, and she could see his desk and one of his hands typing on the keyboard.

Holding her breath, she rushed past the hallway and pushed through the double doors to the front room. Jamie was just taking the chairs down from the tables after vacuuming.

"Jamie!" she whispered. "I need to talk to you."

He rounded on her with wide eyes. "*You* need to talk to *me?*"

"Yes—"

"Are you kidding me? You *slept* with him. You slept with him after I told you not to!"

"Come on. You don't get to tell me who to sleep with."

"I do, too!" he shouted.

Tessa shook her head frantically and rushed at him to put her hand over his mouth. "Be quiet! Eric will hear you."

"Oh, he wants to speak to you, too, believe me." His

words were slightly muffled by her hand, but at least he wasn't yelling.

She set Jamie free and wiped her hand on her pants. "This isn't about Luke."

"Luke," he spat.

"Listen! You didn't call me back yesterday. I talked to Kendall. I think I might be able to get him back on board."

"I— *What?*"

She nodded. "He's agreed to think about it for a few days. But we still need a backup plan."

He looked suspicious instead of enthusiastic. "What kind of backup plan?"

"Something to offer Eric if this falls through. Something that'll help him forget about High West. What about your idea to turn the barroom into more of a pub? Sandwiches and burgers and stuff?"

"Oh, yeah. I forgot you weren't around when I suggested that. He basically told me I was trying to ruin the place and drive us into bankruptcy while I was at it."

Tessa cringed at the leftover fury in Jamie's voice.

"So I don't think that's a suitable distraction."

"Okay," she said, dropping it and moving on to her next idea. "What about that vendor who—" Before she could finish her question, Jamie looked up and coughed.

Tessa turned and found herself facing Eric. He stared at her with icy eyes, and in that moment, Tessa was a girl facing her father. A father who'd seen something he really, really shouldn't have. She clasped her fingers in front of her and swallowed hard.

Eric crossed his arms and stared her down. "I don't know why you snuck past me to talk to Jamie about it. He's just as pissed as I am."

She swallowed one more time, reset her spinning mind, then put her shoulders back. "Neither of you has anything to be pissed about. As a matter of fact, I'm pissed at Jamie." She stepped back so she could keep both of them in her sight, but Jamie was still wearing a leftover expression of confusion from the interrupted conversation. "You had no right to talk to Luke about my sex life."

That got his mind off the discussion of a new deal. Jamie's eyes nearly bugged from his head. "You told me you didn't *have* a sex life!"

"I did not! I've never said a darn thing to either of you about that."

Jamie pointed his finger at her. "You said you weren't engaged in anything."

Eric jerked his chin up. "It's true. You said that."

"I meant I wasn't doing anything that would get me pregnant right at that moment."

"Oh," Jamie snapped, "but you are *now?*"

"For God's sake, Jamie, you don't get to talk to me about saving myself for marriage, all right?" He paled a little and she rounded on Eric. "And you! When was the last time you had sex? We should have an in-depth conversation about it, because apparently I'm supposed to protect you from that."

As if her two brothers were complete opposites

in every regard, Eric's face flamed to bright red. "I don't… You… That's none of your business."

"Exactly."

Eric cleared his throat and examined his shoes. "So… You didn't just let Luke spend the night on your couch?"

"What?"

He shrugged. "I thought there was a chance. Maybe he needed a place to stay."

Good Lord. She really had kept up her charade with too much skill. He thought of her as a seventeen-year-old girl. Actually… Tessa thought back to her senior year in high school and revised the age down to sixteen.

But even though she hadn't been sixteen in a long time, it had seemed easier to hold on to that charade. Easier for Tessa and, more importantly, easier for Eric. "We shouldn't even be talking about this," she muttered.

"I don't want to talk about it, either, but it's not just about you doing…stuff."

Tessa covered her eyes.

"It's about Luke. He's not the guy for you."

"I told you—"

Jamie jumped in. "It's not just his partner. Has he bothered to mention his divorce?"

Tessa tried not to let her shock show. No, he hadn't said anything about a divorce, but was she truly surprised? "We haven't discussed previous relationships. It's not that serious yet."

Eric snorted in disgust.

"His divorce is his business," she insisted.

Jamie and Eric exchanged a look and the weight of it made her uncomfortable.

"Wait, he *is* divorced, right? You're not saying he's married?"

"No," Eric said, but he stared at Jamie until Jamie finally nodded. And then Eric turned and left the room.

"What's going on?" Tessa actually felt afraid. She was starting to worry that his ex-wife had been injured in a mysterious accident involving a malfunctioning brake line.

Jamie dropped into a chair and signaled her to join him. Tessa lowered herself carefully down, perching on the very edge of the seat.

"I didn't want to tell you this."

She made a hurry-up gesture.

"He married a girl he met in school. I don't know anything about the marriage, but a few years ago, she got sick."

"Oh, no!"

"Breast cancer."

Tessa pressed both her hands to her mouth to smother her gasp. "Did she… But you said he was divorced."

"Yeah," Jamie said flatly. "He left her. While she was sick."

She didn't respond for a moment. It was just too ridiculous to take in. What kind of man would do that? Not the kind of man who was eaten up with worry over his partner's pregnancy. "No," she said simply. "It didn't happen that way."

"It did."

"Jamie, you know him. He'd never do that."

"Tessa, I know him as a guy I used to party with. We didn't get into a lot of deep discussions about marriage and morality."

"Well, it's not true," she snapped.

Jamie sighed and pressed his fingers to his temples. "Don't be one of those girls, Tessa. Please."

She'd pushed her chair out, but she froze at his words and put her hands flat to the table. "One of what girls?"

"Tessa." His mouth flattened with disappointment. "Come on. 'It's not his baby, he didn't leave his wife, nobody understands him, he's really a great guy.'"

Tessa gasped in horror. "I'm not that girl!"

"Good, because we haven't raised you to put up with being stepped on."

"Oh, please. You didn't raise me."

Now it was Jamie's turn to look outraged. "Hey, I did my part."

She could see that she'd hurt his feelings and backtracked. "Okay. You're great at being a big brother. An obnoxious big brother."

"Fine," he snapped. "But it'd better fall under big brother duties to beat the shit out of Luke Asher the next time I see him, because that's happening."

Still feeling bad for her careless words, Tessa walked around to the back of his chair to put her arms around him. "No hitting. Stay out of it." She kissed his cheek as he grumbled. "I need to get to work," she said, and let him go.

"Wait a minute! What exactly did Kendall say?"

"Shh!" she scolded as she hurried out of the bar area. Tessa rushed to her office and shut the door, then leaned against it with a groan. When had her life started spiraling? Granted, she was always busy with keeping Jamie happy and Eric calm and her work on track and her love life private. But the reward for all that work was supposed to be smooth sailing, not twenty-four-hour insanity.

And now her stomach burned with anxious hurt over Luke. Could she have misread him so badly? He seemed like such a good guy inside that hard exterior. Was that just an act? She hated to admit it, but Jamie had a point. How many women did she know who refused to see the truth that was so evident to everybody else?

One of her best friendships had been ruined because of stupidity over a man. Over Jamie, actually. Her friend Grace had developed a bad habit of falling madly in love with the wrong men. Jamie had only been in the wrong place at the wrong time. He'd flirted with Grace, as he flirted with everyone, and the girl had tumbled head over heels into stalkerlike love. A few weeks later, when she'd been banned from the brewery for behavior that fell comfortably into the stalking category, she'd finally moved on to a married man who promised he planned to leave his wife soon.

Pure delusion.

Had Tessa picked up that baton and started seeing things in Luke that didn't exist? She was almost sure she hadn't…but that was just another symptom, wasn't it?

She tried to shake it off. After all, she'd had sex with the man; she hadn't married him. Regardless of whether he was an asshole or not, he damn sure knew his way around a woman's body. She'd walked away more than happy. That's all it needed to be.

She smoothed her T-shirt down and took a deep breath, then sat down to go through the invoices awaiting her attention. She processed them as quickly as possible, because she needed to carve out time for some secret number crunching. If Jamie's idea to add food to the bar menu wouldn't make Eric happy, then Tessa had to work extra hard on the Kendall deal. She'd run the High West numbers for Eric months ago, but what if she could nudge them a little bit? Sweeten the pot for Roland Kendall? Excitement urged her on, the feeling that she could make this right. She could fix it. She always did.

Yes, there was definitely some wiggle room in the numbers. Not much, but a little. And if she served them up to Kendall on a silver platter, with garnish, and a big, confident smile…?

A feeling of impending triumph kept her grinning as she closed the spreadsheet. Determined to keep the feeling going, she opened her Twitter feed and read all the compliments women had left for Jamie. The public had a great affection for his bare legs, not to mention a burning curiosity about what he wore under his kilt.

She ignored all that—it wasn't her job to flirt on his behalf—and posted a new message.

If enough people request "Danny Boy" tonight, maybe I'll dust off the old vocal chords.

Ha. He hated that song. She wished she could hang around to see it.

But the lightness of her mood didn't last. The hard strike of a knock on her door wiped her smile clean. "Come in," she said warily.

Eric pushed the door open, but seemed hesitant to walk in. "Hey," he said. He raised a hand to show the stack of envelopes he held. "Bills," he said unnecessarily.

"Thanks."

He stepped in and put them on the edge of her desk, then immediately stepped back.

Tessa was torn. On one hand, she wanted to apologize to him for this morning, to assure him that everything was fine and he didn't have to worry about her. He *never* had to worry about her. That was the point of everything she did.

On the other hand, she wanted to ask for her key and tell him not to drop in anymore. But she knew she wouldn't do that. That house had belonged to their parents. Frankly, it still belonged to all of them, though her brothers had tried to sell her their shares at a laughably low price. How could she refuse him entrance to their family home? Better just to conduct any sexual liaisons at the man's house instead.

"I'm sorry," she said, but Eric only shook his head.

"No, I'm sorry. You're an adult and you don't need my permission to…" He waved his hand. "Do…anything. I've just been stressed out."

"Why? What's wrong?"

"That bastard Kendall has started ignoring my calls again."

Tessa's heart dropped. "Oh," she managed to push out past her closing throat.

"We've already drawn up the final contract. All we need to do is sign it! What the hell does he think he's doing?"

Tessa had to gulp down a deep breath in order to speak. "Maybe he's… Maybe he's not even in town."

"Yeah, he's out of town, but he's not answering his cell phone, either."

"He's probably busy. It's not like he hasn't done this before."

Eric didn't look anything close to convinced. "It doesn't feel right. Before he was trying to make me work for this deal. But now we have an agreement."

"Well, don't keep calling him," she said in a rush. "You're just going to piss him off."

"He's already pissed *me* off," Eric grumbled. "You know what? I think I'll call Monica."

"What?"

Eric's eyes finally focused on her, and Tessa realized that her screech of horror might have been a little suspicious. "What's wrong with calling Monica?"

"Um, aside from a couple of business dinners, all your dealings have been with Roland."

"Yeah, but maybe it's time to take a new tack. She's been much more positive about it from the start."

"He won't like it," she said in a rush. "You know how much he likes to be in charge."

"Well, I'm sick of this shit. I just want to get this contract signed, so we can start phase two."

"Phase two?"

"Full western distribution. We've talked about this."

Tessa felt slightly light-headed at exactly what was at risk here. Eric had a plan and it was lying in her hands right now, already dying, and he had no idea. "Right. Phase two," she murmured. "I just didn't know you had a name for it."

"I'm going to call Monica," he said, already moving toward his office.

"Wait," she squeaked. Then she yelled it louder and scrambled out from behind her desk. "Eric!" She caught up with him as he was sliding into his chair. "Luke came by the brewery last night to talk to you, not me. You should call him."

His hand had been reaching for the phone, but it froze as if she'd hooked him up to a live wire. "What?" he snapped. "Are you insane? You want to get me arrested for threatening a cop?"

"He had news about the break-in."

Eric sighed and ran a hand through his hair. "Damn it, Tessa. I'd rather the brewery be robbed a hundred times than let you be involved with a man who's going to hurt you. So no, I do not want to talk to Luke right now. Or ever. Got it?"

This time when her throat closed, it was with tears instead of anxiety. Everything Eric did, he did because he loved them. He might be difficult and humorless and controlling, but he did it for his brother and sister and he always had. "Okay," she whispered before stepping back. She didn't go to her office, though. Instead, she leaned against the wall and held her breath as Eric picked up the phone. She heard him push the buttons. She even heard the faint chirp of the phone ringing on the other end.

Tessa held her breath and told herself that Monica Kendall wasn't going to tell Eric what had happened. The woman was a businessperson; she couldn't possibly explain what had gone wrong and still maintain her dignity. Still, when Eric started leaving a message, Tessa nearly sobbed with relief.

She walked toward the front room to grab Jamie and shake him. Unfortunately, there were two men at the bar, waiting for Jamie to draw pints. Before he could turn and see that she was upset, Tessa backed up and retreated to her office once again.

Hadn't she just been congratulating herself? Now her life was spiraling out of control again, and she couldn't even lean on Jamie. He'd been convinced from the start that Eric should know the truth. Idiot. She should go to Monica Kendall. Tessa should've done that from the start.

Before anyone came looking for her again, Tessa grabbed her purse and her phone, and headed for the door. The High West offices were near the Denver airport, but she could take the toll road and avoid traffic. And with the new awkwardness between her and her brothers, they might not open her office door for hours.

She drove toward the airport as if she were fleeing something. Not her family, not even Luke, but the weight of the choices she was making. The burden of hoping she was doing the right thing. She wanted it to be right, so she drove fast and hard, playing music so she wouldn't have to think. She rolled the windows down so she couldn't hear the thoughts the music didn't drown out.

The air changed from crisp and cool in the shadow of the mountains to heavy and warm on the plains north of Denver. She could tell a storm was coming long before she saw the black clouds rolling up from the south. She'd get a nice lightning show on the drive home.

Thinking about the weather got her the rest of the way to the High West office, and Tessa walked in without thinking what she would say. The desperation of this act told her everything she needed to know about her chances, but Tessa merely smiled and stopped before the receptionist.

"Hi, I'm Tessa Donovan of Donovan Brothers Brewery. Is Monica Kendall in?"

"She's at lunch at the moment—"

The door whooshed open behind Tessa, and she turned to see Monica Kendall walk in with another woman. They were laughing, seemingly carefree, and Tessa felt a sharp jolt of dislike for Monica. Her black hair bounced as she walked, her head was thrown back and her Hollywood-white teeth glowed as she laughed. How could she be so damned happy? Surely she knew the problems she and Jamie had caused.

Tessa was happy to see Monica's smile falter when they finally locked eyes.

"Oh," Monica said. She waved her friend on, and stopped before Tessa.

"Hi. Can we talk?"

Monica shrugged. "Why not?"

No, Tessa didn't like her at all. She'd met her before, but it had been in an organized setting, and all Tessa had registered was Monica's model-like thinness and sharp beauty. Now she saw that her beauty wasn't the only thing sharp about her.

She strode down a hallway without another word, so Tessa followed, admiring Monica's pale gray linen suit despite herself. A glance down at her own outfit made Tessa wince. Working in a bar, it was easiest to come across as the girl next door, but now she wished she was wearing heels and a dress. Another reason to resent Monica Kendall.

As they walked into a big office, Monica took a seat behind a huge mahogany desk. "What can I do for you?"

Tessa took an uninvited seat in one of the brown leather armchairs and decided there was no point beating around the bush. So to speak. "Your father is ready to walk away from this deal. We both know why."

Monica leaned back in her chair. "And?"

"*And?* And I want you to help me get this train back on the tracks."

Monica just stared at her.

"Don't you want to work with our company?"

"Sure," she answered, as if she didn't give a damn.

Tessa gritted her teeth and tried to hold on to her temper. "Then perhaps you could speak to your father about this. After seeing Jamie leaving your house, your dad isn't exactly eager to do business with us. But maybe you could talk him into it."

Her laughter was back, but this time Monica sounded more bitter than amused. "Why would you think my father would listen to a word I say?"

"Because you're the vice president of High West Air?"

"Oh, sure," she sneered. "I'm vice president, but Daddy's the president."

"Exactly. He made you vice president, so he obviously respects your input—"

"You're kidding, right?"

Tessa blinked. "Noo…"

"Look around, Tessa. Does this look like my office?"

"Um." Tessa glanced around at the dark bookshelves and tall curtains. The artwork on the walls was a little generic and masculine, but…

"My dad designed this office, just like he designed the whole business. He chose the name, the logo, the mission statement, the routes, the planes, the executives, the long- and short-term goals—"

"Look," Tessa interrupted, "I understand what that's like. My brother Eric is the same way. He—"

"No," Monica snapped. "It is not the same thing.

I go to the meetings my dad tells me to. I deal with the clients he wants me to deal with. He ignores my suggestions and scoffs at my ideas. I make no decisions and I make no difference, and he can fire me at any time. Does that sound like your little family business?"

Tessa suddenly couldn't help but be hyperaware of how tiny Monica looked sitting in her tall leather chair behind her giant mahogany desk. Her sharpness now looked less like pure meanness and more like defensiveness. "You and Jamie made a mistake. I get that. But I can't be the only person trying to fix it. I need help. If you could just try…"

"I wouldn't call it a mistake," Monica said. "It was something I wanted to do, and I did it."

That was a little impersonal, but Tessa held out her hands. "Please. Just tell your father that whatever happened between you and my brother will have no effect on the business relationship."

"Sure. Fine. But it won't help. My dad has very rigid beliefs, and he's stubborn as all hell. He's managed to build an empire by being unmovable. How that happened is a complete mystery to me, but there you have it."

"But you'll talk with him?"

"Sure," she said with a smirk. "Whatever you want. But don't get your hopes up."

"Thank you." Tessa stood, but hesitated before leaving. "Um, and if you could avoid telling Eric anything about this? That would be great."

Monica finally offered a genuine smile. "Oh, that's the way it is, huh? Sure. I won't say a word."

Tessa left, and with every step, she told herself she was doing the right thing. She was. She was sure of it.

CHAPTER THIRTEEN

LUKE KEPT A CLOSE eye on Simone as he followed her to the car. Corpses always made him feel slightly sick no matter how many he saw, and with Simone in the state she was in... Surely her skin looked a little gray. But though he kept close in case she wobbled, Simone walked on without faltering once.

It probably helped that the death hadn't been a homicide. They'd investigate further before making a final determination, but the drug paraphernalia surrounding the body indicated a more solitary tragedy.

"I got a message from the tech department," he said as they neared the car.

"Please tell me it's a hit on the video of the keg?"

"Bingo. A white car dropped it off, but apparently the license plate is out of frame."

"Damn," she huffed. "I already checked with the building next door. They've only got video surveillance inside. And the camera on the business across the street is pointed in the wrong direction."

Luke cursed. "You know what we're going to have to do."

"I'm trying not to think about it," Simone said, putting a hand to the small of her back with a grimace.

VICTORIA DAHL   151

There were lots of businesses on the street that fed
to the alley, and most of those places had cameras of
some kind. Every one would have a different angle,
and they knew from bitter experience that every feed
would have a slightly different time stamp, too. Luke
and Simone were going to spend a lot of hours col-
lecting video feed, and unless they wanted to wait a
year for tech to go through them all, they were going
to spend time staring at monitors. His eyes hurt just
thinking about it, and Simone was obviously prepping
for back pain.

But it was a lead.

"We'd better start praying for a fingerprint on that
keg." Simone sighed. She was reaching for the car
door, when someone caught her eye. "Can you wait
a sec? Shelly wanted some advice about applying for
detective next year. I forgot to call her back."

"Sure."

Simone walked over to one of the uniforms and
Luke waited next to the car, staring down at the little
creek that ran through a gully just past the parking
lot.

He opened his phone, telling himself he wasn't
hoping for a message from Tessa. Even when he found
no message, he smiled. She'd put him in a damn good
mood. It didn't hurt that he kept catching her scent.
After using her shampoo, he smelled like kiwi and
citrus, and he'd been sure everyone could tell. Simone
had caught him smiling once and raised an eyebrow,
but she hadn't said anything about his fruity smell.

He should thank Tessa's brother for the drop-in this

morning. If Eric hadn't put a damper on the situation, Luke would be strolling around whistling show tunes and slapping random strangers on the back.

The fact that he hadn't lost any of his good mood after being called to a death scene was a testament to Tessa's powers. Maybe he'd absorbed some of her happiness by sleeping next to her for eight hours. Or maybe having the best sex of his life was enough to cheer a guy up.

Hell, he didn't even regret not waking her up this morning. He'd meant to. He'd even smoothed her hair back from her shoulder and kissed her spine just the way he'd planned the night before. But she'd sighed and curled up like a kitten, and Luke had found himself watching her sleep. In retrospect, that was either creepy or pitiful, or both. But Luke was in such a good mood, he didn't care.

Just as he glanced up to see if Simone was ready, his phone rang and flashed Tessa's name.

"Hey," he said past a grin. "How'd it go with Eric?"

"Ugh. I don't want to talk about it. We reached a truce, but you'd better avoid both my brothers for a little while."

"Trust me, I'll do my best."

"Listen, I'm just about to leave. I figured you were off by now…?"

"We're out on a late call. I've got to check in at the station and then I'm free. Can I take you out to dinner?" *Too soon,* the male ego inside him shouted. *Too soon!* He wouldn't have taken his internal alarm too seriously except that Tessa hesitated over the invitation.

Luke glared at the water that rushed over piles of stones.

Finally, Tessa said, "Sure. I'll meet you at the station."

"Oh." He blinked and glanced at Simone. But what the hell? Simone certainly wasn't going to raz him. "Okay. No problem. You know where it is?"

"Sure, I'm in and out of jail all the time."

"I had my suspicions. All right, I'll meet you at my car in a half hour."

Twenty minutes later, he pulled into the parking lot and spotted Tessa right away. The sight of her in her ponytail and brewery shirt made him smile, but when he realized what he was doing he snapped his mouth straight. It was no use. The smile was back as he walked toward her and saw the way she brightened up when she saw him.

Still, instead of greeting him, she held her hand out to Simone.

"Hi!" she said brightly. "I'm Tessa Donovan."

Luke cleared his throat. "Simone, you remember Tessa from the brewery."

Simone said hello, and when Tessa reached to touch his arm, Simone looked at him with raised eyebrows.

"So," he said, but then he couldn't think of anything more to say.

Simone's eyes twinkled even as her mouth went

suspiciously flat. "I'll go wrap up the paperwork. It's my turn."

"If you're sure…?"

"Oh, it's no problem." Yeah, she was definitely trying not to laugh as she reached for the door. "Nice to see you again, Ms. Donovan."

The whole scene was decidedly odd, and Luke was still trying to figure it out when Tessa stepped back and clasped her hands in front of her. "It's such a nice night," she said. "I thought maybe we could go for a walk."

"Really?" The storm had blown through just an hour before, and the air was still heavy with moisture. It was an odd night—and place—for a walk.

His spidey senses tingled, and Luke realized he'd been slow on the uptake. Great sex had clouded his normal pessimism, but now he could see this whole setup was off. Her hesitation when he'd asked her to dinner, her request to meet him here, even the way she'd reached for his arm a few seconds ago.

Luke tilted his head toward the paved trail across the street. "Sure," he said evenly. "We can walk."

"Great!" Tessa's voice was cheerful. Suspiciously cheerful for anyone else, but her good moods were too frequent to gauge.

By the time they reached the path, Luke was scowling at the blacktop. Tessa didn't say a word; she simply strolled next to him, her eyes touching on everything but him. Only some of the aspens were thick with leaves, but it still felt secluded as they walked farther along the trail, which snaked through a business park.

When Tessa finally spoke, she said nothing. "It's a nice night."

Luke spared her a look of disbelief, but Tessa kept her eyes straight ahead. "You know I'm a cop, right?"

She laughed too loudly. "Of course."

"So it's not hard for me to tell when a woman has something on her mind."

"Oh."

Luke stopped and crossed his arms. "How about we get this over with?"

Her ponytail bobbed when she stopped, the ends of her hair brushing her neck. He felt a sharp stab of regret that he hadn't spent nearly enough time exploring her body, because he had a sneaking suspicion he'd missed his only chance.

Tessa turned and crossed her arms to match his pose. Then she cleared her throat and shifted her weight to the other leg. "Um… About your divorce…"

"That bastard," he muttered. "Christ. I take it you talked to Jamie."

"Is it true?"

"Is what true?"

Her eyes slid away. "What he told me about your divorce."

"I am divorced, yes."

"Luke." She sighed.

But Luke wasn't in a mood to concede anything. He was furious, though he couldn't quite identify the source of his fury. The fact that her brother had been the one to tell her about the divorce. That Jamie had fed her a lie. Or that she might believe it.

Luke narrowed his eyes and clenched his teeth until his jaw jumped.

Tessa finally gave in and spoke. "He said you left your wife."

He waited.

She raised her chin. "When she had cancer."

"I didn't."

"Good!" Her face went bright again. "That's what I told him!"

"But you didn't really believe that."

"I did. I told him you'd never do that."

"Thanks. I wouldn't. But if you didn't believe him, why are you asking me if it's true?"

"Well…because I think you're a good guy obviously, or I wouldn't have slept with you. But I haven't known you as long as Jamie, so…"

"Ah. Well, Jamie and I weren't quite as intimate."

"You know what I mean. You've known him for years."

"No. I knew him years ago. There's a difference. Clearly."

She nodded. "Okay. I'm sorry. So your divorce… It was already happening?"

"I don't want to talk about it."

His words immediately returned the stiffness to her spine. She snapped straight and frowned at him. "What do you mean?"

"I mean what I said. I don't want to talk about it."

"Ever?"

"Well, certainly not right after you asked me if I walked out on my sick wife."

"Luke, that's not fair. Only an idiot wouldn't have asked you after hearing that story."

"Fine. But that doesn't mean I'm in the mood to talk about my feelings right now. Got it?" He spun on his heel and started back the way they'd come.

"Hey!" she called, her footsteps quick behind him. "What was I supposed to think? I didn't even know you'd been married!"

His steps slowed to a stop. Tessa caught up with him and met his gaze. "I don't know what you were supposed to think, Tessa. But I do know, for example, that there's something going on with you and your family. You and Jamie are hiding something from Eric. Something you feel guilty about. But I didn't immediately think, 'Oh, maybe they're embezzling money from the company.'"

"What?" she gasped.

"You see, I like you, so I give you the benefit of the doubt."

"I did the same for you."

"Oh? So why did you make a point of putting yourself in front of Simone tonight?"

Tessa blinked and took a nervous step back. "I don't know what you're talking about."

"Really? Because it seemed like you were making damn sure she saw your hand on my arm, making a point that you had the right to touch me."

Pink floated up her neck, then her jaw. By the time

it reached her cheeks, Luke was resenting just how pretty she looked when she felt guilty.

"So even though you'd already asked about Simone, you weren't quite sure you believed me."

"I'm a woman," she whispered. "And there are some men who'll lie about anything."

"You think I don't know that? Ninety percent of my job is dealing with men like that. So I get a little sensitive about being lumped in with them. And your brother is a…" Luke took a deep breath. "He's protective of you. I get that. But I already told him that story wasn't true."

"So what is true?"

He raised one eyebrow and stared her down. "How about you tell me what's going on with your family? Then I'll tell you about mine."

Her jaw stiffened. "I don't want to talk about that."

"That's what I thought." His anger was losing its energy, and now Luke just felt tired. The breeze picked up on a hard gust, and the bare branches swayed around them, sliding together with eerie sounds. "Come on," he said. "I'll walk you back to your car."

"But—" she stammered behind him, but Luke was moving on. He knew he could just say, "No big deal," and let it go. He could take her out to dinner again, maybe spend the night at her house. Or his.

She was a nice girl, after all. And she was right; it was only reasonable that she would be on guard against someone trying to take advantage of her. He'd be disappointed in her if she wasn't. But he was telling her the truth, even if he'd left out a few grisly details. And right now he just felt…*raw.* Maybe it was unfair to Tessa, but she had made him think of refuge. And now that refuge was gone.

Yeah, it wasn't her responsibility to carry his baggage, but that was just another good reason to walk away.

It only took seconds to reach the parking lot since they'd abandoned any pretense of a pleasant stroll. "I'm sorry," he said, pausing for only seconds at her car. "I've had a bad day, and I'm sorry you had to find out about my marriage that way, but… Our lives are too damn complicated individually, so let's just leave it at that."

She took her keys out of her pocket and unlocked her car. "We'll see." Her clipped words radiated anger, but he couldn't help that.

"Bye, Tessa," he said. She slid into her car without a response, and when she drove off, a little German barmaid bobblehead nodded wildly from her back window.

Good God Almighty, the woman made him smile even when he was breaking it off with her. But this time, the smile edged more toward a grimace, and he was frowning by the time he walked back into the station. There was nothing left to do but work.

CHAPTER FOURTEEN

WHAT A TERRIBLE Tuesday. Truly awful. Worthy of a Monday status, really.

Tessa had way too much to do. She had to call the Kendall Group to find out when Roland Kendall was back in town. Then she had to ask the Donovan Brothers attorney about what it would take to revise the contract if she wanted to change the deal. Lastly, she wanted to call Monica just to check in and see how the conversation had gone with her father. Plus there was all her regular work at the brewery.

So what was she doing sitting in her car in the parking lot of an erotic boutique? Oh, she'd been in the White Orchid before, but she'd never gone in with the express purpose of finding a way to seduce a man. A man who was pissed. A man who'd stared her down as if he didn't feel a thing for her.

Anger had kept her safe as she'd driven away. It had even sustained her long enough for her to stomp into her house and slam the door. But then she'd had a whole night to think. Then another night. Then a third and fourth. All that time alone had let her remember how weary Luke had sounded the first time she'd asked about Simone. Weary and sad. And just plain done.

Now she understood why. Because it wasn't the only lie he was living under.

Tessa knew she hadn't been wrong to ask about the divorce, but she could understand why he'd shut down. Her brothers had taught her a little bit about men, after all, and she knew that their thick skins could be a defense mechanism. They weren't as tough as they wanted the world to believe.

And despite Jamie's assertions, Tessa truly believed what Luke had said about his divorce. She didn't want to be one of those women who believed anything a man said. But she also didn't want to be one of those women who didn't trust her gut. Her gut said not to let it end like this. Her gut said that she should buy some hot lingerie, show up at his door and get him back into bed, quick. Actually, maybe that message was coming from a different body part.

"Whatever," she murmured as she got out of the car and walked into the shop. Happy music and the scent of lilac floated over her as the door closed behind her.

"Hello!" a girl called from behind the counter. Her sculpted bob was glossy black and gorgeous, and her shirtwaist dress was more housewife than sex-toy peddler. Tessa gave her a wave and started to browse.

The toys were in the back room, but if everything worked out well, Tessa wouldn't be needing any toys. So she wandered through the clothing racks, trying to spot something that would rock Luke's world.

She petted a cute red cheerleader skirt for a minute, but decided it might hit a little too close to the old virginity issue for Luke. Considering how he'd reacted to that, he probably wasn't into the cheerleader thing. Then again, he was a man. But it was best saved for another time. She moved on to a gorgeous white lace bustier, but white wasn't going to flatter her skin tone. But again…he was a man. Skin tone didn't really play into it.

Hmm. She held it up to her body, trying to picture herself. It was hot, but it felt a little too contrived. If she was going to wear a lace bustier, she'd have to go all out with big hair and painted fingernails and gallons of makeup. Then Luke would probably arrest her for solicitation.

She put the bustier down and headed for a corner of the store with slightly more muted colors. Suddenly she found herself in a dream world of silks and satins that felt magical under her fingertips. "Wow," she breathed, picking up a little camisole to look at the price tag. She squeaked and put it back down, then picked it up again. The label was something in French that she couldn't pronounce, but the pale pink silk felt almost weightless as she dragged it over her palm. The matching panties were beautifully cut, but maybe a little too modest for seduction, but Tessa couldn't resist taking the camisole to the fitting room, anyway. Maybe she'd buy this just for herself, and get something more revealing for tonight.

But when she took off her shirt and bra and slipped the camisole over her head, Tessa gasped in shock. Yes, the material was expensive and delicate and pretty. It was also erotically thin.

A shiver ran through her and her nipples peaked, and she could see the clear outline of them through the fabric. She could even see the darkness of her areolas. Suddenly she wasn't worried about how modest the bottoms might be. They were the same fabric and they wouldn't leave anything to the imagination. Screw the cost. She was buying the whole set.

She hurried over to the cash register with a big smile on her face. "Oh, my God," the salesclerk said. "Aren't those gorgeous? You've got great taste."

"Thank you. They're beautiful."

"It's a new line our manager brought in a couple of months ago. She's expanding the next order, so be sure to come in again in a few weeks."

"I will."

The girl wrapped up each piece in tissue paper, then looked up in surprise. "Oh, there she is now! That's Beth. She's the store manager."

Tessa turned to see a striking woman walking into the store. She was backlit by the sun for a moment, but that didn't take away from her long legs and curvy hips. This was a woman who didn't wear a size six and knew how to make that a compliment. Then the door closed behind her, and the woman's face came into view. Tessa frowned.

"Hi, Beth!" the salesclerk called. "We were just admiring the new collection. Everybody loves it."

When her eyes locked on Tessa's face, the woman stumbled a little, then caught herself and cleared her throat.

Beth. The name didn't strike a chord, but Tessa was

sure she'd seen her somewhere. She held out her hand. "Hi, I'm Tessa Donovan. Have we met before?"

"No!" the woman yelped.

Tessa dropped her hand in surprise.

"I mean… No. I'm sorry. I'm Beth Cantrell." She grabbed Tessa's hand and pumped it twice. "Thank you for coming into the store, Ms. Donovan."

"Oh, no problem," Tessa said, but she was talking to empty space. Beth Cantrell had already skirted around her and rushed toward the back room.

"Will this be cash or credit?" the girl behind the counter asked. Tessa handed the girl her credit card and frowned at the back room, wondering what had just happened. Weird.

And then something even weirder happened. Her phone rang, and the screen read "Kendall Group."

"Oh, God," she breathed. "I'm sorry, I have to take this." She answered the phone calmly, but her hand shook as she signed the credit slip.

"Ms. Donovan?" an unfamiliar voice said. "This is Graham Kendall."

"Who?" she asked in surprise.

"I'm Monica Kendall's brother. I was hoping we could get together for lunch today. Or maybe dinner?"

"Um…" Her brain spun at a million miles an hour. Graham Kendall. Monica's brother. Roland's son. "I'm sorry. Of course, I'd love to have lunch with you, but what did you want to talk about?" She waved a thank-you at the clerk, then grabbed her bag and rushed out of the store as if he could see where she was over the phone line. Not appropriate.

"Assuming my father refuses to budge on the High West issue—and I think we both know he won't—I might have an opportunity for you."

She thought fast, trying to figure out where Graham stood in his father's company. She couldn't place him. "All right. Sure. I'd love to have lunch with you."

He named a popular high-end place in Boulder and they agreed to meet at twelve. That would only give her two hours in the office before she had to duck out again. She'd wait to call Roland Kendall until after she met with his son. Then she'd get out of the brewery by seven, go home to shower and change and finagle her way back into Luke's arms.

Maybe this didn't have to be an awful day, after all.

THIS TIME, SHE'D remembered to bring a change of clothing to the brewery in case she ended up driving down to the Kendall Group offices again, so she felt completely confident when she walked into the restaurant wearing a sable-brown skirt and heels. It was nice to be seen without a logo attached to her breast as if she'd sold it for advertising space.

And for a moment, when she saw the man who stood as she approached the table, Tessa was glad she felt attractive. He was tall and handsome, and he offered a wide, white smile as she reached to shake his hand.

"Tessa, I'm Graham Kendall. It's a pleasure."

She shook his hand and took a seat, noticing he'd already ordered a bottle of wine and poured her a glass. Despite that she worked at a brewery, she wasn't actually up for a half a bottle of wine in the middle of the afternoon, but the gesture was nice.

In fact, everything about him was nice. He was handsome and perfectly groomed. Their small talk was polite and natural. But something about her first impression was inching away as the minutes passed. His smile was just a touch too wide, and though his skin was buffed and tanned, a slight gray tinge rode beneath it. Yeah, she'd take Luke with his slightly rumpled hair and worried scowls any day.

But dating material or not, this guy might have something she needed. "So," she ventured after they ordered their meals. "What did you want to talk about?"

"I heard my sister might have screwed over your deal with High West. So to speak."

She cringed. "I'm still hoping your father will reconsider."

"If there's one thing both my sister and I can assure you of, it's that my father isn't big on reconsidering."

"Maybe not, but he wasn't inclined to go with Donovan Brothers at first. He changed his mind about that. I don't see why he can't change his mind about this."

"I think it might be because your brother had sex with his daughter."

Yes, now his smile was definitely too wide. Tessa took a sip from her wine and tried to let the awkward moment pass. "Well, if you don't think he'll budge, what is it you wanted to meet about?"

"I'm not sure if you're familiar with all of the Kendall Group holdings, but in addition to some other duties, I'm president of Kendall Flight, which was my father's first foray into air travel. We lease and rent private luxury aircraft. We also offer what is essentially a time-share system that allows people to own partial shares of a private aircraft."

"How does that work?"

"Each individual investor purchases a share of the jet's flight time. Customers can get all the benefits of owning a private jet, without having to pay for the time that it'd normally be sitting in a hangar. Kendall Flight was one of the first companies in the U.S. to offer it."

"I've never heard of that. It's fascinating. How do you think our brewery could fit in?"

"Well, we cater to the needs of our clients, so we couldn't offer to carry Donovan Brothers beer exclusively, you understand. If a customer wants Corona, they get Corona."

"Of course."

"But we could certainly discuss the details of offering your product as part of our jet catering service."

Tessa felt her eyes widen. This might actually be a great idea. It might not offer quite the exposure of an exclusive deal with a nationwide, public airline, but it would get their beer into the hands of a wider audience. "How many customers do you serve annually?"

"We log sixty thousand passengers every year."

"Really?"

"Of course, each flight offers only the menu requested by the lessee, so I can't control which customers would place orders. But I can send you some numbers on other alcoholic beverages we offer."

"Absolutely. I'm intrigued."

"Wonderful," he said with another wolfish smile. This guy was a salesman through and through. "And I'd love to offer a tour of our facilities."

She couldn't tell if that was a come-on or a sincere offer, so she smiled noncommittally.

"There is one more opportunity I could offer…"

The waitress was already at the table with lunch, and Graham Kendall leaned back to give her space, but he kept his smile aimed in Tessa's direction. She grew worried that his next "opportunity" would involve becoming his mistress. Or buying a used car. Roland Kendall might be lacking in charm and smoothness, but Tessa was beginning to think she knew exactly where all the excess had landed.

She took a bite of her pasta and waited for the rest of the sales pitch. It didn't take long.

"Kendall Flight is sponsoring a big charity golf event. This is our second year and it's become my pet project. I've taken it upon myself to organize the cosponsors."

"Oh," she said, trying—and failing—to keep the wariness out of her voice. "We already sponsor a lot of local events. It's one of our main promotional vehicles, actually."

"Ah, but this won't be a local event. It's a golf tournament at a world-class resort in Palm Springs. California," he added, as if she wouldn't recognize the place.

"But we haven't pushed into California yet. It's a pretty crowded microbrew market. I'm not sure what benefit we'd achieve with promotion outside our market."

His smile oozed toward condescension. "Well, obviously this would be a great jumping-off point. If you reached the silver level of sponsorship, we'd serve your beer exclusively. But more than that…this isn't a local 10K or a volleyball tournament. These are business owners, influential people. And assuming you or one of your brothers was there to make new friends and rub shoulders… There's no telling what kind of deals you could open up."

Huh. Tessa was a bit dumbfounded to find herself influenced by his pitch. It actually might be a wonderful opportunity. But it was obviously going to be an expensive one. *Silver-level* expensive.

He pushed harder. "We're talking promo space, a stand or two. Coasters, napkins, the whole nine yards. And you'd be included on all the usual sponsor lists, of course. You'd be included in the brochure. Your branding would inevitably show up in photos of the event."

"It's an interesting idea, though I still hesitate to consider a California event. Why don't you send me all the information, and I can talk it over with my brothers after the dust settles on the High West problem."

"Well, that's the issue. We've already lined up all

the other sponsors. The promotional items are going to press in three days."

"I can't make a decision that quickly."

"Ms. Donovan—"

"Tessa, please."

"Tessa." His tone dripped sympathy. "My father is not going to do business with a man who screwed his precious little girl. I really can't make it more clear than that."

She drew back a bit in shock at this crudeness.

"I'm sorry, but that's the way he sees it, I guarantee you. But I know my sister a little better than my father, and I find it hard to take offense. Your family has a great company, and I think we'd work well together. I'd be honored to deal with you."

"Thank you. But I can't make that kind of decision so quickly. My brothers will need to be involved—"

He raised his eyebrows. "I was under the impression that you wanted to leave your brothers out of this."

"Pardon me?"

"Don't worry. I can keep a secret."

"That's not it at all," she lied. She didn't want this guy thinking he carried her family secret. "I'm trying to resolve the issue with your father before I bring Eric into this mess. That's it."

He held up his hands. "I understand. Believe me. Working with family can be a pain in the ass. My dad and I rarely see eye to eye."

She wanted to make clear that her brothers and her were fine. That they loved one another and she'd never speak about Eric with the kind of bitterness that

Monica had shown toward her father. But there was no way to say that without insulting Graham, so she pressed her lips together and held the words in.

"Regardless, I need to know in two days," he said.

"How much money are we talking?" She braced herself, waiting for a high number, but Graham just smiled again.

"I'll send you the breakdown and a list of the other sponsors. We haven't rolled it out yet, obviously, so I don't have confirmed attendees yet, but I can assure you it will be an impressive group. Names you would recognize. Last year's turnout was pretty spectacular."

"I can't promise anything, Graham."

He wiped his mouth and set his napkin on the table. "I get it. But if you're planning to expand—and I assume that's what you're working on—you're going to have to be more aggressive. Boulder isn't exactly where the big boys play."

"Our goals are obviously not as far-reaching as your family's," she snapped, "but we know exactly what we're doing." *And our relationships aren't nearly as screwed up as yours,* she left off.

"I don't mean to offend you, Tessa. I honestly don't. I just want you to take this opportunity seriously. Don't say no just because it's happening quickly. And all proceeds go to cancer research in honor of our grandmother."

She softened just slightly. "All right. Send me the information, and I'll give it some thought."

"Promise?" he asked, his eyes crinkling with charm.

She was interested in the both the charity event and the idea of supplying Kendall Flight, but Tessa still got out of there as quickly as she could. She fought off the need to stop home for a shower, but just barely.

CHAPTER FIFTEEN

"BRAXTON HICKS contractions…" Luke murmured as he squinted at the first page of the book that covered the third trimester of pregnancy. Did Simone know about this stuff? She'd been raised in foster care for most of her life, so she didn't have any family around to help her out. But he couldn't ask her if she knew about Braxton Hicks because there was no reason Luke should know about them. She'd likely be pissed if she found out he'd bought a few pregnancy books in a moment of weakness.

He glanced around the station room, making sure Simone hadn't magically appeared. She'd already gone home for the day—otherwise, Luke wouldn't have gotten the books out at all—but he had a few minutes to waste before the next DVD of surveillance video was ready. The old computer system couldn't handle viewing them over the network, so the tech department had been burning them in six-hour increments. Luke had already managed to scan three of them. Unfortunately, that wasn't as much progress as he'd like to think. He'd found nothing, and he was only a third of the way through.

Luke turned a few pages of the book, stopping at a

section about birth classes. "Shit," he breathed. He'd been so focused on figuring out who the father was that he hadn't even considered this part of it. Who was going to be there with her when she had the baby? A girlfriend, maybe? But Simone wasn't very social. She'd certainly never mentioned anything about hanging out with friends. Then again, she'd never mentioned a man, either, and clearly she'd been near one.

He needed to let this go, but his gut burned at the idea of stepping back. He'd grown up with a single mom, and he had a soft spot. He'd hated the way his mom had struggled and the guilt she'd felt that Luke's father had left. He could still remember every time she'd apologized to him, and how much he'd hated his father in those moments.

Simone didn't deserve to be alone any more than his mother had. She didn't deserve to be stressed and secretive and angry.

He grimaced in frustration, rolling his shoulders to try to release some tension. The question of who the father was still ate at him. He was a damn detective, after all. It was his job to work through mysteries and solve them. But presented with a very basic question, he proved completely incompetent.

Glancing toward the phone, he resisted the need to call Tessa to talk to her about it. It wasn't the first time he'd had that urge today. Ridiculous to think he could miss somebody he'd only known for a week.

Shaking it off, Luke told himself he was only horny and got back to studying, but just as he turned another page, a shadow fell over him. Luke jumped and looked up into the face of his boss. Sergeant Pallin looked shaken by the sight of the book, and Luke fought the urge to shove it under his papers and wipe his hands on his pants.

He knew the sergeant had heard the same stories as everyone else. The book probably just confirmed the rumors, but Pallin pulled his eyes from it and inclined his head toward Luke's monitor. "Still reviewing tape?"

"Yeah. No hits yet, but it's there somewhere."

"Good. And the Denver files?"

"Still slogging through those, too. There are a couple of things missing from some of them. I'll need to check with Denver again."

"All right. Let me know what you find." His eyes flicked to the book again, but he put his hands in his pockets and walked back to his office. Apparently he didn't want to open up a can of sticky personnel issues.

"Fine with me," Luke muttered. He rolled his shoulders one last time, slipped the book back into his desk and went to go harass the tech department. He'd already got word that there were no usable fingerprints on the keg. It had been wiped clean. So he really, really needed a break on the video. An hour later, he got it. A white car inched through the frame of the surveillance camera from a bookstore. He wasn't sure it was the exact white bumper they'd spotted in the alley, but he jotted down the license plate and immediately ran a check.

"Bingo," he said when the owner's name showed up

in their system. This guy had been arrested four times and convicted twice. A meth head by all accounts. Not the kind of guy Luke would've pegged for a sophisticated robbery, but maybe he'd had a successful life before he'd discovered drugs.

The last address in the system was over a year old. Luke didn't have much confidence the guy had stayed in one place for so long, and it was already six-thirty. He and Simone could bring him in for questioning in the morning if they tracked him down.

He printed out the list of arrests and the accompanying photos, shoved them into a file and looked at the phone again. Good news, bad news...it didn't matter what it was. Everything made him want to call Tessa.

Luke sighed and ran a hand through his hair. He should apologize. He should call and tell her he'd been an ass and she wasn't to blame. But what if she forgave him? Then he'd have to think about how much he'd miss her when it ended for good.

But when he thought about heading home to his empty condo for another night, Luke decided maybe it'd be worth the risk.

"BALLS," TESSA GROANED as she collapsed onto her couch. "Worst Tuesday ever. No doubt." Whatever plans she'd had to seduce Luke had vanished when her afternoon had turned into a jumble of arguing brothers, screwy paychecks and a ridiculously enormous quote from Graham Kendall detailing what sponsorship of the golf tournament would cost. She dropped her White Orchid bag on the coffee table and slumped into the cushions.

There wasn't an inch of seduction in her tonight. At best, she could manage a bath and a drink and a microwave meal. Her pretty lingerie would have to wait.

It turned out that Roland Kendall wouldn't be back in the office until tomorrow afternoon, which felt like a reprieve for Tessa, but Eric had nearly been frothing at the mouth in outrage. Unfortunately, his outlet had been yelling at Jamie for a defective tap that had nearly flooded out the floor behind the bar.

Poor Jamie had been upset enough about the mess before having to deal with Eric's temper, and he'd ended up throwing down his mop and stalking out of the bar. Jamie's walk hadn't lasted long, though. His shoulders had probably itched with the need to get back and get the floor sparkling again. But Tessa couldn't help but take Jamie's brief disappearance as foreshadowing.

Her brothers had gotten along well once upon a time. Jamie had looked up to his big brother as a hero. Eric had played the part of role model to perfection, willingly toting his little brother along to movies and pickup basketball games.

Then their parents had died, and everything had changed.

Eric had become the staid, responsible father figure.

And Jamie had turned into a wild, rebellious teenager who resented being told what to do.

For a while, after Jamie had graduated from college, the relationship had gotten better. They'd almost been friends again. But now… "Oh, God," Tessa groaned, hiding her face behind her hands. The tension hung between them like a permanent cloud, sometimes cracking with lightning and rage. She didn't know what to do anymore.

She let her body slide slowly down until she was lying on the couch, then she closed her eyes and tried to plan her next step. The numbers Graham Kendall had sent were impossible. She couldn't spend that kind of money on her own, and Eric would never make a decision like that so quickly, even if she brought him in on it tonight.

He hadn't yet sent the numbers on beverage sales for the private jet charters. Hopefully they would look good. If they didn't, all her eggs would be in the High West basket, and both Monica and Graham thought that was an impossible dream.

And now…Jesus, now she wasn't even sure they should be in business with the Kendall Group. The family freaked her out. But Eric didn't care about the Kendall family, just the opportunity.

Hopelessness had begun to seep into her cells. It was a foreign, unwelcome feeling. She wasn't normally subject to dark moods, and when they did sneak in, she tried to move too fast to feel them. That was how she dealt with life. She schemed. She acted. She organized. She rushed. But now she was sinking into the couch with exhaustion and there was no hiding from her fear.

Tears were just starting to tingle behind her eyelids when her cell phone rang. She opened her eyes and stared up at the ceiling fan. Whoever it was, it was surely trouble. Eric or Jamie or one of those weird-ass Kendalls. For a moment, she thought of ignoring it, but her conscience wouldn't let her. She reached blindly over and grabbed her phone from her purse.

"Luke," she gasped when she saw the screen.

She hit the button and, holding her breath, raised the phone to her ear.

"Tessa? It's Luke."

"Hi."

"I wanted to apologize for last week. I'm sorry. I lost my temper, and—"

"It's okay. I understand."

"No, really—"

"Luke," she interrupted. "I'm serious. I understand. I sprang it on you out of the blue, and you reacted. It's okay."

He sighed deeply, and his voice dropped to a softer tone. "I really am sorry. Are you all right? You sound funny."

"I'm about four inches deep in my couch right now, so I might be a little muffled."

"You're tired," he said.

"Yeah."

"Me, too."

"Want to take a nap together?"

She'd meant it as a joke, but when he replied, "God, yes," Tessa realized she hadn't been joking at all. Her eyes slid to the white shopping bag sitting on the table.

The pale gray script promised discretion and pleasure. Tessa found that she still had a tiny bit of energy left inside her. Oh, yeah.

Still, instead of jumping on the possibility, she smiled at the bag and waited. They'd argued and he'd broken it off. She wasn't about to invite herself over. The ball was in Luke's court.

"But," he finally said, "I'd settle for dinner if you'd be willing to see me again."

"Hmm. I don't know…"

"I'll let you call me detective."

Laughing, she pushed herself up from the couch. "Deal. Can you give me half an hour?"

"Take forty-five minutes. I need to make a reservation and change into a suit."

"A suit?"

"I thought I'd take you someplace nice. Unless you're really too tired?"

Oh, no, she was over her exhaustion at this point. And this was something to do, something to take her mind off her problems. Tessa hung up, grabbed her new lingerie out of the bag and raced for the shower.

Granted, she didn't need to seduce Luke anymore, but there was nothing wrong with trying to blow the man's mind.

LUKE'S HAND TIGHTENED on the steering wheel when he heard the beep of his cell. He didn't want to think about work tonight, not that he was in much danger of being distracted from Tessa. She looked beautiful.

His eyes slid over her bare arms as he grabbed the phone.

"Hello?"

"I just wanted to see if you were still mad at me."

He cringed. "Hey, Mom." He stole a look at Tessa to find her eyes wide and curious.

"Well? Are you?"

"No, you know I'm not."

"Are you sure? You haven't called since Eve left."

He cleared his throat. "I'm sorry, Mom. I can't talk right now."

"You're still working?"

"No," he said, bracing himself.

"Oh," his mom said. Then, "Ohhhhh! You're on a date!" The last sentence came out as a loud screech, and Tessa smothered a laugh.

Luke fought the urge to turn on the radio so she couldn't eavesdrop. Instead, he hurried his mom off the phone. "Have a good night, Mom. Bye."

Tessa grinned at him. "You're adorable."

"Why? Because I talk to my mom?"

"No, just because you're cute. Detective."

He stared straight ahead, afraid he'd blush or grin or blurt out, "Aw, shucks," if he looked at her.

"Where are we going?" she finally asked.

"You don't know?" There was only one restaurant at the end of this road that wound up the mountains, but Tessa shook her head. "You've never been to Flagstaff House?"

Her squeal startled him so much that he nearly hit the soft shoulder of the road. He came even closer when she leaned in to press kisses to his jaw. "Jeez. Maybe I should've saved this for a bigger apology."

Flagstaff House was the grand dame of expensive dining in Boulder, maybe even in the whole Denver area. It was also a clear sign he was trying too hard, but when her lips parted against his neck, Luke was glad he'd chosen it.

"I can't wait," she whispered against him, and the searing heat of her mouth turned ice cold under her breath. Luke bit back a shiver. A pleasant heaviness in his cock threatened to become something more substantial.

Jesus, he was glad he'd called her.

They rounded a hairpin turn and there it was, a glass-and-wood triangle plunked down on the rugged mountainside. The sun had sunk behind the mountains and deep twilight had settled over the parking lot. After Luke parked and opened her door, Tessa pulled him up the stairs to the deck that overlooked the city.

"I'm sorry," he said. "I asked, but there's no outdoor dining yet."

"No," she whispered. "It's beautiful."

The whole town was spread out below them, and Denver rose in faint peaks of buildings beyond that. As they watched, streetlights and houses blinked to life like fireflies.

Her fingers slid between his.

He squeezed her hand. "Do you want dinner, or should we stay here and watch the stars come out?"

When she turned to him, Luke felt an ache wind

through his heart. It touched every chamber like a cruel hand. His chest felt too small.

Tessa rose on tiptoes to kiss him, and he drew her close. They kissed for long seconds, and he couldn't help but run his hands along her back. The black dress was made of some soft, slinky material, and he felt nothing but her body beneath the fabric.

Alone in the dark, standing above the sky, Luke touched her in slow motion. He smoothed each fingertip down her spine, shaped her hips, cradled her ass in both hands. He smoothed one hand up to her ribs, then gently cupped one breast. Her nipple pushed against his palm. Nothing but this paper-thin fabric separated him from her skin.

Tessa sighed into his mouth. "I missed you," she said, the words barely a whisper.

The lurch of his heart scared the shit out of him. "You're just using me for my body," he joked in defense.

"I know." She sighed. "It's so great."

His huff of laughter strangled on a groan when she snuck her hand down to press against his cock.

"You'd better button your coat, Detective."

"You're not helping." He jerked his head toward the view. "Look. The moon's rising." She took her hands off him long enough for him to take a few deep breaths while she oohed and aahed over the view. "Are you hungry yet?" he managed to ask.

She looked over her shoulder to run her gaze down his body. "Starving."

"Stop it," he growled, knowing he'd spend the whole

meal thinking about her mouth. Laughing, she led him into the restaurant like he was a puppy on a leash. Luke didn't feel even a twinge of shame. She could put a leash on him if she wanted as long as that path led to being deep inside her body.

Ninety minutes later, he was trying valiantly to focus on the conversation. It wasn't that she bored him. Not at all. It was that she'd just swiped her finger through the last of the sauce on her plate and was now surreptitiously sucking her finger. "Sorry," she said, totally mistaking his frown. "You'll probably never take me to another nice place."

"No," he said hoarsely. "Please." When he gestured toward the béarnaise sauce on his own plate, Tessa laughed as if he were kidding. But a suitable replacement arrived in the form of the dessert tray. Tessa gasped and immediately ordered tiramisu, but Luke saw her eyes coveting the caramel cheesecake, too, so he ordered that.

He poured the last of the wine into her glass, his mind registering that he'd only had one glass and she must be getting pretty tipsy. Then he went back to staring at her. Her dress dipped low enough to show off her cleavage, and it draped perfectly over her breasts, drawing his eye to every sweet curve. One slide of his hand and she'd be exposed to him. The thought haunted his every second.

"...and I do want to talk about it. If you promise not to say anything."

Luke blinked and forced his eyes up. "What?"

She slumped a little, pushing her dessertspoon

around on the empty table. The plates were gone. "It doesn't matter, anyway." She sighed. "It'll all be over in a few days."

Good God, what had he missed? "Tessa—"

"Don't look so worried. It's nothing huge, just... I shouldn't say anything, but I don't want to keep any secrets from you, and the wine's helping."

"You don't need to—"

"Eric has been working on a big deal with the Kendall Group for months, and I think Jamie has managed to screw the whole thing up." She took a deep breath and let it out in relief. "There."

"Oh. So Eric doesn't know?"

"No. I'm trying to fix it. There's still a possibility..." She trailed off, as if even she didn't believe it. "There's so much tension already. You don't have any brothers or sisters?"

"None."

"God, it's so complicated."

He curved his fingers over hers and cradled her hand. "So what's going to happen?"

"If the deal falls through? I don't know. I'm trying to pull something else together."

"By yourself?"

She nodded, looking a little sick, but when the waiter approached with the desserts, her face brightened. "Oh, wow."

And then Luke was lost again, between the moaning and licking and sparkling eyes. He could picture her exactly...on her knees, wetting her lips, humming with pleasure.

"This is so good." Tessa moaned.

"God, yes."

She rolled her eyes. "You haven't even tried it yet."

No, but he truly hoped he would. Soon.

CHAPTER SIXTEEN

TESSA HAD NO IDEA how close they were to Luke's place, but she was counting the seconds down like a rocket launch. At the beginning of the drive down the mountain, Luke's hand had been on her knee. Then it had slid a little higher, just to the edge of her dress so that her hem brushed his knuckles. After five minutes of torture, she was sure the heat must have imprinted his fingerprints into her skin permanently. She'd flexed her thighs, edged her knees apart, but he'd taken his sweet time moving higher. And he'd stopped well before he'd reached any interesting places.

Now her purse was crumpled in her clutching hands, but Tessa refused to ask for more. He was in the driver's seat tonight. She was just going to sit back and enjoy the ride. Unfortunately, they seemed to be stalled.

She wanted his hand between her legs. Wanted him to stroke her right here in the car. She wanted him to shove his hand down the top of her dress and take terrible advantage of her before they even made it home. But then her pretty underwear would be wasted, wouldn't it?

She had to be patient. Patient. Good things come to those who wait.

As if in affirmation, Luke's hand tightened on her thigh. For a split second of joy, she thought he was pushing his hand higher, but then his hot grip disappeared, and he put both hands on the wheel as he slowed and turned into the driveway of a town house.

Thank God.

He'd done nothing at all worth noting, but she was already shaky with need. Wet with waiting for him to touch her. She had no idea what it was about him that drove her wild, but just watching him walk around the car to open her door made her shiver. She'd dated quite a few guys in her life, but they'd all seemed vaguely like overgrown college students. Maybe it was this town. Or maybe that's what men in their twenties were like. But Luke inspired all sorts of different feelings in her. As if she could lean on him and he'd never falter.

A strange reaction to a man who sparked the kinds of rumors he did. But that didn't stop her body from embracing it.

The steady night breeze brought goose bumps to her skin when he helped her out of the car, but she barely felt it. She was too busy counting the steps to the door, cursing the time it took for the key to find the lock. He stepped aside to let her in, and even his politeness now seemed just another torturous delay.

He tossed his keys on a table. "Can I get you a drink or..." His words trailed off when she turned to face him and his gaze slid down her body. Her nipples were tight from the cold, and she knew that this dress didn't hide that in the least.

"You're driving me crazy in that dress," he said hoarsely.

"Really? I couldn't tell."

His eyebrows rose at the challenge in her voice, and when he took a step toward her, she took a step back. Another step brought her to the wall, and then Luke was on her, his mouth harsh with lust.

He'd never kissed her so roughly before, and she loved the edge of wildness in his touch as he cupped a hand over her breast. His thumb flicked her nipple. His teeth scraped her lower lip. She was glad she'd played coy. The waiting had been even harder on him.

He didn't hesitate for a second before reaching for the straps of her dress and pulling them down. The dress slithered down her body and pooled around her heels. Luke touched the silk beneath and pulled back to look.

"Jesus," he said. "You're gorgeous." Slowly, he touched his fingertips to the silk, tracing a delicate circle around her tight nipple. The feel of the silk caressing her areola made her shudder. He traced even slower, his breath coming louder in the quiet room. She watched his fingers, the way his roughness caught at the silk, the way he worshipped her…. Then his head bent, and Luke sucked her hard into his mouth. The silk went warm and wet against her. His mouth pulled.

Tessa cried out and wound her fingers into his hair

to stop him from escaping. He tightened both hands on her hips to make sure she didn't escape, either. As if she would move an inch away from him when her sex tightened with every draw of his mouth.

"Oh, Luke," she groaned past clenched teeth. He drove her mad. Everything about him drove her mad.

His mouth lifted, and the silk was sheer where he'd wet it. He went to his knees, his gaze on her breast, on the drawn bud of her nipple straining against the fabric. His eyes rose to meet hers, and his gaze was fierce and wild as he dragged a thumb over the spot he'd kissed. Spirals wound down to her belly. Her clit throbbed.

As if he knew just what was happening, he lowered his head and kissed just below her navel. Then lower and lower still, until he put his mouth over her covered sex and sucked just as he had at her breast.

Tessa cried out and her knees nearly buckled. She spread her hands against the wall, fighting the urge to let gravity pull her down as his tongue pressed wet silk against her clit. "Yes." The heat was so good. So wet. And then he lifted his mouth and there was ice pressed against her when he blew.

"You're so fucking perfect," he whispered, his eyes devouring the sight of her through the underwear. When he put his mouth back to her, the kiss was lighter this time, slower. She found herself whimpering within seconds, curling her nails into the wall while her heart soared up.

When she closed her eyes and pressed her head to

the wall, Luke's hands slid to the tops of her thighs. His thumbs traced along the edge of her panties, over the tight tendons of her thighs, down to the hollow just below her sex. His tongue feathered against her sex, an incessant pleasure that never ended.

"Oh, please," she whispered. The edges of his thumbs eased beneath the silk. "Please, please, please."

He rubbed the plump flesh. His thumbs caught her wetness and dragged it over her.

"Oh, *God,*" she gasped in desperation. She was so close, but he couldn't get deeper, the fabric was too tight.

Thank God he wasn't so controlled tonight. He didn't torture her. In fact, Luke barely lifted his mouth when he yanked the underwear down, and then his tongue was parting her, licking her, his fingers sliding along the seam of her body until they sank deep.

Tessa angled her hips toward him, urging him deeper. His tongue worked magic and she gasped his name, then screamed it, then threw her head back in a wordless cry. The floor seemed to roll beneath her, but the wall held her up as her body shook. When the pleasure finally fell away, Luke put his mouth to her thigh, then her hip, her belly, her waist. All she could do was breathe until the dark spots in her vision faded.

As Luke stood, she kicked the pile of clothing off her feet and fell to her knees.

"Tessa—"

"Shut up." His back thunked against the wall when

she swung him around, but before he could protest, she'd worked his buckle open and reached for his zipper. That kept him quiet. In fact, he struggled out of his jacket and pulled his tie free. He was still unbuttoning his shirt when she wrapped her hand around his thick cock. The skin was so hot and tight, stretched over his hardness. She gave a little hum of pleasure as she drew him free.

"Ah, damn," Luke breathed, working his shirt down his arms. She heard the tick of a button bouncing across the stone tile when he yanked the sleeves past his hands.

She was glad he'd gone to the effort. When she looked up at him, he was one long expanse of lean muscle. She met his gaze past her lashes. His eyes blazed. His jaw clenched into a furious line. And then she kissed him.

WHEN HER MOUTH touched him, it wasn't a tentative taste, but a hot, openmouthed kiss that took half of him deep into her throat. Luke choked back a groan and tangled his fingers in her hair. Tessa's moan of approval thrummed through his cock as her mouth tightened.

He wanted to close his eyes and press his skull back against the wall so he could concentrate on every press of her tongue, but he couldn't look away from her. Her flushed cheeks and golden hair, her pink lips sliding over him. The glistening moisture on his shaft when she pulled back before taking him deep again.

"Tessa… Christ." The idea of her innocence had

clung stubbornly to his psyche, and this felt wrong. Forbidden. He had expected her to be tentative. Maybe even nervous. He hadn't expected her to take him deep, to feel her throat tighten around him.

"Mmm," she purred.

Shit, he was lost. There was no hope for holding out. He'd have to prove restraint and stamina later. Because right now her tongue was rubbing and her mouth sucking and…this was so wrong. This was *Tessa*.

Yet the feeling was better than any fantasy he could've spun about her. His cock grew even harder until every draw of her mouth made him grimace with ecstasy. It only took a few moments of that pleasure before his control slipped. Luke cursed and his fist tightened in her hair.

In response, she dug her fingers into his thighs and pressed so close that her mouth touched the base of his cock. He couldn't stop from thrusting into her as his orgasm slammed through him. He couldn't stop the low shout of primal joy that rumbled from his throat as she swallowed him down.

Nothing—nothing—had ever felt so good as her mouth working him until the very last second of pleasure crashed down his spine.

"Tessa." He sighed, finally letting his head fall back against the wall. "Tessa," he repeated, just to remind himself that it was really her. Because even after that, it seemed impossible.

"Luke?"

"Mmm?" God, he'd make an effort at pillow talk if

she wanted, but he felt drugged. The sheets were crisp and cool, her body was one long line of heat against him, and his skin still buzzed in some strange limbo between numbness and heavy pleasure.

"What's this?"

He opened his eyes expecting her to be looking toward some picture or random knickknack in his room, but then he felt her hand touch his side. Oh.

He closed his eyes again.

"Is this where you were shot?"

"No. That's where I was stabbed."

"Stabbed?" Gasping, she pushed herself up to stare down at him. He was still trying to ignore her, but he opened his eyes to take in the view of her breasts.

"Luke!" she slapped his chest impatiently.

"What?"

"How did that happen?"

He sighed when he realized all his lethargy had vanished. Tension crawled back into his muscles like swarming ants. "I was stabbed." When she started to growl, he added, "During an arrest."

"Oh, my God, were you okay?"

He watched her breasts as she bounced with emotion. "I'm alive, right?"

"Luke. Up here."

He shook his head. "If you want to have a conversation, I suggest you lie back down. Or put on a shirt. But preferably lie down."

She flounced down, her elbow pressing into his ribs until her arm finally settled its warmth across his stomach. Her fingers feathered against the scar.

"It was pretty bad," he said matter-of-factly. "Hit the intestines. Sepsis. All that." *All that.* He'd been in the hospital for weeks. He'd nearly died.

"I'm sorry," Tessa said, her words whispering over his shoulder. "Was it here in Boulder?"

"No. L.A."

"Oh." She didn't ask any more. Didn't press him. And maybe that was why he said it, answering her unspoken question without really answering it.

"My mom came out. She stayed with me, so I wasn't alone. I moved out here a few months later." Of course, Tessa couldn't know what he meant, but her hand flattened and covered the scar as if she could heal it. It had been the lowest point of his life, lying in that hospital bed. He'd known he was close to dying. He'd felt death pushing him into that thin mattress, holding his limbs down. In that moment, he'd wanted one person with him. Just one person. And she hadn't come. After everything they'd been through, she hadn't come.

Tessa kissed his shoulder. He closed his eyes.

"Do you want to talk about it?" she asked. He shook his head. He didn't want to think about Eve. She had no place here.

"Where were you shot?"

"In my back, across my shoulder blade. It was minor."

"Another arrest?"

"Yeah. It was my first week on the job."

"You're kidding."

He felt a smile tug at his lips. Thank God he could laugh about it now. "I'm not kidding. I wasn't even supposed to be in danger. I was in the hallway of an apartment during a big bust. One of the dealers fired his gun and the bullet came right through the wall and grazed me. You can't imagine the kind of shit I took for that. My nickname for a while was Magnet."

Tessa's head popped up. "Magnet?"

"Bullet Magnet. They joked that I wasn't safe to stand near. It was no big deal, but I was a rookie, so it took a while to wear off. Hurt my pride."

"Oh," she said. He cracked an eye open to find her frowning down at him.

"Really, it wasn't that bad. After a while."

She smiled and laid back down. "Poor baby," she crooned, and Luke chuckled and pressed a kiss to her head.

"I had to work hard to prove I wasn't a bad luck charm."

"Well, you make me feel safe," Tessa said softly.

"Safe from what?"

"I don't know. Safe from myself."

He drew his chin in to try to look down at her, but she shook her head.

"I feel like I don't have to think with you."

"I'm not sure that's a compliment."

She smiled against his skin. "It is. I'm glad I came over."

He squeezed her closer. Her mouth brushed a kiss to his shoulder. He was sinking again. Tingling with relaxation. "Me, too," he whispered, then as an after-thought, "Maybe we should do it in the bed sometime."

She was still chuckling when Luke closed his eyes and slept, the sound of her laughter nothing more than a soothing dream.

CHAPTER SEVENTEEN

TESSA SMILED AS LUKE kissed her again. The big cot-tonwood in her backyard shaded them from the dim morning light. She didn't want to get out of his car. Didn't want to go into her empty house. They'd finally managed to have sex in the bed that morning, and she would've spent all day there if she could, curled against him, lying under him.

But there was work. And family. She groaned and reached for the handle of her door.

"I'll call you later," he said.

"Be careful today, all right? No shootings or stab-bings or anything."

"I'll do my best."

She started to get out, but he touched her arm.

"Come by tonight? I'll make you dinner."

"Do you cook?" she asked.

"Well, I grill. And I make salad."

She kissed him one last time. "I'll bring the beer."

"You're a male fantasy come to life, you know that?"

"Ha. Don't think I haven't heard that before."

She floated across her backyard, smiling at the way

Luke's car stayed parked as she dug her keys out. He'd pulled into the alley as if he was protecting her reputation. Now he was watching to be sure she made it safely inside, because 8:00 a.m. on a Wednesday was such a dangerous hour.

Her grin held as she dropped her purse on the kitchen counter. The smile stayed in place as she walked into the dining room. And it disappeared like a popped bubble when she saw Eric standing by her couch. He was staring in horror at the White Orchid bag as if it had sprouted fangs and clawed hands. He turned toward her, mouth open in shock.

"Okay." Tessa sighed. "Give me your key."

"Where have you been?" he barked.

"Where do you think I've been?"

He gestured to the bag, his face turning bright red, his jaw working as if he couldn't make any words come out. "Jesus!" he finally yelled.

"Oh, for God's sake, Eric! You have to give me the key to the house. Or at least promise to only use it in an emergency."

"It was an emergency! Your car was in the garage and you wouldn't answer the door. I forgot my phone at home… I was scared to death."

"Eric…" She dropped her head and took a deep breath. "Look, I know I've never talked to you about men or dating, but I'm fine. I know what I'm doing."

He glanced at the bag again, then crossed his arms and edged away from it.

Tessa rolled her eyes. "So why did you come by?" *Again.*

"Jamie and I talked."

Her heart immediately jumped into a frantic race for oxygen. "What?"

"He told me you two spoke about Luke Asher. I was worried about you. But...I guess my concern was unwarranted. Or maybe it was fully warranted." Oh, he sounded bitter, but Tessa was so busy trying to calm herself down that she didn't respond. Jamie hadn't told him about Monica Kendall. Yet.

"What are you doing, Tessa?" His words were heavy with disappointment.

"I'm fine, Eric. Please trust me. When have I ever let you down?"

They watched each other for a long moment, and she held his gaze with pride. She knew she'd never let him down. She'd made damn sure of it.

He finally looked away. "You know how proud I am of you. I just don't want you to be hurt."

"I know how to deal with pain, Eric. We all do."

He bowed his head. "That's the reason I don't want you hurt again. Isn't it obvious?"

"That's impossible," she said, even though she understood perfectly what he meant. She wanted the same thing for him and Jamie. For everything to just *work out*. "I'll be hurt one day. And again and again after that. But I'll still be happy. Anyway, I'm telling you that Luke isn't who you think he is. Not at all. I'm not afraid of pain, but I wouldn't ask for it." Hell, he wasn't even a babe magnet, just a bullet magnet.

She heard him sigh. His shoulders stayed tight. He wasn't moved. They would go around and around about this and he'd never give in. But then Eric shook his head and stepped forward to pull her into his arms. "Are you serious about this guy?"

"Not serious," she said, but when her heart lurched, added, "not yet."

"Give me some time to get used to it."

She pressed her ear to his heart. "Okay."

"But I'll make him regret it if he hurts you. And I still don't like it."

Tessa smiled and said "okay" to that, too. When she pulled back, she narrowed her eyes at him. "Maybe it's time to come clean about your dating. How come I never see you with anyone?"

"Because I'm never with anyone," he answered, but she noticed the way his eyes slid quickly away, and wondered what he was hiding. Still, she had too many secrets to make any point of his.

"Can you wait fifteen minutes while I shower? We can get that breakfast we talked about."

She'd been trying to avoid him, but that had been a mistake. Half an hour later, they were digging into their diner breakfast when Tessa dared a question. "Have you ever met Graham Kendall?"

"No. Why?"

"I ran into him the other day. At Starbucks."

"Oh? Did he say anything about why his father won't take my calls?"

"No, but we spoke about Kendall Flight a little. Have you heard of it?"

"Sure."

"It seems like maybe it's another good opportunity for us. He's going to send me some numbers."

"Great. Let me know when you get them."

He continued eating, his eyes still distant and dark.

"He also suggested a sponsorship of—"

"You know what? I don't even want to hear about another deal with a Kendall Group company until this bastard gets back to me. I'm beginning to think these people are just screwing around with us."

She swallowed a suddenly cementlike piece of pancake. "Are you having buyer's remorse?"

"I'm sick of this. Maybe I should've taken the hint from the start. If I didn't think this was the best path to expansion…"

There. There was one small crack in his unwavering support for this deal. There was that tiny bit of promise she'd been hoping to grab on to. If she kept a tight hold, and tugged it carefully…

"Then maybe you shouldn't worry," she said. "Maybe it's a sign. If he backs out, he backs out, and we'll concentrate on an even better opportunity."

"No, I've put too much work into this. He's just being inconsiderate. As usual."

"I'm not sure we can trust him," Tessa said on a rush, surprising even herself.

He shrugged. "That's what airtight contracts are for."

"He's slimy."

"Regardless, people are excited about his airline. And when will we ever have an opportunity to get *paid* to advertise our beer to a captive audience of new customers?"

That was just it. The brass ring she couldn't reach with any other company. Yes, there were other opportunities, but they were only opportunities to squeeze Donovan Brothers beer onto the shelf next to a hundred other bottles.

"Well, we're doing fine," Tessa said quietly. "Everything's good, with or without Roland Kendall."

But Eric didn't respond, he only scowled at his phone as he scrolled through something on the screen. Something work-related, obviously. As far as she knew, he didn't have a life outside the brewery, but maybe he was as good at keeping secrets as she was.

She nodded her head toward his phone. "Hot text message from your new girlfriend?"

"No, it's an email from—" His head whipped up and he narrowed his eyes. "Very funny."

"You should think about getting laid. Then maybe you wouldn't be so focused on my sex life."

"I am not focused on your sex life. That's ridiculous. And creepy. And I'm not… That is…" He shook his head. "Never mind."

"What?" she pressed, curious now, despite her teasing.

A heartbeat passed in silence, then two. "Let's go," he said abruptly, pushing the bill and some cash closer to the edge of the table. "The brewery won't run itself."

Their father had said that. Not often, only on the rare days when he'd been too tired to be excited about his business. *That place won't run itself,* he'd say with a wink and hard stretch. Now she couldn't believe he hadn't been dead tired all the time. There were three of them running the place now. He'd had only himself and the ghost of his brother.

Then again, after the accident, Eric had only had himself and ghosts, too. She'd been amazed by him as a teenager. Now she was in awe.

She bumped her shoulder against his arm as they walked out of the restaurant. "Why don't you take some time off next month?"

"We've got the brew show in Santa Fe next month, then the Denver one after that."

"So? That's two long weekends."

"Plus all the prep work."

Tessa sighed, wondering when he'd last taken a vacation. She couldn't remember. Hell, she couldn't remember when she'd last taken one. A few days here and there. A few side trips during brew shows.

She slid into Eric's car. "Maybe I should go to the beach."

Eric got in and closed the door. "Did you say something?"

"No," she answered without hesitation. "But you know what? You should go to the beach. Florida."

"Florida? Me?"

A sudden image flashed in her head of Eric strolling the beach in a black Speedo. "Okay, maybe Oregon. Or Maine."

"Yeah," he said. "Maybe." But his tone said there

was no chance. He was already back to worrying about the brewery.

Weren't they all.

CHAPTER EIGHTEEN

SIX HOURS. THAT WAS how long it had taken them to track down one measly thief. Six hours of knocking on every damn door of every place he'd been rumored to hang out. Finally, Luke and Simone had doubled back to his grandmother's house and found him eating macaroni and cheese and homemade corn bread.

The grandmother had seemed neither surprised nor dismayed to see them again. She'd just shrugged one shoulder and shouted, "Frankie, the cops are back!"

He'd bolted. They'd chased. And now he was slumped over the table of the interview room, one hand pressed to his skinned forehead.

"I think you're going to live, Frankie."

"Why'd you have to throw me into that stupid fence, man?"

"You made my partner run. Not cool."

"I didn't know she was pregnant! What am I under arrest for?"

"You're not under arrest. Yet."

Frank Valowski looked up and met Luke's eyes. "I'm not?"

"Not yet. But you're on probation, so this could all go south for you real quick."

"Look," Simone said, her voice understanding and soft, "you can call your lawyer and clam up. That's your right. But we know you're not the brains behind this operation."

His eyes widened by the smallest fraction. His fingers began tracing circles on the table. "You saying I'm not smart enough?"

"No. Are you saying this robbery was your idea?"

"What robbery?"

Luke smiled. "We've got surveillance tape connecting your car to a robbery at Donovan Brothers Brewery. Does that ring any bells?"

Oh, yeah, it did. Frank's fingers pressed hard against the scarred tabletop. "I want my lawyer," he grumbled.

"You got it. But when she brings up the idea of a deal, I suggest you listen carefully."

Despite his own words, even Luke was surprised when Frank's lawyer and the D.A. reached a deal within the hour. If he cooperated fully in the investigation, his probation would be extended two years, but he'd see no jail time. Fair enough. All they really had was proof that Frank had gotten his hands on the keg somewhere. They certainly couldn't pin all these robberies on him. But in the end, the deal led to nothing but mystery.

"I never saw the guy. He called and asked me if I wanted in on a deal. Said he got my number from a mutual friend. Normally I wouldn't go for something like that, but…"

"But what?" Luke asked.

Frank shrugged. "I don't know. It seemed like nothing. He said when I got there, the door would be unlocked and he'd give me the alarm code."

"When did he call you with the alarm code?"

"That night. Told me to head on over."

Luke leaned closer. "Did you recognize his voice?"

"Nope. Just sounded like a regular white guy, I think. Nothing special."

"How did he pay you?"

"Said he wanted the computers and I could keep anything else, and I figured that was good enough for an easy job. But there wasn't anything else. Not even twenty bucks in the till. That fucking keg was my whole payment, and then I saw the story in the newspaper and I thought, 'Shit, I've gotta get rid of this, too.' I should've dropped it in the creek, but I figured if I left it in the alley, some loser would take it home."

"He did," Luke said.

"So what the fuck happened?"

Luke smiled. "Bad time for a traffic stop."

"Shit," Frank groaned.

Simone gave him a few seconds to wallow in his misfortune before she spoke. "How did you make the drop?"

"The what?"

Luke gritted his teeth in impatience, but Simone was as cool as always. "How did you deliver the computers?"

"There's a fence behind the brewery. The guy had already loosened the boards. I just pulled them off, put the computers on the other side and jammed the boards back up. I guess he picked them up from there."

"Are you kidding me?" Luke asked.

"Nope. I told you it was easy. I didn't even need a truck."

The lawyer cleared her throat. "All right, I think Mr. Valowski has been more than cooperative here—"

"We need the phone number," Simone interrupted.

The guy offered his cell phone, but they all knew it was hopeless. A man who'd put that much thought into a robbery would've used a disposable cell. Even the dumbest criminal knew that much.

"Did he ever call again?"

"I wish. This shit's been nothing but trouble, and I'd like to give him a piece of my mind. I'm out, man. I'm straight from now on."

Likely story. Even Frankie's lawyer rolled her eyes.

Luke had one last question before they cut him loose. "Who's the friend who hooked you two up?"

"He didn't say."

Simone and Luke left Frankie and his lawyer to work out the details with the probation officer.

"Jesus," Luke muttered. "That was a waste of a fucking day."

"At least we know the guy's method now," Simone countered. "It wasn't a complete waste."

"Maybe we should look at the employees again. It sounds like someone on the inside helped out. The lock and the alarm code… Then again, it's not as if there's a common employee that links all these businesses."

"Maybe the guy has a way with people. Or maybe he blackmails them into helping."

Luke frowned as they reached their desks and sat down. "Too much exposure, though. He's careful not to put himself at risk. No real contact with the accessories. No chance he'll trip an alarm and get caught. No way anyone will stumble upon him crawling out a window with the stolen property. He's good. I can't see him leaving a different witness at every site."

"Yeah." Simone leaned back in her chair, resting her head so she could stare at the ceiling. A burst of laughter exploded from one of the offices. She scowled. "It's too damn noisy to think in here." Luke watched the way she rubbed at her holster where it cut into her shoulder.

He was surprised by the sergeant's voice when it came, but not as surprised as Simone. "It's time for you to think about desk duty, Detective Parker," he said from past Luke's shoulder. Simone wrenched forward, her chair squealing in protest as her eyes popped open.

"Excuse me?" she gasped.

"You look tired."

"It's this chair that's hurting my back," she snapped. "I'll go on leave when it's time, but I'm not going to volunteer to sit on this torture instrument for eight hours a day. Sir."

Luke kept his mouth shut. He didn't like to see Simone mixing it up with criminals, either, but he knew better than to step into that mess. Simone was quiet, and her bite was *way* worse than her bark.

Maybe the sergeant had realized his mistake, because he stayed silent behind Luke before he finally walked away. Luke sighed in relief. Simone closed her eyes again.

"So what are you thinking?" Luke asked.

"I don't know. One more month. I'm not waddling like a penguin yet."

"No," he said startled. "I meant…" He let his words trail off. Was she really talking to him about this?

"Plus, it knocks them off guard," she added.

"Who?"

"The suspects. Haven't you noticed?"

Yeah, he'd noticed. Of course he had. It was exactly what he liked so much about her. She wasn't big and tough and threatening, and she worked it to her advantage.

"Listen," Luke said. "I've got to call Ben Jackson in Denver and find out what the hell's going on with these files. Then why don't we check out of here on time for once? We'll head to my place and brainstorm for an hour. Like we used to."

She rubbed her temples and shifted uncomfortably in the chair. "Yeah. Let's do that. I need a milk shake."

"What?"

"I'll stop and get one on the way. I'll see you there." She pushed up awkwardly and stretched again. "You want a shake?"

"Um. No, thanks. I'm fine." *Fine* was a good word

for it. Simone was finally opening up. Sure, it wasn't much, but it was something. Luke found himself smiling down at his desk for a good ten seconds, and then he picked up his phone and got back to work.

"COME ON, WALLACE!" Tessa shouted over the loud male voices that surrounded her. "Jamie did not say your stout was garbage! Calm down!"

"He implied it!" Wallace yelled back. "You think I don't know what I heard?"

Jamie threw up his hands. "All I said was that I thought the end note was a little bitter. Pull back on the chocolate, man."

"Fuck you!"

Eric just stood there with his arms crossed. Silence fell over the kitchen, though it was marred by the loud sound of Wallace's furious breathing. Once that slowed, Eric raised his chin. "Are you done?" he asked calmly.

Wallace just grunted, but Tessa could tell the storm had passed.

"Jamie's right," Eric said. "And you know he's right. So try again. It's a winter brew—you've got plenty of time to play with it."

Wallace grunted again, but he didn't disagree.

Jamie, seemingly unaffected by the argument, gave Wallace's arm a friendly slap. "Try that other chocolate you were talking about, man. The one from Mexico. That was the one you wanted, anyway."

Wallace shrugged, so Jamie slapped him again. "If

anyone can do it, you can. You're a fucking wizard, man."

"Okay," Wallace finally agreed. "All right. I'll try again."

Tessa wrinkled her nose in disgust. "Good Lord," she said as she left them to their weird bonding. She might understand men, but that didn't mean she had to like them all the time. Sometimes they were just giant, obnoxious children wrestling around until someone cried uncle.

Actually, that was kind of how she felt it was going with Roland Kendall, too. But she'd cry uncle a million times over if it would get him to budge. She closed her office door and waited for the call. The last time Tessa had called, the receptionist had sighed and said that Mr. Kendall would call back around five. It was 4:59 p.m.

When the phone rang, she snatched it up.

"Tessa! Good to hear your voice. It's Graham Kendall."

Graham Kendall? She pulled the phone from her ear and glared at it. He started talking again.

"…surprised you didn't show more interest in the offer—"

"I'm sorry," she snapped. "I really can't make that kind of financial decision so quickly."

"What if I could give you a few more days?"

"Sure. Whatever. I just can't talk right now, okay?"

"I'll call you on Monday!"

"I thought you were going to send those numbers on the catering over to me."

"I'll get them to you as soon as I can. Let's get this golf tournament ironed out first. That's our top priority."

Tessa hung up with a huff. The phone rang two seconds later. "Hello?"

"Ms. Donovan," a much rougher voice said.

Her heart stopped with an excruciating lurch. Roland Kendall. This was it. She could feel the destruction of her family barreling at her like a freight train. "Mr. Kendall," she whispered. Horrified at the weakness of her own voice, she tried again. "Welcome home. I hope your trip went well."

"It was fine."

"I hope you—"

"Look, Ms. Donovan, I'll put you out of your misery. I was leaning toward a Denver brewery last month, and I've decided to go with them."

"No," she whispered. Her hand fell to her desk, the knuckles clunking hard against the wood, but Tessa didn't feel it. All she could feel was the hand the phone was in, and the way the edges cut into her fingers where she squeezed it. "I understood that Monica was going to argue in our favor...."

"My daughter hasn't exactly shown good judgment where the Donovan family is concerned. I disregarded her opinion on the matter."

"Have you finalized the deal yet?" she asked in panic. "Did you sign a contract?"

"No, but—"

"What if we..." Tessa considered the numbers. They were right there at the front of her brain on constant display. Then she thought of her monthly salary. Then the value of her car. Finally, she added in her savings account. "What if we supplied High West with enough beer to cover your customer demand for the next six months?" She swallowed the heavy lump in her throat. "At no cost to you."

"Pardon me?"

"We'd require the two-year contract, of course. The last eighteen months at the rate already negotiated by you and Eric."

Silence greeted her words. Tessa clenched her eyes shut and breathed. In and out. In and out. She could swing this. If it meant that her brothers would be happy, she'd pay for the beer herself. She didn't need her car. She only lived a block from her work and Boulder had a great bus system. But her brothers… they were irreplaceable.

"If you can come through on that deal, Ms. Donovan, I think we can put this little incident behind us."

"Really?" Tessa pressed her hand to her mouth to keep from sobbing with relief. She should've known from the start that money would trump ideals with this man. She should've offered him an outrageous deal from the very start. Despite that she was about to start leaking money like a sieve, Tessa felt a surge of power burn through her muscles and settle in her bones.

She wasn't a fool. She was the one who'd run the numbers in the first place. This deal wouldn't cost her more than four thousand dollars a month. That would be well worth the priceless return.

"I'll speak to Eric," she said, "and I'll have the contract to you next week."

When she hung up, Tessa clasped her shaking hands together. She'd done it. She'd fixed the unfixable problem. Granted, she'd thrown a big chunk of money at it to get the job done, but the cost would be well worth it, long-term. After all, her brothers had already sacrificed more than her, Eric most of all.

But the shaking wouldn't stop. Maybe she should grab another sample of Wallace's chocolate stout. Failed or not, that brew had a high alcohol content. But her stomach turned at the thought.

Tessa closed her eyes. She listened to the familiar late-afternoon sounds of the brewery. Their dishwasher, Henry, was filling a pail with hot water, preparing to mop the floors. Eric's voice filtered faintly through the office wall as he talked on the phone. His voice floated on top of the muted hint of music from the front room. And even at this early hour, laughter from customers occasionally crept through the walls.

She identified each and every sound, and it soothed her. This place was as much their family home as the house they'd grown up in. And she would lie, cheat or steal to hold on to that.

Well, maybe not steal. Luke might frown on that.

She managed a smile, though adrenaline still pooled in her stomach like acid.

This was good. She had nearly a week to work out the details of how to keep this deal from her brothers.

VICTORIA DAHL   217

She'd have to hide it. They'd never, ever support it. But she could handle it. She had to.

As if in reward for her positive thoughts, her phone beeped out a text alert.

I'm heading home. Why don't you stop by later?

Luke. This was a slightly more pleasant shot of adrenaline. Her muscles went warm instead of sizzling. Her stomach did a slow, lazy turn. Tessa finally felt steady enough to rise to her feet. She found Jamie behind the bar.

"What the hell was that 'Danny Boy' crap last night?" he asked when Tessa sauntered over with a smile.

"Oh, that? How'd it go?"

"You know I hate that damned song."

"But did you sing it?"

His scowl told her that, yes indeed, he'd sung for their patrons. "That wasn't the worst of it. The worst of it was having to listen to everyone else hum it for the rest of the night."

"Sorry," she said, making sure he knew she wasn't the least bit sorry at all.

"You're a brat."

"Maybe, but I'm a brat who just saved your butt."

He raised an interested eyebrow, but he had to break off the conversation to fill pint glasses for the people who'd just arrived.

Tessa noticed the empty space that had been cleared

in the far corner of the room and got out her phone to tweet a reminder about the band who'd be playing tonight.

Normally, she'd hang around to help out or just enjoy the music, but tonight she'd be otherwise occupied. Occupied good and hard, if she had any say in it.

"What the hell are you blogging now?" Jamie snapped.

"It's called tweeting. And it's nothing to do with you."

"Liar. So tell me how you supposedly saved my ass." Tessa beamed up at him, which seemed to make Jamie nervous. "Tessa. What did you do?"

"I salvaged the deal."

"What deal?"

"What deal do you think?"

His eyes widened by slow degrees. His jaw dropped.

"Exactly," she drawled.

"There's no way. Kendall wouldn't even… No."

Tessa shrugged with ill-concealed pride. "A two-year exclusive fulfillment deal just like we wanted. You can call me a miracle worker if you want. I won't object."

Instead of calling her anything at all, Jamie put his arms around her and lifted her off the ground.

She squealed and squirmed, trying to get her arms free so she could hug him back. But when he twirled her around, she just gave in and laughed.

"How the hell did you do it?" he asked when he finally set her down.

"I talked to Monica. I talked to Kendall. Gave him a little time to calm down."

"And what about Eric?"

"Oh, I don't think Roland Kendall's going to say anything, do you?"

Jamie pulled a white towel off his shoulder and twisted it around one hand. Not a good sign. "It's still not right, Tessa. Everybody else knows about this."

"No," she said flatly. "I did not do all this just so you could give your confession and get it off your chest. How is it going to help Eric to know about you and Monica? How will that help anyone? He'll be pissed at you and Monica, number one. And he'll be pissed at me and Kendall, too. Leave it alone."

He wound the towel tighter.

"I'm serious!"

His eyes rose to meet hers, and Tessa was shocked at the hardness in them. "So am I."

"No, Jamie. Not this time. Please. If you want to own up to your mistakes and make some sort of confession, do it the next time you screw up. Not this time."

"The next time, huh?"

He was ruining the good news, and Tessa grew impatient. "Or don't mess up again. Whatever you want. But this is not the time for getting it off your chest."

"We're not kids anymore, Tessa. And Eric isn't our dad."

She waved him off. "I don't want to have this conversation right now. It's over. Be happy."

He held her gaze for what seemed like an eternity, stubbornness written all over his jaw, but finally he relented with a nod. "Fine. You're a miracle worker. We'll leave it at that."

"Thank you." She gave him another hug and added a kiss for good measure. "Now stay out of trouble."

"I should be saying that to you," he said quietly.

Tessa braced herself for another lecture, but even though she saw worry flash through his eyes, he just tossed the towel over his shoulder and went back to work. That was one nice thing about brothers. They rarely wanted to talk about feelings. That suited her just fine.

"Looks like a great night," he said, glancing out at the tables that were already filling up. And the conversation was officially over. Tessa was free to escape and she started back to her office.

A careful hand on her arm stopped her. "Is Wallace here?" a soft voice asked.

Tessa looked down to see a woman so petite that half her height seemed to be made up of her perfectly round afro. "Hi. Yes, he's in the back. I'll get him for you."

"Thanks. I'm Faron, by the way. If he asks."

Tessa knocked on the door of the brewing room before she opened it, just in case Wallace was making love to one of tanks. "Wallace, there's someone named Faron here to see you!"

The brewmaster popped up from crouching next to one of the mash tuns. "Faron's here?"

"She's in the front." Tessa could've sworn he licked his lips when he glanced toward the barroom. "Do you want me to bring her back?"

"No, I…"

She watched in shock as the foul-tempered behemoth tried to smooth a hand through his bushy hair, then gave up and patted it down. "No, just tell her I'll be out in five minutes. Comp her a beer?"

"Um, yes. Of course. Absolutely." Well, this was new. Wallace's dates were normally the nervous ones. He always stayed steady as a thousand-year-old tree. Until now.

More than a little curious, Tessa took Faron's order herself, surprised when the woman ordered a porter. Faron looked like she had the appetite—and bone structure—of a bird. She wasn't chatty, though. She took her beer with a simple thank-you and retreated to a table in the corner to sit quietly.

"Wallace's date," Tessa whispered to Jamie.

"That man is a god," he said with complete sincerity. "He's the one who should be tweeting. In his own name, I might add."

"Hey, I gave you the chance to do it. You weren't interested. Suck it up."

"Get out of my bar," he growled, and Tessa left with a laugh.

She made one last phone call, confirming with the human resources vendor that everything still looked good with the Social Security numbers. No alerts had been triggered. They'd dodged a bullet. Well, actually… Tessa had made a move toward stricter information protection. That hadn't been dodging a bullet at all. It had been ass-kicking forethought.

She shut down her computer and headed for Luke's house on a cloud of triumph. Tessa Donovan, protector of families and savior of breweries. Oh, and defiler of men, if she had anything to say about it. Yes, indeed.

CHAPTER NINETEEN

"So WHAT's MISSING from the files?" Simone asked, but Luke was distracted from answering. Instead, he frowned at the way she shifted in her chair, her hand going to her side.

"Are you okay?"

"I'm fine," she said, but he watched her ease slightly to the right. "What's up with the files?"

"A couple of the later cases have references to interviews with a witness, but I can't find the records. I called Ben. He's going to look into it."

She made a thoughtful noise. "So I thought Frankie was being truthful."

"Me, too. He was already on for another two years of probation. No reason he wouldn't want to bring the other guy down with him."

"No reason except fear, and I didn't get any of that."

"I'll swing by and check out the fencing behind the brewery tomorrow. See if that part checks out. Do you know what the layout is back there?"

She shook her head but fired up her laptop to access satellite images. The results weren't promising. A neighborhood street dead-ended right behind the

brewery. It was unlikely anyone had installed surveillance cameras at all, and certainly none that pointed
at the street. They'd have to knock on doors, and the
lieutenant likely wouldn't want to alarm the commu-
nity over a property crime.

Luke put his feet up on the table. "So let's assume
there wasn't an insider helping out. How else could he
have gotten the code?"

"A source at the alarm company?"

"Huh. I kinda like that idea. But it still puts him in
an identifiable position, if you assume he's using the
same guy every time. Did we already check on the
alarm company?"

"Yep," Simone said. "Three different companies
for the last four robberies."

"Shit. But you know what? Maybe these days he
doesn't need any inside help. Maybe he could just set
down a tiny camera in the back room to record the
code. That would take, what? Two seconds?"

Simone nodded, but she shifted again and eased
her hand behind the small of her back. Luke frowned
until she shot him an irritated look.

"What?"

"You're not having Braxton Hicks, are you?"

"What?"

"It's early yet. You should call your doctor."

"Um, Luke? Have you lost your mind?"

"Look, I'm sorry. I know you don't want me involved, but I can't just pretend you're not pregnant.
And if you're starting to have contractions, then—"

"I'm not having contractions. My back hurts. That's all."

"Sometimes back labor can masquerade as—"

"Are you kidding?" she interrupted with a screech. "Since when do you know anything about back labor or Braxton Hicks?"

"I've…read stuff." Luke didn't like the way she was staring at him, and now he was the one shifting in his chair.

"You've read *stuff*. About pregnancy."

"Let's get back to the case." He bent over the computer and pretended to study the satellite map, but Simone pushed to her feet with surprising speed and headed toward his bedroom.

"Hey!" Luke jumped up and chased after her, but she was more agile than she'd been in weeks, and Simone slipped into his bedroom before he was even halfway down the hall. "Hey!" he shouted again. At first, he was mostly worried he'd missed one of the condom packets from this morning. Or that Tessa had left some lacy thing behind on his bed.

But when he finally burst into the room, he found that Simone had ignored the rumpled bed and was standing at the small desk under the window. She picked up a book and turned it over, then reached for another.

"You're reading baby books?" Her soft voice swelled through the room and pressed against his brain.

"They were on a table at the front of the bookstore," he said, but that was only a half-truth. Yes, the first book he'd bought had been an impulse buy. But the second and third and fourth had been a mission. Luckily, half of his purchases were still at the office.

She flipped one open and paged through it, then set both books down with a sigh. "You can't do this, Luke," she whispered.

"Do what?"

Simone just shook her head and edged past him to head for the door. But this time he was on her heels. "Do what, Simone?"

She snapped her computer closed and stuffed it in her bag, but he followed her all the way to the front door. Her hand touched the doorknob, but then she stopped and slumped. "You can't save me from this, okay? You can't fix this."

"Aw, hell, Simone. I don't even know what I'd be saving you from. Maybe the dad's in the picture. Maybe he's not. Maybe you went to a damn sperm bank. I don't care anymore, all right? I just want to help."

"You can't help."

"Yes, I can! Everybody has help. Women have husbands and sisters and moms and friends. I just… Maybe you have girlfriends. Maybe there are five women at your house every night making sure you know about preeclampsia and…and early labor, but I don't think there are."

"Luke…" She dropped her head and stared at the floor for too many heartbeats. When she pressed her hand to her eyes he worried she was crying, but he made himself hold his ground. He wasn't going to back down. She needed him, whether she wanted to admit it or not.

"Preeclampsia?" she murmured, shaking her head.

"It's pregnancy-induced high blood pressure that—"

"I know what preeclampsia is, you freak. I just can't believe you do."

"I'm a detective. I like to know things."

"Luke—"

"I just want to be there for you. And for the baby, if you're keeping it. Shit, I don't even know if you're keeping it."

Both her hands went to her belly. "I am."

His heart tightened at the thought. She was going to be really good at this, but he could feel the uncertainty crawling beneath her skin. "Are you scared?"

"I don't know," Simone breathed. "It's just… It doesn't matter if I'm scared, does it?"

"It matters to me. That's what I want you to know."

Nodding, she took a deep breath. "Okay. I've got it."

"Listen, I know you were in foster care for a long time, so I assume your family isn't in the picture. Does someone go to classes with you?"

She adjusted the bag on her shoulder and let her eyes slide away from him. "They start next week. I have a doula. She'll be there for the birth."

"Okay, good. Just know that I'm here for you, if you want me. You and the baby. All right? I don't know anything about babies, but…"

"Neither do I," she said with a tiny laugh, but the laugh turned into a gasp that sounded suspiciously teary.

Luke put his arms around Simone, moving carefully in case she didn't want to be touched. He hadn't put his arms around her since that one night when they'd had too much to drink and made a stupid mistake. But this wasn't anything like that. This wasn't a mistake, and she leaned into him, her forehead pressing to his shoulder. He expected her to sob then, to break down completely, but that wasn't Simone. She was strong, and she simply let her breath out on a slow rush.

"We'll figure it out together, all right? I know you can do this on your own, but you shouldn't have to."

She took another deep breath and nodded. Luke felt a startling relief spread through his chest. After he patted her back over and over, they both stepped awkwardly apart at the same moment.

When she smiled, Luke realized it was the first true smile he'd seen from her in a long time. He didn't give a damn who the father was. He didn't even care if people thought it was him, as long as Simone would be okay.

TESSA STOOD AS QUIET as a mouse on the tiny front porch of Luke's condo. She hadn't meant to eavesdrop, but it had started out innocently enough. She'd walked up and raised her hand to knock, then realized the voices she was hearing were coming from Luke's place.

She hadn't dared interrupt. Luke and Simone were

finally talking, and the open window next to the front door didn't offer any disguise as to the topic. Tessa had frozen. She didn't want to walk away or even breathe too loudly as Luke had begged Simone to let him help. He was so good. So...noble. No wonder he'd always wanted to be a cop.

Silence fell inside, and Tessa's skin started to crawl with anxiety. She backed down the step, took two more steps backward, and then she heard the doorknob began to turn.

"Oh, God," she whispered, backpedaling until she stood just in front of her car's bumper. When Luke's door started to open, she lurched forward as if she'd been in midstep.

"Hey!" Tessa called out to Simone. "How are you?"

Simone's nose was slightly red, but she managed a smile and a few moments of small talk before heading for her car.

"Crap," Luke cursed from the doorway when his gaze fell on Tessa.

"Nice to see you, too, Detective."

"No, it's not that." As if to prove it, he stepped down and gave her an enthusiastic kiss. The taste of his mouth evoked all kinds of lovely sensory memories for Tessa, and she melted into him like a schoolgirl with her first crush. She draped herself against him, winding her arms around his neck, taking his tongue against hers like the taste of something perfect.

When he broke the kiss, he was breathing almost as hard as she was. "Jesus, woman."

"Not disappointed to see me anymore?"

"No, but I forgot about dinner. I'm sorry. I was thinking about work."

"Hmm. Should I take my beer and go?"

"I was kind of hoping you'd give me a minute to shower so I could take you out."

She dragged her gaze down his body, then back up again. "All right. But only if you promise to put out later. Can you do that, Detective?"

"What kind of boy do you think I am?"

Tessa leaned so close that her lips brushed his ear when she spoke. "The kind who got on his knees for me last night. And this morning."

"Ah. That kind."

"Go on." She gave him a tiny shove. "I'll put the beer in the fridge. You shower."

"Yes, ma'am."

But the minute he was gone, Tessa regretted sending him away. Now that she was alone, it was too easy to replay Luke's conversation with Simone over and over in her head. Something about it niggled at her brain, though Tessa couldn't say why. It didn't contradict anything Luke had told her. Not really.

But Jamie's words hung over her, haunting like a brotherly ghost. *Don't be one of those girls.*

Tessa heard Luke's shower start up as she put the bottles in his fridge. She thought of the way he'd asked to help Simone…and her baby.

He couldn't be the father, could he? Surely if Simone were carrying Luke's child, she wouldn't be so welcoming of Tessa. But even if he wasn't the dad, did he care too much about his partner?

She paced the kitchen for a few seconds, pressing her fingers against her lips. "No," she murmured. That couldn't be it. The dynamic wasn't strange enough, was it?

Tessa tried to shake her brother's words from her head. She didn't want them there, not tonight. Tonight was her reward. She'd earned it.

But just as she managed to put it from her mind, Tessa wandered back to Luke's bedroom, and her eye was drawn immediately to the books on his desk. Her stomach dropped, and for a moment she felt the whole evening slip away from her.

But no. She wouldn't let it. She might be stupid. She might be delusional, but she wasn't weak. Luke was what she'd come here for, and goddamn it, Luke was what she'd get.

The books seemed to glow against the dark desktop, so Tessa took steps to rectify the problem. She took off her jeans and shirt and laid them over the books. Then she took off her underwear, grabbed a condom from the bedside table and headed for the shower. This moment was not going to get away from her, even if she had to force herself on Luke. Once his hands were on her, she'd forget everything else.

So Tessa left the questions and complications behind and stepped into the clouds of steam that hid Luke Asher's body. The rest of the world fell away as soon as the glass door snapped shut.

CHAPTER TWENTY

HE JUMPED WHEN the door closed, twisting around with a speed that made her heart flutter in admiration.

"Oh," he said, his eyes quickly transitioning from alarm to appreciation. He started to smile, started to make a witty remark, but Tessa pressed herself against him before he could speak.

The feel of his body shocked the breath from hers. He was hot and solid, but his skin slid over hers with such liquid heat that her pulse swelled to immediate arousal. The shower hit her back in a tingling spray as her breasts flattened into his chest, slipping against him with delicious pressure.

Whatever he'd been about to say, he let the water wash it away. Instead of speaking, he molded his hands to her back, shaping her ribs, her hips, her spine. He explored her in one unbroken touch that seemed like creation, as if she'd been formless before she stepped into him.

She touched him as well, echoing his movements, closing her eyes so she could concentrate on the feel of him. His skin was slick with water and soap, his muscles barely yielding beneath the push of her hands. Then he would tense as he shifted or moved, and those muscles would push back against her fingers like flex-ing steel. She opened her mouth against his shoulder, drinking the water that flowed from his skin to her tongue.

His cock stirred against her belly. She felt it swell against her, felt it rise up and press into her flesh. She pressed tighter, loving the way it slipped against her, relishing the pleasure he must feel at even the smallest shift of their bodies. Putting her teeth to his shoulder, she pushed her hips harder, sighing at the way his shaft slid along sensitive skin.

His fingers dug into her back with a force close to pain. She licked water from his shoulder, his collar-bone, wishing she could swallow him inside her. Her own urgency frightened her. She'd never felt anything like this desperation.

When her mouth found a trickle of water, she followed it down to his chest, licking her way over his nipple and down to his ribs beneath. She bit the muscles of his stomach, making them twitch in shock before she went to her knees before him.

Blinking water from her eyes, she looked at him, at his thick, straight cock, at the rivulets of hot water that snaked down his stomach…and finally at his face as he watched her. His eyes glittered as his jaw bunched with tension. Water dripped from his wet hair. He put one hand to her head, and the other against the wall.

Tessa smiled wickedly up at him, but his expres-sion didn't budge. She nibbled her way down the gor-geous V of muscle that angled down from his hip. But she teased him, dragging her open mouth down to his thigh, kissing her way back up with sweet, slow deliberation.

Luke's fingers stayed loose on her head, but his breathing quickened. His shaft grew even thicker.

Humming in anticipation, she nuzzled her mouth beneath the base of his cock, sucking gently at the tender flesh.

He hissed. His fingers wound into her hair. She sucked and licked him until he finally groaned and tugged her higher. As he urged her up, she let her open mouth drag along his shaft; she pressed her tongue to the sensitive skin, pushing her heat into him.

Finally, she closed her mouth around the flared head, but she wasn't done with her teasing. Instead of taking him deep, she ran her tongue around the ridge, then sucked with just enough pressure that he'd be dying for more. Sure enough, only a few moments passed before he groaned her name.

But today, Tessa wasn't interested in giving him what he wanted. She was selfish, and she'd only been prepping him for what *she* needed. She gave him one last slow kiss, then reached for the condom she'd set on a ledge by the door.

Luke looked dazed as she slowly rolled it down. Her heart thundered with wild anticipation as she pushed to her feet and turned her back to him. She braced herself against the wall and looked over her shoulder. "Fuck me."

His muscles jumped as if she'd slapped him, and the vicious lust on his face looked like anger as he reached for her.

Her boldness paid off. She didn't want him to make love to her tonight, not as if he cared. She needed to be taken, and Luke obliged.

He grabbed her hips with rough hands, and Tessa smiled. She'd never been one of those girls that men went wild for, but Luke was wild now. He growled low in his throat when she set one foot on the tiled ledge of the shower.

She felt his shaft slide along her, and then he pushed into her and Tessa sighed with happiness. "Oh, God, yes," she moaned as he pulled out and pushed deeper.

She eased forward until her forehead rested on the tile and she watched her hand spread wide against the cool white surface.

"Jesus Christ, Tessa," he muttered. He found a rhythm as she arched her back and tilted her hips. He slid against her, inside her, pushing everything else out, and Tessa closed her eyes and relished every thrust. The tile was so cool under her, and his cock so hot inside her, and the water flowed around them, warm and wet.

He squeezed her hips, holding her tight as he took her harder. *Yes,* she thought, *this.* He was so big. So strong. His shaft so thick that she gasped at the feeling of being stretched too tight. Before, he'd treated her like she was innocent, but not this time. Not now. Now he used her like she was made for this.

His hand moved up to cup her breast. He squeezed her, tightening his fingers around her nipple.

"Ah!" she cried out, turning her head to the side, pressing her cheek to the tile. "Yes. *Yes.*"

"Tessa, fuck… You're so damn tight."

The thrill of his words twisted through her, spiraling deep into her belly, winding around her sex. She felt the moment he lost control. His thrusts grew as ragged as his breath. His fingers tightened on her breast and her hip. Tessa smiled as he jerked against her, a rough groan echoing against the glass walls.

When his shudders passed, he stayed tight inside her, and the hand at her breast slid lower. When his fingers brushed her clit, she cried out sharply.

"Your turn, sweetheart," he whispered, tracing circles against that tight bud of nerves.

She bit her lip, straining against him, her brow tightening as the pressure built. Despite that, for a moment, she thought it wouldn't happen. She was trying too hard, desperate to lose herself. But her tangled worries couldn't stand up to the skill of Luke's hands. They were as miraculous as ever, and all of her tension coalesced into that one spot. Her fingers curled into tight fists.

Her body went tight as a bow and she cried out a broken scream as her sex pulsed around his cock. The orgasm crashed through her whole body, rocking her heartbeat into thunder. When it finally faded, Tessa slumped into the wall.

"Holy shit," Luke whispered.

"Yeah," she agreed. "Definitely."

He pulled out of her and collapsed against the other wall. "Are you okay?"

"Yes," she whispered, because she wanted to be. This deal she'd struck with Kendall was scary. And falling for Luke was scary, but sometimes maybe it was okay to be afraid.

"I'M SORRY," HE SAID. "I know this isn't very romantic."

Tessa shook her head and followed Luke as he walked along the fence line of the brewery. "It's fine. The nice thing is that Jamie's busy inside the bar, so our date won't be interrupted."

He tugged on another board. "Maybe we should stop in for a drink."

"Oh, sure. That'd go over great."

As he moved on to another board, he shot her a cautious look. "Are we going to sneak around for a while, you think?"

She felt strangely reluctant to commit to that, so she just smiled and pretended not to notice that he'd asked a serious question. Luckily, the next board tilted out when he tugged on it, and Tessa breathed a sigh of relief as Luke turned his full attention to the fence.

He pulled again, and the board popped off. Luke slipped latex gloves on and tested the next board. It slid out so easily it almost slipped to the ground.

"Sorry," he said. "I just need one second."

"Carry on. You're hot in detective mode."

"Oh, yeah? Maybe I'll show you my handcuffs later."

She knew it was just a slightly distracted joke, but

Tessa felt a shiver of nervous delight at the thought. Maybe indeed.

One last board slid loose, and then Luke disappeared to the other side of the fence. She peeked through to see him take a few pictures with his phone. He walked slowly around the dead end, then bent to pick up a crushed cigarette box. As if he carried a portable crime lab with him at all times, he tugged a clear plastic bag from the pocket of his coat and dropped the box in there. A few minutes later, he stepped back through the opening and began knocking the loose boards back into place.

"Could I ask one more huge favor?"

Tessa would've gladly said yes to anything at that point. Her knees were still weak. Her sex still swollen.

"Could we stop by the department for just a minute? I want to have this printed."

"Absolutely." In all honesty, she was curious about his job. Who wouldn't be? The man solved crimes for a living.

But she tried to act dignified when they got to the police department. She tried not to grin at the uniformed police officer who manned a desk near the door. And she hid her gawking behind casual glances around the big station room as they filed past the few people working the evening shift.

"You can sit at Simone's desk. This'll just take a second."

Tessa sat down and tried not to clap her hands and squeal. Instead, she leaned back in her seat and clasped her hands in front of her, pretending to be a cop. She watched Luke past her lashes as he marked up the evidence bag he'd brought in, then walked off to grab some paperwork. None of his charm was on evidence here. He frowned, his gaze far away and cool. Tessa couldn't help but think of him in the shower, and how rough he'd been just when she needed it.

She shivered and rocked farther back in the chair.

She couldn't imagine working in an office like this every day. She'd never done anything like that. Before turning twenty-one she'd occasionally worked weekends at restaurants, just to get the feel for it, but even that hadn't been common. Mostly, she'd taken care of her brothers. She'd learned how to cook and bake when she was fourteen, and she'd made a meal for them nearly every night, because that's what their mom had done. The idea of letting that kind of thing go...it had terrified her. Eric had been living in his own place, but he'd moved back home to live with them. He'd given up his privacy and freedom, the least she could do was feed him. She'd begged, cajoled and browbeaten Jamie into doing the yard work. They hadn't had a mother and father, but they'd had a nice home. And she'd managed to graduate with straight A's in high school, and nearly a 4.0 in college. But this kind of a normal nine-to-five office life was foreign to her.

Not that it was nine to five, obviously. Luke wasn't the only one here at 7:00 p.m. Tessa glanced over at the guy two desks to the left and found him staring at her. "Hi," she said.

He lifted his chin in greeting, then shot Luke a

narrow look when he walked back into the room. "Got a date, Asher?"

"None of your business," Luke replied without looking up from his papers.

"You sure she should be sitting in your partner's place?"

Luke's eyes rose to meet Tessa's for a second, then he turned a snarl on the other detective. "Watch your mouth, Morrison."

Tessa started to get up. "I can move. I didn't know I was—"

"That's not what he meant, Tessa."

"Oh." Oh. The other cop was referring to the rumors about Simone's baby. She felt a hot flush climb up her neck.

"Hey, Morrison, how about you apologize for being a dick?"

Morrison just grunted and bent back over his work.

"Asshole," Luke muttered as he stapled papers together and copied something from the paper onto the evidence bag. After digging through his drawer for something, he closed it and came around to Simone's desk. "I'm sorry," he said.

"It's no big deal."

He reached past her to open a drawer to her right, but after digging around for a few seconds, he froze. She heard him murmur something too soft to hear. He lifted out a paper and stared at it for a long moment before tucking it back in and closing the drawer. His face had gone tight with an emotion he didn't want to let out.

"One more thing and then we can go."

He stalked out, and as soon as he disappeared around a corner, Tessa eased open the drawer. She leaned to the right, angling her head for a better view inside, and then she saw it. An ultrasound picture. One of those 3-D ones she'd seen on the news. The baby's face was clearly outlined in shades of gray, and that one glimpse told her what the emotion on Luke's face had been...sadness.

Tessa felt all her fears return.

She closed the drawer and looked up at Morrison, but he was done with her. He'd said his piece. He'd made his feelings known. His fellow cops thought Luke was the father, and Tessa didn't know what to think. The way Simone acted toward her...Luke couldn't be the father. So why the hell did Tessa feel terrified that she was being lied to?

SHE'D BEEN QUIET since the station, and Luke was more than sorry he'd taken her there. Fucking Morrison. He was the worst of the whole lot, because he was one of those assholes who thought female cops were nothing but trouble, and anyone who worked with one must be sleeping with her, too. What a mouth-breathing cave-man. Ironically, the only one who hadn't treated him with suspicion was the other female detective in the major crimes division. She seemed content with the idea that it was nobody's business but Simone's. Or hell, maybe Simone had confided in her. Maybe they'd gossiped and giggled about the guy over the bathroom sink. Yeah, right. As if Simone ever giggled.

But that wasn't Luke's concern. His concern was the way Tessa kept worrying her bottom lip with her teeth. The way she kept staring at her water glass while they waited for their meal at her favorite diner.

"Is everything good at the brewery?" he asked.

"Yep. Everything's great."

"Really? I detect a lighter tone. Did you resolve the issues with that deal?"

Her smile started out small, but it soon spread to an all-out grin. Luke's heart responded with its typical lurch.

"Actually, I think that's going to work out."

"Just like that?"

Her smile twitched a bit, but she nodded. "Just like that."

"What about the sticking point? How did you smooth that over?"

"Um, we just agreed to set that aside."

The nice thing about Tessa was that she was a terrible liar. She practically squirmed in her seat, and when the waitress approached with their plates, she leaned back with a sigh of relief. Luke let her take one bite of her omelet before he pushed again.

"So the thing that Jamie screwed up had nothing to do with the negotiations?"

She swallowed her omelet as if it were made of cement. Luke raised his eyebrows and waited.

"It didn't… Um…" She took a sip of water. "The

disagreement didn't really have anything to do with the deal, per se."

"I don't understand."

Tessa looked to the side, as if someone else were listening. "Jamie slept with Roland Kendall's daughter."

"Roland Kendall being the 'Kendall' of 'Kendall Group'?"

"Yes, exactly."

"Christ." Luke shook his head. Jamie had been pretty wild in college, but Luke had been under the impression that he'd calmed down slightly in later years. "How did her father find out?"

"It's a long story. He found out and he called off the deal. I managed to talk him back into it."

"Have you told Eric yet?"

"Nope. And I'm not going to." She popped another bite into her mouth.

Luke set down his fork. "You're not going to?"

"There's no reason to."

"Tessa, everybody else knows. He's going to find out somehow, and then he's going to be extremely pissed that he was kept in the dark."

"I know my brothers, Luke. Eric doesn't need to know, and if I can keep it from him, I will. He doesn't need more stress."

"And Jamie agrees?"

She stabbed her omelet so viciously that the fork clanged against the plate. "Sure. Why would he want to say anything?"

Another lie. Did she think he couldn't tell? Sorting truth from lies was half of his damn job.

But he let it go. It was her family, her secret to keep. And hell, maybe Eric wouldn't want to know. He'd certainly been happy to maintain his ignorance about Tessa's social life. Boy, her brother had been way off on that one.

Strangely, Luke felt almost nervous around her now. When they got back to the car, he didn't know whether he should open the car door for her or hit the locks and molest her in the front seat. Both, maybe? She was a nice girl. And she was a wild woman. She was vulnerable, yet she didn't need him. She was so sunny, but she'd faced more tragedy than he ever would.

This was a dangerous situation. There couldn't be anything *more* dangerous than a combination of fascinating personality and smoking-hot sex. Luke had been fooling himself thinking they could see each other casually and he'd be fine. He'd have to hit the brakes on this fast.

But instead of slowing it down, he took her home. He'd pull back soon, though. After this weekend. Or after he solved the case. Soon, but not now.

He opened two beers and handed her one. "Now we've reached that critical point where we find out if we have anything in common."

She perched on one of the kitchen stools. "In what way?"

"Music or a movie? More importantly, which music or movie?"

"And here I thought you were going to show me your handcuffs."

He started to smile, but there was still something off about her. Something too light, even for Tessa. And earlier, in the shower…she'd been desperate, not happy. "Are you okay?"

"Sure. Why?"

"You're just acting a little…odd."

"Jeez, all I did was ask about the handcuffs."

"Look," he said with a shrug. "I get it. Girls like handcuffs. That's not what—"

"What do you mean 'girls like handcuffs'? How many girls?"

"I just mean that women have brought it up before. Not that I've—"

She set the beer down so hard that foam bubbled over the top and slid down the sides.

"Now you're acting *really* weird," he said. "What's going on?"

She shook her head, then pushed up from the stool and crossed her arms. "I'm just…worried."

"About what?"

"Lots of things."

"Okay. Like what?"

Tessa cleared her throat and tossed her hair back. Luke set down his own beer and braced himself.

"I know we've already talked about it, but this thing with Simone—"

"Damn it," he barked. "I knew I shouldn't have taken you to the station."

"It's not just that guy. I, um, accidentally heard you and Simone talking. Tonight."

"Okay." He thought back, but he couldn't figure out what she might have misunderstood about that.

"You swear you're not the father?"

"I already made that very clear."

She held up her hands. "I believe you. I do. It's just that you seem so close. You're so… I have this horrible feeling you're in love with her, Luke."

Pissed as he was, Luke couldn't help but laugh at that. "If I am, I've sure got a funny way of showing it."

"Yeah, well, remember that Madonna-whore complex? What if I'm the whore?"

"What?" he yelled.

"I'm just saying—"

"How many psych classes did you take in school? Stop pinning these weird diagnoses on me."

"Fine! But you care about her a lot. A *lot*. And I don't want to be the idiot caught in the middle of that."

Luke threw his hands up in the air. "What am I supposed to say? I'm not in love with her. I care about her because we've spent the past two years working side by side together. We don't have those kinds of feelings for each other. Why can't you believe that?"

"I don't know. It scares me."

"Why?"

"Because…" When she swallowed, Luke finally registered that she was close to tears. "Because I don't want to be that stupid girl who falls for someone awful!"

His anger didn't leave him, exactly, but he felt it sink into his body until it was drowned by his rushing blood. "I'm not looking for a relationship," he said quietly.

Tessa looked startled, and she put her hand to her mouth as if she'd just realized what she'd said. "I didn't mean… I know this isn't—"

"So let's take it easy on each other, all right? We'll be careful."

Her hands paused in midair. Frowning, she narrowed her eyes at him. "Careful about what?"

"Falling. If we're going to fall, let's be careful."

She drew in a soft, steady breath. Luke held her gaze, hoping that she'd see he was feeling the same thing. The exhilaration and the fear. He'd never say it, but it was there.

She let out her breath so slowly that he could barely see her chest move, but her pulse beat madly in her throat.

"In case you can't tell," Luke said, "I don't have the best track record. I might not be long-term material."

Tessa shrugged. "We don't have to talk about that now. As long as you promise you're not lying to me."

"That's a promise. I'm not in love with Simone. It's just that…I don't know. I became a cop because I like to look out for people. And Simone…she's like a sister. Plus…"

"What?"

"I guess kids kind of scare me."

"Kids *scare* you?"

He knew it sounded ridiculous. It was hard to put into words. "They're so fragile. The idea of her raising a baby on her own…"

"They're not that fragile. Kids bounce back from almost everything."

Luke shook his head. "People say that, but it's not true. Being a cop in L.A…. Jesus, it was a nightmare, dealing with kids. Like seeing ruined lives playing out in front of you every day. Babies addicted to drugs. Kids left alone because their moms had to work. Kids into trouble just because they had no guidance. Girls out on the street because their dads treated them like shit. They don't bounce back, Tessa. We just tell ourselves that. One wrong step and sometimes that's it."

"But that's not going to happen to Simone."

"Hopefully not, but it can't hurt if I'm around to help, can it?"

Tessa took his hand. "No," she whispered. "That wouldn't hurt at all."

"The world is a cruel place."

"I know," she murmured, and he knew she was thinking of her parents.

"I'm sorry, Tessa."

"Okay," she whispered. "But that's enough talking."

"Yeah?"

"Let's watch a movie. Enough saving the world for one day. Let's just relax. And maybe…fall. Very carefully."

Luke smiled and picked up his beer with a hand that would've shaken if he hadn't moved so carefully. "You got it."

CHAPTER TWENTY-ONE

TESSA FELT LIKE she'd slept half the week away. Granted, not everything she'd done in bed had been sleeping. But she'd obviously been more stressed than she'd thought. She'd spent the night at Luke's a couple of times, but the nights at her own place she'd slept like the dead for nine hours at a time. Now she was wide-awake, clear-eyed and realizing that she hadn't solved her problem at all.

How the hell was she going to get this contract past Eric? She'd put off talking to the lawyer as long as she could. But tomorrow was Monday and she'd have no choice.

She sipped her coffee and stared out the window to her tidy backyard beyond. The trees cast dancing shadows on the brick patio. It was cold today; she could see the hard frost on the grass that hadn't felt sunlight yet. But the bright morning still tempted her. Maybe a walk would help.

Tessa bundled up and hit the sidewalk, trying to force her mind to think. But despite all her sleep, her mind still felt fuzzy, blurred at the edges with her impatience to set this aside and get back to thinking about Luke.

She was in full-on crush mode, a state she hadn't suffered since she'd fallen for Bryce Stevenson in high school. But Bryce had never so much as kissed her. Luke, on the other hand… Oh, Luke offered so many more delicious ways to fall head over heels. She didn't know who she thought she was fooling; there was no careful way to do it. And she wanted to enjoy every reckless moment. That couldn't happen until she solved the problems with this deal.

Tessa walked past the bike shop on the corner of the block, then past the brewery. She kept going, hoping an idea would come to her. Five minutes later, she passed Eric's apartment, ducking her head to hide her face as she walked.

Luke was wrong about keeping this from Eric. Jamie was wrong, too. Eric didn't need to know. One, because he'd be pissed at Jamie for years. And two, because he'd never let Tessa sacrifice her own financial health for the sake of the brewery. Neither would Jamie, but she didn't know who else to turn to.

Though he lived farther from the brewery than anyone else, Tessa found herself heading toward Jamie's place. She didn't go there much. More often than not, when she saw Jamie outside work, he was at her place for dinner or at one of their kickball games.

For a few years after college, he'd shared a place with friends, but last year he'd found an old house being converted into a split duplex, and he'd bought the first-floor unit. She stepped onto the covered front porch and knocked on Jamie's door.

It was ten o'clock and he could still be asleep. Even

if he wasn't asleep, he might not be alone, but Tessa was willing to brave the embarrassment. A full minute later, he hadn't answered, so she knocked again, hoping he'd suddenly appear.

She felt…lonely. She missed just having brothers, the simplicity of those relationships. Jamie couldn't help her figure out what to do about the contract, but maybe they could just sit and catch up on each other's lives.

But he wasn't home.

She didn't know why she felt lonely. She'd certainly gotten lots of attention from Luke this week. Then again, Luke was the source of her uncertainty. What she felt for him was scary. Even assuming he'd been completely honest with her, it was scary. She'd never felt more than friendly affection for any of her other lovers. It had been easy to like them and easy to walk away. But with Luke… God, with Luke she felt like she was standing on a cliff looking out over the ocean. It was beautiful and thrilling and she never wanted to leave, but one more step and she'd have nothing to hold on to. If she let her guard down, she'd plummet.

Tessa stuck her hands in her pockets and started for home at a much slower pace than she'd left it, but she stopped when she got past the corner of Jamie's house. Cocking her head, she frowned at the sidewalk. A rhythmic thunking sound floated from the back of the house.

"What in the world?" she muttered.

Hoping she wasn't sneaking up on the other owner's side of the yard, she tiptoed down the stone walkway and put her eye to the space between the privacy fence and the gate. It took her a moment to locate the source of the sound, but she finally spotted Jamie at the back of the property, wielding some sort of tool.

Tessa eased open the gate, then stood straight and frowned. "What are you doing?"

Jamie jerked to the side with a pickax poised above his head. "Oh, Jesus. It's you."

"Who did you think it was?"

He raised a sardonic eyebrow. "Someone walking through the gate of my yard without invitation?"

"Ha! Silly."

Jamie took off his gloves and wiped his forehead on the sleeve of his shirt. "What's up? Is everything okay?"

"Sure." She turned in a slow circle, taking in the transformation of his yard. "When did you have the yard landscaped?"

"I've been working on it for a while. I started it last fall."

"*You* did this?"

He shrugged and walked to the deck to grab a bottle of water.

Wait a minute… "You've got a *deck?* But I was here… When was that? In January?"

"Yes, I cleverly hid my activities beneath a thick blanket of snow, but you've found me out now. Want some coffee?"

"Sure," she breathed, still taking in the landscaping. Not only was there a big wooden deck, there was a Jacuzzi set into a little gazebo, a rock path that wound through a garden and…whatever he was working on in the back corner. She squinted toward the giant pile of dirt and rocks, trying to figure out what it might be.

"Here," Jamie said, gesturing with a cup of steaming coffee. "Sit down."

She took in the brand-new planks of the deck under her feet, then lowered herself into a red Adirondack chair.

"Sugar and milk," Jamie murmured as he handed her the mug.

"Thanks. What are you making back there?"

Staring toward the pile of dirt, he sipped from his coffee. "Water feature."

"What does that mean?"

He sighed and cut a sideways look at her. "A waterfall."

Tessa's coffee went down the wrong pipe, and she coughed and hacked until her eyes teared up. "A waterfall?" she finally gasped.

"Just a little one. And a lily pond."

"That's…" She searched for a word. Uncharacteristic? Unexpected? Bizarre? "Great," she finally finished.

He rolled his eyes. "With the yard split down the middle, it's long and narrow. I wanted it to lead to something instead of just looking like half of a lawn."

"Okay, but…since when do you do landscaping?"

"I bought some books," he muttered.

Tessa reached past the space between the two chairs

to take his hand. "It looks like something out of a magazine, Jamie. It's amazing."

"Thanks."

"Is that an apple tree?"

Jamie cleared his throat. "Why'd you stop by?"

"I just wanted to see you."

He let it rest at that, and they sat and drank their coffee in silence, watching a flock of blackbirds pick through the garden. And then Jamie ruined it.

"So you're determined to screw around with Luke, huh?"

She huffed and shot him an exasperated look. "Yeah, I'm pretty determined."

"If you want to explore your wild side, I guess you've got a right to that—"

"You *guess?*"

"—but can't you find someone else to do it with?"

Tessa opened her mouth, tempted to channel the screechy outrage of a teenage girl with a brutal crush. But a split second before her tirade spilled out, she saw Jamie's face. Really saw him. And he didn't look arrogant or high-handed. He looked miserable. Tense with worry…over her. Her anger cooled so quickly that she shivered.

"He tried to walk away, you know," she said softly. "When you told him I was a virgin, he tried to end it. He's not a heartless user. He's a nice guy."

"How can you be sure?"

"I don't need to be sure. I'm not marrying him. We're just dating. I'm not a kid anymore. If I'm going to make mistakes, let me make them."

Jamie laughed. "You're seriously telling me that? Fine. I agree. We're too old to sneak around and cover shit up. We've got to make our own mistakes."

"I meant in our personal lives!"

"I know what you meant, but you're wrong. I'm not hiding anything anymore. Eric's not going to ground us. He's not going to cut off our allowance. Hell, he can't even fire us."

"He can leave," she snapped.

Jamie pulled his chin in. "What?"

"He's put in his time. He did what he had to do. But he doesn't need us or the brewery."

"Tessa." He huffed out a startled laugh. "What are you talking about?"

"Nothing," she answered, surging to her feet. "Thanks for the coffee." She set the empty mug down on the deck and rushed away.

"Hey," Jamie called. He stood just as she hit the gate and pushed through.

"I'll see you tonight!" she shouted, speeding up to a jog.

"Tessa!" he called, but she kept on going. It was ridiculous to talk about this stuff. What was the point of that? Talking wouldn't keep anybody close. Maybe Luke was perfect for her. He didn't want to talk about anything, either.

Strangely, that thought actually cheered her up as she rushed down the street. He seemed to take her for who she was, in all her craziness. And she was determined to show him the same courtesy regarding his. Tessa dialed his number and slowed to a walk.

"Good morning, Detective," she said when he answered. "Did you miss me last night?" She'd missed him, but she'd felt too vulnerable spending four nights in a row with him.

"Oh, I missed *something*."

Tessa snorted. "Dirty."

"Speaking of dirty, are you coming over tonight?"

"Actually, I'm busy tonight. That's why I called."

"Are you trying to confuse me?"

She grinned. "Maybe. I've got a kickball game tonight, and I wondered if you'd like to come watch."

"Pardon me?" His voice suggested she'd gone mad.

"The brewery has a team. Tonight's our first game of the season. Do you want to come watch me kickball some ass?"

"Did you just say 'kickball some ass'?"

"What? It's the lingo."

"Okay, I'm going to go ahead and say yes before you scare me away. But what about your brothers?"

Crap, she hadn't even thought about her brothers, which was ridiculous. They were a quarter of the team. "Well, Eric has agreed to stand down, though I'm not sure he'll ask you to join the team. As for Jamie… hopefully he'll be okay as long as we don't dry hump in the outfield."

"Um. Yeah. I think I can manage to avoid that."

"Deal. I'll see you there. It's at six-thirty. The baseball field two blocks past the brewery."

WHEN LUKE GOT to the baseball field he realized his mistake. He shouldn't have promised not to dry hump her in the field before seeing her outfit. Tessa looked like his junior high wet dream.

She wore tube socks that ended just below her knees, then it was a long stretch of smooth, golden thigh right up to her nylon gym shorts. Above that, she wore a tight T-shirt with the brewery logo emblazoned across her chest in eye-catching red. Or maybe the color wasn't eye-catching, but the canvas beneath it. Of course, she'd topped it all off with a high ponytail that glinted gold and bronze in the late-afternoon sunlight.

Luke's chest ached every time his heart beat, and he sat down quickly in the bleachers before her brothers could see how he was ogling her. What the hell were they thinking letting her wear something like that, anyway? He glanced around at the other people in the stands, expecting to see men taking pictures on their phones and posting them to the internet. But the vast majority of the spectators were women. Which made sense, he supposed. There was only one other girl on the team. He recognized her as a server from the fingerprinting they'd done. Otherwise, the rest of the team seemed to be Jamie, Eric, Wallace and the young dishwasher. Eric looked unhappy to be there, but Jamie seemed to be having a good time chatting up two gorgeous women who jiggled a lot when they got excited. But Luke's eyes barely skimmed over them. Tessa was stretching her hamstrings, after all. He had to memorize this for later playback.

When she looked up and saw him, her face caught the sun and her mouth broke into a smile that hit him in the gut. He was starting to get used to it, or at least he accepted the wave of panic that swept over him. Ignoring the daggers Eric's eyes were throwing his way, Luke beamed back at her, then watched every single bounce of her body when she turned and jogged toward the outfield.

The game was on. Luke had no idea what happened as the innings progressed. All he knew was that Tessa jogged closer, and then jogged far away again. Sometimes she jumped up and down at home base a few times. Sometimes she kicked the ball. Luke watched, not thinking about any of his open cases even once. He simply felt the warm sun and the cool breeze and watched Tessa have a great time in her indecently wholesome outfit. It was the best time he'd had in years.

Scratch that. It was the best time he'd had in *public* in years. Of course, the private times were now covered by Tessa, too. And Christ, he couldn't wait to get her someplace private tonight. He prayed to God everybody wasn't going out for drinks and pizza afterward. Luke would go mad if he had to sit next to her thighs at a table with her family.

"Stop staring at my sister that way," a voice said from right beside him.

Luke jumped and reached a hand toward the spot where his gun normally lay. "Jesus," he cursed as he spun toward Eric. "Where the hell did you come from?"

"I'm up last," Eric said, gesturing toward the line at home plate.

Luke hadn't registered anything except the fact that Tessa was only fifteen feet away and she was at the back of the line, providing a fantastic view. "Sorry," he muttered, not even bothering to deny his ogling.

"You'd better not be lying to her."

"I'm not."

"If you are, cop or not, I'll find a way to make you miserable."

"Understood." Luke wasn't going to argue with the man. Eric had every right to worry about Tessa. She looked vulnerable as a fucking lamb out there. "I promise that what you've heard about me isn't true. None of it."

Eric surprised him by saying, "All right. I'll accept that. Until I have a reason not to. I don't want her hiding things from me, so let's call a truce."

Though he nearly choked on his tongue at Eric's words, Luke reached out and shook his hand. Tessa, not hiding things? That'd be the day.

Eric bounded down the bleachers to rejoin his team, and Jamie glared at both his brother and Luke. Strange to think his old friend could still be so pissed, but maybe it made sense. Luke hadn't been an angel in college, and Jamie knew that.

As Tessa moved up to base and waited for the kick-ball pitch, Luke's phone rang. He pulled it from his pocket, keeping his eye on the play. "Asher," he said.

"Asher, it's Ben Jackson down in Denver. You in the middle of something?"

Tessa connected with the ball and raced for first, but she was tagged out before she got there. "Nope,"

Luke said as he stepped down to the ground and circled behind the bleachers. "What's up?"

"I'm pulling a slow weekend shift, so I checked into the records for you. It's strange. Those interviews are definitely missing. I called the investigating detective—he's over in violent crimes now. I figured the case was still fresh, but he claims not to remember anything about the interviews. Says they must have been nothing, since it didn't lead to anything else."

"You sound doubtful."

"Hell, man. I don't know. They're just robberies. I can't imagine anyone would put effort into a department-wide cover-up. Think about how many people it would've taken."

"Could it have been the detective on his own? Maybe a nephew or cousin was involved."

"I could try to track down his partner, if you want." But Ben sounded more than a little reluctant. "He's not the one who signed the reports, though."

Luke shrugged. "I'm sure it's nothing. And thanks."

"All right. Call me if you think of anything else."

When he circled the bleachers, he almost ran straight into Tessa as she stepped around. "Oh, hey!" she said. "Important phone call? Big murder investigation?"

"You're not supposed to look so hopeful."

"Oh, sorry. Right." But she still looked up at him with bright eyes.

"No, it's not a big murder investigation." He let his eyes dip. "By the way, you look…"

She flexed her biceps and posed. "Sporty?"

"No, that wasn't what I was going to say."

She tried on a tough look. "Kick-ass?"

Luke slowly leaned close and set his lips against her earlobe. "Please tell me you're wearing plain white panties, because that would really complete this fantasy for me."

Tessa yelped with laughter, then pressed a hand to her mouth. "What?"

"You look like every cute girl I ever fantasized about in my ninth-grade gym class."

"Ooooh…" She pulled back to raise an eyebrow at him. "Well, well, well, Detective. You do have a filthy side, after all. What is it you imagined these girls doing?"

"Aw, hell, Tessa. I was in ninth grade. By the time I got to the part where I imagined a girl without panties on, it was all over."

Grinning, she took a step closer and put her own mouth to his ear. "So you just need me to lie there and let you slide my panties down? That's all?"

"Honestly? I'm ashamed to say that just might do it."

"Really?" She wiggled her eyebrows. "Let's find out, then."

Luke was wearing a Cheshire grin when he looked up. Unfortunately, his self-satisfied smile was aimed right in Jamie's direction before Luke could wipe it from his face. He stiffened.

"Oh, God," Tessa breathed. "Is one of my brothers standing behind me?"

"Yeah."

"Balls," she muttered.

Luke jumped back and pointed at her. "You *did* say 'balls' that day!"

"What?"

"Never mind," he said before spinning her around to face Jamie. "Great game, man," he offered feebly.

Jamie glared at him before looking at Tessa. "I'm off tomorrow. Chester's coming in to cover me. Call me if there's any problem with that. Or anything else."

"Sure," Tessa said. "I will."

He frowned at her as if he was waiting for something else. "Or come by my place and talk if you want."

She nodded, and Jamie turned and walked away without another glance at Luke. Tessa stared after him.

"I'm sorry," Luke whispered. "I don't want to cause any trouble between you."

"No, it's lots of things. Thirteen years' worth, I think." A deep breath raised her shoulders up, but when she turned to him, she was smiling again. "Come to my place. I'll make you dinner. I'm actually a pretty good cook. And then…maybe I'll let you get to second base."

"Oh, yeah? Maybe I can steal third."

Her smile said she had a better idea. "How about sliding into home?"

Luke groaned at the joke and told her she wasn't funny, but he was secretly giddy as a damn schoolgirl. And falling even faster than before.

CHAPTER TWENTY-TWO

TESSA THOUGHT SHE'D found a way around the problem of the contract. If she wrote up a second contract agreeing to cover the cost of each shipment of Donovan Brothers beer to High West Air for the next six months, Roland Kendall could simply sign the contract that Eric had already had drawn up. That would be the contract her brothers would see.

The only problem with this plan was that Tessa would feel like a scheming, underhanded crook of a sister who'd pulled multiple people into the deception of her family. But she'd already done that, hadn't she? She'd already let half a dozen people know that she was willing to go behind Eric's back to advance her cause.

Well, she'd be the bad guy if she had to be.

Tessa called up the brewery's lawyer and asked if she could put him on retainer for herself personally. It was the only way to keep him from blabbing to Eric.

"Tessa," he said when she finally told him what she wanted drawn up. "What the heck are you doing here?"

"I've made an arrangement to keep the deal alive. That's all."

"But this is… You'll be personally liable for this. I can't allow that."

"Come on, Richard. You're my lawyer, not my boss. Write it up with some safeguards and limits, all right? You have the estimates we worked out with High West, don't you?"

"Yes."

"Protect me from ruin, then, but I know what I'm doing."

"You have the money to cover this?"

"I do as long as you can find a way to limit it to around thirty thousand. I don't want to lose the house."

He sighed in a way that told her Richard was also an older brother. "And I assume Eric and Jamie have no idea you're doing this?"

"I'll counter that with a question. Do I know everything that Eric does?" He didn't answer. She'd known he wouldn't. "When can you get this to me?"

"Wednesday," he said gruffly. He wanted to say no—she could feel that coming through the phone like the pull of gravity—but he likely didn't want to take the chance she'd go to another attorney and do it badly. Richard was a nice guy—compared to anyone, not just other lawyers. She'd have to buy him a beer when this was over.

"Eric!" she called when she got off the phone. He didn't answer, so she walked to his office and knocked on the half-closed door. He waved her in as he finished up a phone call and hung up.

"I just talked to Monica Kendall!" she said.

"Are you two friends now?"

Oh, God, no, she wanted to groan, but she ignored the question. "She said Roland still intends to go forward with the deal. Has he called you yet?"

"No." He looked doubtful. "I don't know, Tessa. I heard through the grapevine that he was talking to a competitor in Denver. I'm beginning to think something isn't right."

"I'm sure it's fine. She said he hasn't signed the contract yet, but he intends to. Maybe he was just doing some last-minute comparisons."

"It's beer, not a defense contract." He frowned and leaned back in his chair. "If this doesn't go through, I'm going to have to revamp our marketing strategy for the next two years. I've worked everything around this."

She nodded frantically. "I know. But let's wait and see. I've got a good feeling." He shot her a doubtful look. Tessa shifted, her heart pattering with nervousness.

"Well, hopefully he'll deign to call me before I head to Santa Fe."

"Oh, is Santa Fe this week?"

"I leave Friday."

For a moment, she'd hoped Eric would be leaving for the microbrewery festival earlier in the week. That would give her another whole week to make sure everything was perfect. But this was for the best. She needed to get this over with.

"I'm beginning to think we might need to hire a full-time marketing person," he said.

"Really?"

"The ad agency is great for promotional stuff, but they can't do the shows personally, and Jamie and I are getting spread thin. I've got Santa Fe this weekend, and he's got Durango in two weeks."

Tessa felt her fingers curl around the arms of her chair. "I could help."

"No, we need more than that."

He wanted to hire another full-time person? Where would they work?

"And if we're going to start adding new states every year, we'll probably need a dedicated distribution person. And more bottling space."

Tessa shook her head, speechless. They didn't have room for all this. "Eric, those are big plans."

He waved a distracted hand. "Yeah, I know. I'm just thinking ahead. We'll work it all out. Thanks for the heads-up on High West."

"Sure," she whispered, getting up to move slowly back to her office. She'd known he wanted to expand, but somehow she hadn't really considered what that might mean. They'd grown a lot in the past few years, but the adjustments had been so gradual that it had felt natural. Normal. But this... She hadn't thought about *this*. If they started adding multiple states at the same time... If they started growing exponentially...

She'd been trying to keep things from changing, but what if *everything* changed? What if she'd helped bring about her own worst fears? She didn't like change. Not at all. Apparently, even less than Eric did.

Trying to ignore this new fear, Tessa put her head

down and made herself see to her normal brewery duties. She paid invoices, issued her own and painstakingly worked her way through yet another change of coverage notice from their insurance company. She found a new review of their amber ale and tweeted a link to it, then updated the website. An email about a delay of a barley shipment probably wouldn't affect production, but she forwarded it to Eric and Jamie just in case.

Fifty other things managed to fill up most of her day, but it didn't clear her mind. In the end, she still picked up the phone to call Jamie, trying not to feel guilty for disturbing him on his day off.

"What's wrong?" he answered, his voice hoarse and sleepy.

"I'm sorry. Did I wake you up?"

"No. What's going on?"

"Has Eric talked to you about his plans for expanding the business?"

"We've discussed it."

"He wants to hire more people, add more bottling space. Where are we going to get more bottling space? This lot is barely big enough for the parking lot as it is."

Jamie cleared his throat. "Yeah."

"We can't move! This is our brewery. It was *Dad's* brewery."

He stayed silent, but the shushing sound of fabric told her he was getting out of bed.

"I'm sorry. Are you alone? I don't want to—"

"Look," he snapped. "I thought you were determined

to give Eric everything he wanted. Why are you
spooked now?"

"I'm not doing this for Eric! I'm doing it for us. All
of us!"

"Tessa." He sighed. She heard a door open on Jamie's side of the line, then the faint brightness of birdsong. She pictured him outside on his deck, looking
out over his yard. She hoped he'd put pants on. "What
the heck's going on with you?" he finally asked.

"Nothing! I just don't want you two fighting! And I
don't want to move. And I don't want five new people
taking over our offices. Things are fine the way they
are."

Her heart dropped so quickly she put a hand flat to
her desk to steady herself. When her pulse found its
way back to her chest, it beat so hard that it invaded
her throat and her skull. Oh, God.

"I can't go on just being the bartender for the rest
of my life. Is that what you want for me?"

"No! Of course not. Eric wants to hire someone
to do distribution full-time. Maybe you could take on
more of that, and we'll hire another bartender."

Tessa rubbed her eyes. "Do you think we should be
making this move with High West?"

"You're asking me this now?"

"You're going to give me a damned ulcer." She
heard him collapse into one of his deck chairs, and
Tessa held her breath. "No, I don't think we should be

involved with these people. I don't like them. But Eric wanted it, so you wanted it. What was I supposed to do?"

Tessa gasped. "Did you sabotage the deal by sleeping with Monica?"

"That is *not* what happened," he ground out.

"All ri—"

"I don't sleep with women to... I'd never... *Jesus.*"

"I'm sorry. Really. I shouldn't have said that."

His breath left him on a long hiss. "This has become crazy, Tessa. All of it. I should've taken my knocks. We should've let this deal go. I don't like these people. Any of them."

"It's not final yet," she whispered.

"He's got the contract. It's done. We'll deal with it."

"Yeah," she murmured.

"It'll be okay, sis. Don't worry."

Tessa agreed, but she couldn't shake her bad feeling. And a few minutes later, her bad feeling became even more justified.

Henry knocked on Tessa's door. "There's a guy in the barroom to see you. Says his name is Graham."

She popped up so quickly that Henry jerked back. Good thing or she would've had to push him out of the way when she rushed past. Eric's door was closed, thank God.

"Graham," she whispered as she approached him. "What are you doing here?"

He had his hands stuffed in his pockets and was

looking over the barroom with condescending good cheer. "I like your place. Very homey."

"Thanks. But what can I do for you?"

"I sent you another email."

"I know. I'm sorry I didn't have time to respond. I'm afraid the answer is still no. We can't afford that kind of sponsorship, and even if we could, we'd need more time."

"You're making a big mistake. There won't be another tournament for a whole year, and in the meantime, you're going to miss out on all that networking, all those possibilities...."

"I know, but—"

"Is your brother Eric here?"

She stepped back. "Why?"

"Because I thought he might be interested in what I have to say." This time his smile wasn't the least bit fake. It was slimy with self-satisfaction and bright with threat.

Tessa's heart beat a hundred miles an hour. "No," she said, willing herself not to glance toward the door. "He's not here. He's prepping for a show in Santa Fe."

"Too bad. Maybe I'll try again later."

He walked out, whistling a perfect rendition of "Happy Talk" as he sauntered through the door. Tessa could only stand frozen with horrified shock. He'd threatened her, hadn't he? What kind of charity tournament was this?

Jamie had been right. These people were bad news. All of them. As soon as she could force her feet to move, she walked back to her office and called her attorney. "If I back out of this deal now, would there be any legal repercussions?"

"Thank God," he murmured, then cleared his throat and carried on. "The only possibility is that Kendall could claim he passed up another opportunity on the basis of your promised deal. But as you're only supplying a product, and he could go with another vendor at any time, his case wouldn't have merit."

"Good. Don't do anything right now, okay? I need some time to think." And plan. And maybe cry a little.

"IT'S ONE DAMN fingerprint," Luke grouched at the technician.

"Yeah, well, you're one detective among thirty. Get in line."

Luke set his head against the doorjamb and banged it a couple of times. "Okay, I'm sorry. Can you give me the status?"

"It's dusted and scanned and the computer is working on it right now. It could be a few minutes. It could be an hour."

"Why didn't you say that first?" he growled as he turned and stalked out. "I'll be at my desk," he tossed over his shoulder. *"Waiting."* He'd sent a team out to sweep the area behind the fence and they'd come up with a few more scraps of trash, but he was focused on the cigarette package. It was an empty packet of Dunhills. Not the most common brand. Dunhill was a high-end English brand, and whoever had bought the pack must have purchased them in a smoke shop, not a grocery store. An odd piece of trash to find next to the lonely curb of a dead-end street.

But if someone had pulled up to the curb and opened the back door of an SUV to load up stolen goods… Even the lightest breeze could've blown that empty pack out of the truck.

Ah, crap, it was a long shot, but what the hell. Maybe he'd get a hit on someone with a record. Maybe the guy's mug shot would come up with Criminal Mastermind Leader stamped across it.

He chuckled, thinking that Tessa would love that.

"Did you get a hit?" Simone asked as he dropped into his desk chair.

"Nothing yet."

"So why do you look so happy?"

He glanced up in surprise. "What?"

"You're walking around here with a smile on your face, Asher. It's freaking everybody out."

He stole a glance around the room, but no one was even breathing in his direction. Simone winked. "Gotcha."

"You're funny. Speaking of, what are *you* so happy about?"

"I don't know," she said, surprising him. He hadn't expected an answer. "I feel better. Not so lost somehow."

Luke sat up straighter in his chair. "Really? That's great."

Her eyes slid down, and he realized she was holding something.

"What's that?"

"Nothing," she said, but when she slipped the small square back into her desk, he recognized it as one of the ultrasound pictures he'd found the other night. "It's a girl," she said softly.

He felt his eyebrows climb.

"The baby," she clarified, as if he might have no idea what she was talking about. "I've decided I'm really happy about that. That's less complicated, I think. Easier for me."

"Because the dad won't be around?" he ventured.

"Yeah."

"You're sure?"

She swallowed. One of her thumbs moved slowly over the top of her belly. "It's…not possible."

That could mean any number of things. Luke's mind started turning over the possibilities, poking holes into the great mass of questions he had. But he forced his mind to step back and let it go. There was a father somewhere. Someone she loved or didn't love. Someone she'd met once or known for years. It didn't matter. It meant nothing. "I'm glad you're feeling better," he said simply.

"Thank you."

A girl. Maybe Tessa would help him pick out a gift.

"Asher," a voice said just before a hand dropped an envelope on his desk. "Your print."

He was still muttering a thank-you when he ripped open the manila envelope and pulled out the paper. The name caught at him like barbed wire dragged across his mind. What the hell? He knew this name. How?

Almost frantic, he typed in the name and pulled up everything he could find. Still confused, he tossed the paper to Simone. "You know this guy?"

She shrugged and shook her head. "I don't think so."

"Shit."

The guy had been processed at some point. He'd been fingerprinted, obviously, but there were no charges, just tickets. A few traffic tickets. One for drunk and disorderly years before, another ticket for possession of marijuana. Probably the guy had gone to the U. Is that why the name struck a chord?

He tapped a pencil against his forehead for a full minute. When that didn't shake any thoughts loose, he pulled up Google and typed in the name. And the results hit him like a freight train.

Shit. This was serious. And he couldn't say one word to Tessa. "I've got to call Denver."

"What is it?" Simone asked.

"It's a whole crapload of trouble, is what it is. And I think I know why those case files lost some of their contents."

CHAPTER TWENTY-THREE

"YOU'RE QUIET TONIGHT," Tessa said as she pushed her fried chicken around on her plate. "Big murder investigation?"

He managed to crack a brief smile. "Nah. I just can't seem to shut off work."

"I understand. It's hard to maintain interest after a full two weeks of dating."

"Sorry," he said, making an effort to relax. He aimed a pointed glance at the one lonely drumstick on her plate. "You're pretty quiet yourself. Tired of me?"

"We'll see. Maybe it's your turn to bust out the fancy lingerie."

"Did those Wonder Woman panties you had on yesterday count as fancy lingerie?"

"They seemed to do the trick for you, so they count."

His smile lasted a lot longer this time. "I'll try to step up my game, then."

She laughed, but she still didn't eat more.

"Dinner was great," he said. "Thanks for cooking for me. I'm impressed."

"More confirmation that I'm the perfect woman?"

"You bet."

She stood and took her plate to the sink. Luke didn't like the tense line of her shoulders, so he followed her and snuck his arms around her waist while she rinsed the plate. When he kissed her neck, she leaned into him with a sigh.

"Are you still worried about the deal?" he asked, hoping she'd yell, *Yes!*

Nodding, she turned off the water, but didn't move away. "I don't know what to do," she whispered.

Relief stabbed him like a blade, but he tried not to let it show. "I thought the deal was finalized."

"Not yet. I'm having second thoughts. I think I can still get out of it."

"Why do you want to get out of it?"

"It's just… The Kendall Group is a big, success-ful company. I think the deal could make us money. I think we could expand. But what if I don't want to expand?"

"What do you mean?"

"I like things the way they are."

He turned her around and kissed her forehead. "You know you can't make this decision on your own. That's a serious conversation you need to have with Eric *and* Jamie."

"I've already talked to Jamie. He agrees."

"He doesn't want to expand?"

"I'm not sure he cares either way, but he doesn't like the Kendall family any more than I do."

Luke stepped back, his hands still on her shoulders

as he watched her face. "The Kendall family?" He'd been afraid he'd have to bring this up himself.

"Yes, Roland Kendall and his daughter and his son. There are others we haven't met, but… At first they seemed normal. Now they all seem slimy."

He dropped his hands and paced across the kitchen, then back to her, trying to figure out a way to tell her something without telling her anything. "There's one piece of advice I give to any crime victim who asks. You have to trust your gut. If you're thinking that something is off, then something is off."

"Always?"

"Every single time. I'm serious. You can't ignore that."

Tessa chewed on her thumbnail. Luke ducked down to meet her gaze. "If you can back out of this deal, then do it. At least put off the decision for a few days."

"Okay."

There was that blade of relief again, gutting him open. "In fact, why don't I do a little research for you? See if I can turn anything up."

Her face broke into a smile. "That would be so great. Thank you."

"It's the least I can do. Just don't make a decision until I get back to you, all right? Promise?"

"Promise." She hugged him and gave him a kiss before pulling away to grab his plate and finish cleaning. "So how's Simone?" she asked.

"I'm still not in love with her, if that's what you're asking."

Tessa laughed. "That's not what I was asking."

"She's great, actually. She's talking about the baby more. Doesn't look so tired. It's a girl, by the way. She told me today. Maybe you'll help me buy some stuff? I don't know anything about, uh, pink."

She grinned at Luke until he cleared his throat and looked away. "You're sweet."

"Yeah, right."

"Do you want kids?"

He shrugged. "I've never thought much about it."

"Not even when you were married?"

His body turned to steel. How the hell had he stumbled into this conversation? "We were young," he said, adding nothing else.

"But you must have had plans. How long were you married?"

Luke crossed his arms. "Three years."

Tessa crossed her own arms and glared at him. "I'm not interrogating you, Luke. You don't have to get so defensive."

"I'm not defensive," he snapped. "I just don't like to talk about it."

"I hardly asked anything at all."

"Okay, but we both agreed there were places we weren't ready to go."

"I know, but I've talked to you about my brothers. I just thought…"

Oh, he couldn't believe this. As if he didn't have enough on his plate. "Is that the way you think it works? Tit for tat? Fine, then. You tell me about your worst breakup. Go ahead."

She rolled her eyes at his challenge. "I would, but I've never been through a bad breakup."

"Come on, Tessa. I'm not one of your brothers. It's pretty clear you've been in relationships before."

"I'm not pretending I haven't dated. I've dated plenty. It's just never gotten serious."

He took a step back. "Really?"

"What?" she snapped. "I've been busy."

"Doing what?"

"Working."

His eyebrows rose. "In a mine?"

She glared at him with enough heat that he felt singed. "I haven't exactly had a normal life. I've been a small-business owner since I was fourteen. And in high school and college, I didn't have time for a boyfriend. I had a house to take care of. A family."

Oh, shit. He'd stumbled into her parents' death again, with all the grace of a raging elephant. "I'm sorry. You're right."

"Well, I wasn't raised in a foundling home or something. Don't look at me like that."

"Sorry," he said again, his gaze sliding to the floor.

"Dating has been fine for me. I just didn't have the emotional stamina for anything else, okay?"

"Sure. I understand. But I want you to understand, too. I've never talked to anyone about my divorce, and I'm not going to start talking about it like this. I'm not going to be poked and prodded like I'm in therapy."

"I only asked a few questions! You're overreacting."

"Probably," he managed past his tight jaw. "Look, I've got to get back to work."

Tessa drew herself up in outrage. "Since when?"

"Since I can't stop stressing about work and I'm obviously not fit company tonight. I'm sorry. I'll call you later."

She put her hands on her hips and glared at him.

"I'm sorry," he said again, not much of an apology to offer as he grabbed his coat and left.

Tessa must not have thought it was much of an apology, either, because he heard her mutter, "Asshole," just before the front door closed.

He should go back. He should apologize. But Luke felt so guilty that his body didn't seem to fit inside his skin. He rolled his shoulders and cracked his neck, then headed straight back to the station.

How could he have been so insensitive about her love life? Of course she was closed off. She must've had a pretty ideal childhood until the day her parents had died. She'd been adrift afterward, surely…thrust into thinking about things other teenagers didn't think about. Hell, when Luke had been fourteen, all he'd thought about was himself. And girls, but only when those girls had to do with him.

He also felt bad that he'd lashed out about the divorce. She couldn't know how hard the divorce had hit him. She couldn't know that it had both broken his heart and shamed him to his bones. He could try to explain it to her, but then she'd be ashamed for him, too, wouldn't she? How could she accept that he'd been so bad at being a husband that Eve would've rather died alone than stay married to him? He'd felt… Jesus, he'd felt *desecrated* by the time he'd left California. How could he let Tessa see that?

But at the moment, his sharpest regret was having to lie to Tessa about Graham Kendall. He didn't have anything solid yet. Just a fingerprint and a hunch. He could not tell the victim of a crime that an acquaintance might be responsible, not until he had proof. And he couldn't blow up this deal without evidence.

Thank God she had good instincts. That alleviated some of his guilt, at least. She was sharp as hell, and she'd figured the important parts out for herself.

As Luke pulled into the station parking lot, he dialed Ben Jackson in Denver one last time. Ben hadn't answered his phone all day, so Luke assumed he was off, but maybe he was pulling a night shift tonight. Or, like Luke, he could've come into the office to hide from personal trouble. It was a pretty common ploy among cops. Criminal investigations were problems that could be solved. Emotions were way more messy. It was so easy to tell yourself that solving a murder was more important than resolving an argument about the checkbook.

The call went to voice mail, so Luke hung up. Maybe Ben had figured out how to have a good life outside the job. Luke hoped he was getting there, too. It was easier in Boulder, which had been his main goal in coming here. Being a cop in L.A. had been too brutal. It separated you from everyone else. It had certainly separated him from his wife. Then again, according to her, they'd never been very tightly connected.

Christ, he had a headache, but he couldn't blame that on his ex-wife. It was this damn case.

Graham Kendall ran a private jet company for rich men. By all accounts, he was rich himself. In addition to being president of Kendall Flight, he was on the board of the Kendall Group. So why would he be orchestrating local break-ins?

Determined to find out more about Graham Kendall, he called up the FBI's national crime database for the third time that day. There wasn't much on Kendall, but what did pop up was strange. A moving violation in Las Vegas, and another in Denver. Nothing unusual for a man who likely owned sports cars, but the fact that such minor infractions showed up on the national database…that made no sense. It was almost as if they'd once been associated with something else. An arrest. A warrant. Something that had been wiped from the system.

His cell rang, and Luke hoped it would be Tessa, but Ben's name shone on the screen. "Speak of the devil," Luke said when he answered.

"Sorry I missed you. I was interviewing a witness."

Luke bit back the impulse to ask if it was a big murder investigation. Tessa had invaded his brain. "I think I've got a lead on our robberies."

"Great!"

"Have you ever heard of a guy named Graham Kendall?" Luke listened closely in case Ben knew something he wasn't planning to reveal, but he sounded relaxed when he answered.

"I don't think so. You want me to check into something?"

"Yeah. I want everything you've got on the guy." Luke handed over every relevant detail he had on Graham Kendall, then settled in for a long wait. He was just opening Google when his phone rang again. "That was quick."

"I think you were expecting someone else," his mom said.

"Oh, hey, Mom. How are you?"

She talked about her garden and her work as a part-time substitute. As usual, she brought up going back to work as a full-time teacher, and Luke did his best to talk her out of it. Then the conversation took a more significant turn.

"So...how's Tessa?"

He had to smile at the way his mom said Tessa's name as if she knew her. "Fine."

"Still seeing her?"

"A little," he said, glancing up at the ceiling to brace for a lightning strike.

"Well, I'm sure she's nice."

"Funny, you don't know anything about her."

"I'd like to. What does she do?"

"Let it go. If it gets serious, I'll tell you more."

She gave a little sigh of displeasure. "I'm just curious."

"All right," Luke muttered. "Fine. She owns her own business."

Her gasp sounded suspiciously happy.

"Now," he said quietly. "Why don't you tell me why you're suddenly so curious about my personal life?"

"There's nothing sudden about it." Her voice turned high at the end of the sentence.

He let his head fall back to the top of the chair. "Spill it, Mom."

"Spill what?"

"When's Eve getting married?"

Utter silence met his question. He couldn't even hear her breathe. That was all the answer he needed. "What do you mean?" she finally whispered.

"She shows up to visit. She looks better than ever. You tell her I'm seeing someone just to be sure she knows I'm not still stuck on her. You're suddenly invested in my personal life. She's remarrying, right?"

"She brought your ring back," his mom said on a rush. "She said you wouldn't take it when you moved out, but she couldn't keep it any longer because… She met someone. They're moving in together and… making plans."

Luke let all the air ease out of his lungs as his chest tightened. "I see." He waited for the hot pain. For the betrayal. For the violent hurt she'd once caused him. The sense of failure. But the worst that he felt was a sort of irritated curiosity. Had she fallen for someone like Luke despite her best intentions? Or had she found someone who could truly make her happy? To his surprise, he hoped it was the latter.

"I'm okay," he said to his mom, though he was speaking the words to himself, as well. "It's fine. You don't have to worry."

She drew a shaky breath. "I loved her. Maybe it wasn't right to still love her after the divorce, but I did. But I hated what she did to you. Don't ever doubt that."

"I know," he said, but he wasn't sure he had. Regardless, it was over now.

"I'm glad it's behind you, Luke. It's been a long time."

It had been. They'd been divorced longer now than they'd been together. What a strange thought. No wonder the wounds had healed. "All right. Just so you don't worry... Yes, I'm still seeing Tessa, but we're taking things slow. It's complicated."

"Taking things slow, huh? That's sounds pretty serious."

He laughed as he said goodbye. It was serious. And scary as shit. But if it turned out bad, he was ready for that. If it turned out great... Well, maybe he was ready for that, too.

Turning back to Google, he typed in "Graham Kendall" and tried to work through the thousands of hits. When he got to the fifteenth description of the same aeronautics event, he gave up and tried an image search. There were plenty of pictures of planes and airports, but there was a third type of image that stood out. Graham in Las Vegas. Graham surrounded by neon lights and scantily clad women. Graham gambling.

Maybe it meant nothing. The guy was seemingly wealthy and only thirty-four years old. Vegas was a natural watering hole for a man like him. But it could just as easily become quicksand.

Ben called back a few minutes later. "I don't know," he said.

"You don't know what?"

"Something is rubbing me wrong about this one. His file is pretty thin, but there's a note in here. Something about an interview, but there's no record of an interview."

Bingo. "What did they want to talk to him about?"

"No idea."

"I'm getting weird hits on the national database, too. You know the case files I was asking about yesterday? The ones with the holes in them?"

"You think it's related."

"I've got this guy's fingerprints outside a robbery scene. His file's incomplete, those robbery files are incomplete."

"Yeah."

"Will you give me the other detective's name? The one whose partner moved to violent crimes?"

"He's a pain in the ass," Ben warned. "A real battle-ax. I only call him as a last resort."

Luke smiled. "I'll leave it till morning, then." But come morning, he was going to nail Graham Kendall to the wall.

CHAPTER TWENTY-FOUR

LUKE STARED AT Graham Kendall through the tiny square of reinforced glass in the interview room door. The guy was cool as a cucumber, still neatly pressed and groomed in his expensive suit and silk tie. He didn't look like a man who'd been interrogated by the police for two hours. He looked like an executive humoring his managers with a meeting. His lawyer was a little more tense, but Luke didn't think that had anything to do with the situation. The guy looked like he had a stick up his ass 24/7.

They weren't getting anywhere with the questioning, so Simone was trying out her good-cop routine, even encouraging Graham to flirt with her. Graham was clearly a man used to manipulating women if he expected clear-eyed Simone to believe he'd be interested in a date with a significantly pregnant woman.

What a slimeball.

Luke reached distractedly for his phone and dialed Tessa's number.

"Hello, Detective," she answered after only one ring.

Her voice snuck through the phone like a seductive hand. "Hello, Tessa."

"Did you call to apologize?" she prompted.

"I do apologize. I was preoccupied last night. And tense. I'm sorry."

"It's okay," she said easily.

"But that's not why I called. I need to see you and your brothers immediately. We've got a lead on the robbery, and I need to ask you a few more questions. Do you think you could get everyone together?"

"Sure, everyone's here right now. What kinds of—"

"I'll be there in five minutes." He raised a hand to get Simone's attention, then tilted his head toward the hallway. She was still rising when Luke opened the door. "Gentlemen, if you'll excuse us. We've got an emergency, but we should be back in an hour."

"Detective Asher," the attorney said, his words rigid with the knowledge that his client wasn't yet under arrest. "You can't expect my client to remain here all day. He has no knowledge of the robbery and you have no reason to suspect him—"

"Aside from the print."

"There's no proof he's even been on Donovan property. He's answered every question, and now he needs to get back to his work. If you could—"

"We only need a few more—"

"We're leaving," the attorney snapped. Graham Kendall's mouth rose in a confident smile.

"It's one o'clock," Luke interrupted. "How about if you take Mr. Kendall out for a nice lunch, then stop back in and see if we have any more questions."

"Nonsense."

"I'd hate to find that we had difficulty locating Mr. Kendall after lunch. We might be forced to call his associates, his employees, his clients, just to track him down."

Kendall's smile stiffened.

"Are you threatening my client, Detective?"

"Of course not. I'm just worried about the time I'll lose making phone calls if Mr. Kendall leaves Boulder before Detective Parker and I can finish this interview."

The attorney darted a look at his client. "Fine. We'll be back in an hour. But this is the end of my client's generosity. Much as he'd like to help, he has important duties as president of Kendall Flight. I'm sure you understand."

Luke followed Simone into the hallway. "We're heading over to the brewery. Let's find out what the Donovans know about this guy."

"That guy's so slimy I feel like I need a shower," Simone muttered. "You should've seen the way he leaned closer after he checked out my empty ring finger."

"What? Desperate single moms are hot."

"Bite me."

Luke smiled, but it was halfhearted. His gut churned with adrenaline. It was the normal excitement of getting so close to an answer that he could taste it, but that excitement was mixed with the anxiety of breaking this news to Tessa. But he'd been a cop a lot longer than he'd been her lover, and he owed it to this job to do it the right way.

"You okay with this?" Simone asked.

"I think so. I've got no choice, regardless."

"I could do it alone."

"That'd be worse, wouldn't it?"

She shrugged. "Probably."

"Let's just get it over with. Hopefully they'll tell us something that'll trip him up." Luke was hopeful, but not expectant. This case was too convoluted to allow for planning.

As he and Simone headed for the door, their sergeant stepped out of the records room and nearly smack into Simone's path. He stumbled back with an alarmed look at the stomach he'd almost rammed. "Excuse me."

Simone brushed past him.

Once they were out of earshot, Luke leaned close to her ear. "You two still arguing about desk duty?"

"Yes."

"Don't you think he has a point?"

"No. I'm pregnant, not disabled."

"But the baby—"

"Luke, I swear to God…"

He raised his hands and fell back. "All right. I got it." But this time she didn't give him the silent treatment. Not that she was ever chatty, but they talked over the interview with Kendall and agreed that neither believed a word he'd said. The man was behaving like any upstanding businessman brought in on a charge of robbery. What he didn't know was that Luke had finally spoken to the other guy who'd worked the robbery cases in Denver. And he now knew just what had been cleared from the records.

"I assume you want me to stand on the sidelines?" Simone asked as they pulled up to the brewery.

"At first. But jump in if I miss anything."

"You think you'll be distracted by an outraged girl-friend?"

"Good possibility." Luke didn't bother correcting the girlfriend title. There was nothing dangerous in letting that stand when she might not even speak to him after today.

One o'clock on a Tuesday apparently wasn't a busy hour as there were no other cars in the parking lot. He'd almost been hoping for witnesses to keep the mayhem to a low level, but no such luck.

As soon as Luke opened the door, Eric strode forward, wiping his hands on a towel. "You've got news?"

"I do. Is everyone here?" Before Eric could answer the question, Tessa pushed through the swinging door and held it open for Jamie. Jamie lugged a keg through the door and set it behind the bar. Tessa met Luke's eyes with a smile. Last night's argument seemed to have been forgotten. Luke would've felt relieved if he hadn't been facing this next few minutes.

"Why don't we all sit down?" he suggested. Only Tessa's face registered the correct amount of wariness at his words. She lowered herself slowly to a chair and placed her hands flat on the table.

Luke folded his hands in front of him. "We picked up someone this weekend who was involved in the break-in."

"Involved?" Eric asked. "How?"

"He walked in, took the computers and the keg and walked out."

"Walked in?" Eric snapped. He shot an ice-cold look at Jamie. "What do you mean, he just walked in?"

Luke held up a hand. "Someone contracted him. Told him not to worry about the door or the alarm."

"I locked that fucking door," Jamie growled. "I set the alarm."

Tessa touched his hand to calm him down. "Who contracted the thief?" she asked. Ah. Here was the sticking point.

"The guy got an anonymous phone call. If he did the job, he could keep anything else he wanted. The caller just wanted the computers."

Tessa frowned. "For the Social Security numbers."

"Yes. The thief left the computers on the other side of your back fence. Aside from the phone call, he had no contact with the caller."

"So that's it?" Jamie asked. "That's all you've got?"

"Not quite. I found a cigarette pack on the other side of the fence. We got a print."

Jamie made an impatient hurry-up gesture. Luke played the coward and held Jamie's gaze instead of looking at Tessa. "The print belonged to Graham Kendall."

Tessa gasped. Loudly. But her brothers both just frowned. "Kendall?" Eric asked. "As in Roland Kendall's son?"

"Yes."

"Graham," he muttered. "The guy who runs Kendall Flight. That makes no sense."

Luke finally dared a look at Tessa. Her face was pale as snow, her lips still parted in shock.

"I know at first glance it must seem like an odd coincidence," Luke said. "But I have reason to believe that—"

"When did you get that print?" Tessa blurted out.

Luke cleared his throat. "I picked up the print on Wednesday, but we didn't get a hit until later."

"How much later?" she pushed.

"Yesterday."

"Yesterday." Her mouth barely moved. "You had Graham Kendall's name yesterday."

He held her gaze and didn't say a word.

Eric waved a hand. "What the hell does that matter? I want to know what all this means."

Luke nodded. "We need to know which of you knew Graham Kendall. How you know him. How much time he's spent in the brewery."

"We don't know him," Eric insisted. "Well, Tessa ran into him once."

"I went to lunch with him," she clarified.

"What?" Eric asked. Luke tried not to assume the same outraged expression.

"It was just lunch. He wanted to discuss that charity event."

"What charity event?" Simone asked at the same time Eric barked, "When?"

Luke was more interested in the timing question. "When?" he repeated, pretending it had to do with the investigation and not the sharp stab of jealousy in his gut.

"Last week," she said. Yeah, that was jealousy.

"Why didn't you tell me about this?" Eric asked, again echoing Luke's thoughts.

"We spoke about the promotional opportunity. We decided not to pursue it."

"Don't you think I should've been invited to that lunch?"

"I don't know, Eric," she snapped. "Do you invite me to every business lunch you have?"

He pulled in his chin. "That's not the same."

"How is it different? I met with him. He was slimy, and he wanted us to make a decision about a $55,000 promotional sponsorship in two days. I told him to take a flying leap."

Simone spoke up again. "What was the name of the charity event?"

"I don't remember. It was in California. He sent me an email. I'll print it out for you if you want."

Luke nodded. "Was he ever in the brewery?"

Eric shook his head, but Tessa said, "Just once. He stopped by yesterday afternoon. He was never here before the robbery, as far as I know."

Luke nodded, but he noticed that Jamie's face had turned a sick shade of gray beneath his tan. "Jamie, you were working that night. Was he here?"

"No." His voice was raspy with tension.

"But you've thought of something."

He swallowed hard, his eyes darting toward Eric.

"Jamie," Tessa said quietly, and Luke realized what

was going on. The sister. She'd been here. He almost blurted it out right then, but Tessa's eyes were wide with horror as she stared her brother down. "Jamie," she said again, his name nearly a whisper. Luke held his breath and hoped he wouldn't have to force the issue.

"I have to tell them, Tessa," Jamie said. "You know I do."

Eric looked back and forth between his siblings. "What the hell is going on here?"

Tessa held up her hands as if she could stop the tide, but Jamie granted her no mercy. "Monica Kendall was here. The night of the robbery. She was here when I locked up."

That night. Shit.

Eric scowled in confusion. "She came to the brewery? Why?"

Jamie cleared his throat, but Luke's eyes were on Tessa. Tears turned her eyes to green pools. Her mouth opened several times, but she didn't speak. He wished he was just her boyfriend, wished it was that simple. But he was here as a detective, and he couldn't say or do anything that would stop the flow of information. His hands fisted. He dug his fingers into his palms, wishing his nails were long enough to cause pain.

"She said she wanted to try the beer," Jamie said. "She came by around seven."

"And she stayed until close?" Eric asked. Luke already knew that answer.

"Yeah," Jamie said. "She stayed until close."

Luke stepped in to cut off any more of Eric's questions. "Do you think she could have seen you enter the alarm code? Would she have had a chance to unlock the door after you locked it?"

"Not the back door. Maybe the front, I suppose."

"And the alarm?"

Luke saw the answer in Jamie's eyes. Apparently so did Eric. His face had lost its shock and now fury sharpened his features to stone. His blue eyes turned to platinum. "She was here when you locked up. She saw you enter the code, which means she left with you. Right? That's what you're saying? Despite everything that was riding on this deal, you fucked her, didn't you?"

Tessa flinched, but Jamie met his brother's gaze head-on.

"She said she was feeling tipsy. She asked me to drive her home."

"And that's all you did." There was no question in Eric's voice. His words dripped with scorn, and Jamie finally looked away.

Tessa drew a breath that caught in her throat, and despite his intention to approach this impersonally, Luke reached a hand out to touch her arm. She jerked away.

Simone stepped forward. "So tell us exactly what happened as you were leaving."

Tense silence ruled the room for a few heartbeats before Jamie nodded. "There was one table left at closing time. Normal for a Monday. I shooed everyone out, but Monica stayed behind. She said she didn't think she could drive. Asked if I would drive her home. She'd been drinking sample glasses, trying out the different beers, but she'd had six or seven, and she's skinny, so I didn't think anything of it." His eyes cut to Eric. "If a woman says she can't drive, I take her at her word."

"So she stayed behind," Simone pushed.

"Yeah. I warned her it would take a few minutes to close up. I locked the front door, turned off the signage lights, finished cleaning the front room."

"Then what?"

"Then I carried the glassware to the back, and turned off the office lights."

"So she could've unlocked the front door then."

"I guess so. I didn't recheck it."

Luke nodded. "The cameras didn't catch anyone in the front lot, but if someone came from the back and stayed close to the wall, I think they could've slipped by the camera." He gestured for Jamie to continue.

"I was finishing up when Monica came in back to join me."

"So you didn't even go back to the front room?"

"Just to turn off the lights and glance around. That's it."

"And then she left with you via the back door?"

"Yes. She was…she'd been flirtatious. She was definitely very close when I set the alarm."

"So she could've watched you."

"Yeah."

Tessa sounded like she was choking. "This doesn't make any sense," she whispered. "They're rich. They're successful. Why would they risk everything to steal a few computers from us?"

"I'm not sure it's that simple," Luke answered. He watched her arms cross and hold each other and wished she'd let him touch her.

Simone leaned close. "Monica Kendall," she whispered. Luke nodded. They needed to interview her as quickly as possible. If they could get the sister to cooperate, Graham would be under arrest soon enough. Luke stepped back to call the station to have a check run on Monica. He avoided the radio, unwilling to let a reporter get ahold of his story before it blew up. As he waited on the phone, Luke watched Tessa lean in and speak in a low voice to Eric, but Eric pushed up from the table and walked away. Tessa followed, but Jamie stayed in his seat, his shoulders relaxed, his face peaceful. He'd obviously wanted to confess, but Tessa looked grief-stricken.

"I'll grab the print kit," Simone said, pointing toward the lock high on the front door. Seconds later, a dispatcher informed him that Monica Kendall had no record in Colorado, not even an outstanding parking ticket. He hoped this was her first interaction with the police. She might panic and blurt out a confession before her lawyer arrived. They couldn't stop a person from incriminating herself if she wanted to.

Simone pulled prints from the lock. Eric disappeared into the offices while Tessa stood looking helpless.

"Let us know what you find out, man," Jamie said as he slowly rose to his feet and rolled his shoulders back.

"I may have to ask you a few more questions about Monica, but only if the need arises."

"I understand." Jamie's eyes slid toward Tessa. "I'll be in the back," he said. Simone packed up the kit and went to wait in the car. They were finally alone. He was surprised when Tessa spoke first.

"I can't believe you," she said dully.

"I couldn't tell you."

She raised her chin. "Legally?"

"Not legally, per se, but ethically."

"Then what you're saying is you *wouldn't* tell me."

He'd been expecting this and didn't even cringe. "If that's the way you want to look at it, fine. I tried to warn you—"

"Warn me? With little hints and pretend sympathy?"

"That wasn't pretend. And I wasn't sure of anything. If I'd—"

"Just…" She held up a hand, closing her eyes. "I don't want to talk about this now. I need to go try to save my family."

"I think you're overstating the—"

Her growl interrupted him, and Tessa stomped from the room without another word. Luke wanted to go after her, but he needed to work the lead. And perhaps that was for the best, as his impulse was to chase her down and tell her she was being ridiculous and melodramatic. He was better off getting back to work.

When he got into the driver's seat, Simone shot him

a questioning look. He ignored it just as he ignored the painful lurch of his heart as he pulled from the parking lot.

TESSA HEARD THEIR VOICES before she even pushed past the swinging doors. They weren't yelling yet, and she felt a brief moment of hope that stabbed through her like a knife, but the knife turned when she saw them, squared off in the middle of the kitchen. This wasn't a friendly conversation. Eric's hands were fists, and Jamie's face was twisted into a snarl. Wallace leaned against the door to the tank room, looking as if he were settling in for a long movie.

"Unbelievable," Eric snapped. "Really, truly unbelievable. How many times did I warn you to stay away from her?"

"I did stay away from her."

"Oh, really? Then how did you end up between her damn legs, Jamie? Huh? How did that happen?"

"I said I drove her home. Why do you automatically assume I slept with her?"

"Didn't you?" Eric yelled.

"That's not the point."

"It's exactly the point. Goddamn it, there was a reason I didn't want you to meet her. You both treated me like I was crazy, but look what happened!"

"I didn't mean to—"

"Oh, you never *mean* to. But you never manage to exercise a second of self-control in your life. Not one."

Jamie stepped into Eric's face. "That's not true. I've never punched you in the damn face, have I?"

Tessa rushed forward. "Stop!"

"Come on, Tessa." Eric laughed gruesomely. "Maybe Jamie needs a good ass kicking."

"Just calm down," she begged, grabbing both their elbows. "The deal is back on. Nothing was ruined."

Eric stood straighter, taking a step back from Jamie so he could look at her. "What do you mean, the deal is back on?"

Ice swept over her body. "I meant the deal is fine."

"No, that's not what you meant."

Jamie shook off her hold and stepped back, as well. "Give it up, Tessa. I'm telling him the truth."

"What truth?" Eric barked.

"Roland Kendall caught me leaving Monica's place in the morning. He called off the deal."

A tiny sob snuck past Tessa's throat when she saw Eric's face go blank with shock. "It's back on," she whispered past the tightness.

Eric shook his head. "When did this happen?"

"Two weeks ago," Jamie said. "The day after the break-in."

"Roland Kendall called off the deal two weeks ago, and you two hid this from me? You lied to me? Both of you?"

"I'm sorry," Tessa rasped.

"Tessa… You…"

"I wanted to fix it," she explained.

"Fix it? Christ, how could you leave me out of it? All of our plans…our expansion…?"

"I didn't want you to be mad."

"Be *mad?* Jesus, what are you, twelve years old? This is a business!"

"It's not!" she yelled. "It's not just a business. It's our whole family!"

"Oh, it's nice to know it's so easy for you to lie to your family, then. Tessa, I'm starting to think I don't know anything about you."

Jamie stepped in. "Come on, man. Leave her alone."

Her panic tripped to a higher level. Now Eric was mad at both of them. Furious. A vein pulsed in his temple. His eyes were pale as ice. Tessa's heart radiated pain with every beat. She pressed a hand to her chest. "I'm sorry. I wanted to fix it. I *did* fix it."

"That's not the point," Eric said. "You've been hiding this from me for two weeks, going behind my back to Kendall and God knows who else."

"I'm an owner of this company, too. You conducted the initial negotiations on your own. You can't fault me for talking to him."

"Can't I?"

She pressed her chest harder. "But it's all good in the end, isn't it? We don't even want this deal now, do we? He didn't sign the contract yet. And now we know the whole family might be insane."

"Then it'll be a perfect partnership," Eric snapped.

"You can't seriously think we're going forward with High West."

"Why not? It's about money and our future."

"Money!" she yelled. "Money has nothing to do with our future. We can't get involved with these people. They're sick and dishonest, and both Jamie and I saw that. If you'd only talked to us about this plan, we'd never have gotten involved with these people!"

A voice called, "Hello?" from the front room and Jamie cursed under his breath. "Shit, I've gotta work the bar. Tessa, come with me."

"No!"

"I don't want you two tearing each other limb from limb. Come on."

Eric let out another ugly laugh. "Don't worry about it. I'm leaving."

"Eric, wait," Tessa started, but Eric was already out the back door, leaving nothing but a flash of bright sunlight echoing through the kitchen.

Jamie cleared his throat. "I told you—"

"Stop!" she yelled. "I don't want to hear it."

"Fine. We'll talk about it tonight. All of us." Jamie grabbed a clean towel from a rack and tossed it over his shoulder. "Don't worry yourself sick in the meantime."

But Tessa's tension only got worse. Her shoulders pulled tight, her stomach even tighter. Eric had never walked away from her like that. Never. And Jamie… he acted like he didn't even care. Even Wallace eventually gave up on the show and retreated into his glass cave.

Tessa walked slowly to her office, grabbed her purse and went home to cry.

MONICA KENDALL SMILED at them from behind the vast expanse of her giant desk. She was pretty, Luke supposed, though there was a sharpness about her that turned him off. Still, she had the type of in-your-face beauty that lots of men admired. Maybe Jamie had gotten caught up in that.

"Did you say you were from the *Boulder* Police Department?" she asked. Her smile slid even higher, but there was no joy in it. Her fingertips were white where they pressed against the desktop.

"Yes," Simone said. "I'm sure you heard about the break-in at the Donovan brewery?"

"No," Monica answered. "I hadn't heard about that." She looked only at Luke. It was his turn to play good cop.

He smiled and leaned forward a little, establishing intimacy. "It happened the night you were there." Her eyes widened, and Luke eased back, giving her psychological room. "With Jamie," he clarified. "Did you notice anything strange?"

"Oh, no." She sighed, tension leaving her on a deep sigh. "No, I didn't notice anything. He locked up and drove me home. That's all."

"And when did you make it back to the brewery that night?"

Her smile eased toward flirtation. "I didn't. Jamie drove my car that night. I dropped him off at his car the next morning."

"What time?"

"Around seven-thirty."

Simone interrupted their friendly talk with a far

colder tone. "And what about that night, Ms. Kendall? What did you see before you left with Jamie?"

"What do you mean?" She'd already lost her fear. Her natural arrogance had returned, buoyed by Luke's appreciative look.

"What do I mean?" Simone asked. "I mean I'm going to get a call in a few minutes from the tech unit, and I'm pretty sure they're going to tell me your prints are on the lock of the brewery's front door."

The color fell from Monica Kendall's face as if someone had opened a drain. "What?"

"I also expect your cell phone records will show that you called your brother just before the robbery took place."

Her eyelids fluttered. "I talk to my brother all the time."

"Really? Is that when you two plan the robberies?"

Monica's sharp inhalation punctuated the end of Simone's sentence.

"Hey," Luke soothed, holding up his hands. "Let's calm this down a little. Here's what I think…" He set his hands on her desk and pondered them solemnly. "I don't think you're in charge of this crime ring."

"I'm not!"

"I think your brother pulled you into this. You're obviously not a bad person. But he's your brother. What are you supposed to do?"

Her eyes darted toward the phone.

"I have a brother," Luke lied. "If he asked me to do

him a favor… No big deal…just head into a business once or twice a month. Do a little flirting…"

"That's not how it happened! I mentioned that I was going over to the brewery. Graham asked me to do him a favor. That's it. I didn't know what he planned to do!"

Well, that part was a lie, but the rest of it looked like the god's honest truth.

"I don't want to go down for that idiot," she grumbled.

Luke nodded sympathetically. "It's not like it's the first time he's gotten into trouble."

"That little shit is going to—" At that moment, it all hit her. Luke saw the exact millisecond that her fear turned to calculation. Her face remained pale, but her slack jaw tightened. She closed her mouth and narrowed her eyes.

He dropped his voice to a near-whisper. "We could arrest you right now." He angled his head toward the cruel and unyielding Simone. "We've got all the evidence we need to take you in."

Her irises flickered, her gaze bouncing back and forth between Luke and Simone. "Or we could call the D.A., call your lawyer, and we could all have a friendly chat up in Boulder."

"If you arrest me, what happens?"

"Oh, we'll take you downtown and book you into jail. You'll be photographed and fingerprinted and searched. Then you'll be put into lockup."

"Lockup."

"Until your lawyer gets you out. It'd probably be no

time at all, though. A day until your bail hearing. Two at the most."

"And there'd be mug shots?" she breathed, seeming most horrified at that.

"Yes."

She gingerly patted her hair and frowned at something beyond Luke's shoulder. He turned to see a portrait of Roland Kendall on her wall.

"I'll talk to the D.A., as long as you can guarantee I won't be arrested."

"You'll need to discuss immunity with the D.A. and your attorney."

She nodded, her gaze getting colder the longer she looked at her father's portrait. "He deserves to be embarrassed," she said, as if she were convincing herself. "He always treated Graham like the golden child. The son who loved football and baseball. The son who liked to fish and golf. But Graham was playing him like a damned violin. He always was. It's time for dad to wake up."

"Why don't you call your attorney and gather your things? We'll meet you at the police station in Boulder."

Simone leaned close as they walked through the wide double doors of Monica Kendall's huge office. "We'll take her 'downtown'?" she whispered, nudging Luke with her elbow.

"What? That's some great imagery."

"So do you think she's as innocent as she claims?"

"Oh, not that innocent," he said. "Are they ever?" Tessa immediately came to mind. Tessa against the wall. Tessa in the shower. He checked his phone to be sure she hadn't called.

"Your girl was pretty pissed," Simone said. He jumped like he'd just been caught looking at dirty pictures.

"Huh?"

"Back at the brewery. Did you two make up?"

"No, we definitely did not."

"Give her time. She'll calm down. You two are cute together."

Luke paused in the act of opening the car door and glared at Simone. "We're *cute* together?"

"Well, she's cute and you're, you know...gaga."

"I am not gaga," he huffed in disgust as he got into the car and started the engine with a hard crank of the key. "Your condition is making you emotional."

"Really? I thought *your* condition was making you emotional."

"Ridiculous," he muttered. But Simone's look said she didn't believe that any more than he did. He was worried. He'd never seen Tessa look so serious. It gave him a bad feeling. Maybe he'd underestimated her anger. In her mind, he'd damaged her family, and her brothers meant everything to her.

Christ, he wanted to go to her. His muscles ached with the need to take action. If he could only explain himself and apologize again, if he could only have some time with her. She'd understand. She'd have to.

"Come on," Simone said. "Let's get this over with so you can go buy some flowers."

"Flowers. Right. You think that'll work?"

"It'll work," she assured him.

Luke took a deep breath. Yeah. It'd definitely be fine.

CHAPTER TWENTY-FIVE

THE WALLS WERE CLOSING in on her. Even in this house with too much space and too many rooms, the walls were squeezing in, making it hard to breathe. "Where is he?" she whispered.

"Stop pacing," Jamie ordered. "Eric will be here."

"He was supposed to be here ten minutes ago. Eric's never late."

"Well, he's had a hell of a day. Cut him some slack."

She stopped in her tracks to glare at him. "How can you be so relaxed?"

"Tessa," he groaned, letting his head fall back on the couch. He put his feet up on the coffee table and stretched out. "I *wanted* to tell him, remember?"

"But that was stupid! He's so angry, just like I said he would be."

"Well, right now, he's angry because we lied to him."

"Oh, he's pissed about you and your magically disappearing pants, too."

He opened one eye, but closed it without responding. Tessa resumed her pacing, trying to draw a steady breath to keep the walls at bay. "Fifteen minutes," she said when the clock ticked to six-fifteen.

"Well, I hope he hurries up. Chester can only cover the bar until seven."

She breathed in and out, in and out. She knew he wasn't gone. Eric might leave at some point, or Jamie might leave, but they'd say goodbye before they left. They wouldn't just disappear.

Jamie raised his head. "Are you hyperventilating?"

"No. I'm breathing. I'm calming myself."

"Sounds more like wheezing. Cut it out."

Tessa grabbed a throw pillow from the chair and chucked it at him.

"Hey!"

"Stop being so calm!" she screamed.

"Jesus Christ, Tessa. You're losing it."

"I know I am!" The sound of a car door slamming snapped her out of her breakdown, and Tessa rushed for the door. Eric stalked up the front walk, his face a mask of cold fury.

Folding her hands, she backed away from the door until her legs hit the coffee table. Eric stepped through the door and gave both of his siblings an equally quelling look. "Well?" he snarled. "What did you two want to discuss?"

Jamie slid his gaze toward Tessa. "You'd better ask her."

"You know what we need to discuss. Both of you. We need to figure out what we're doing here. What's going to happen."

"Nothing's going to happen," Eric countered.

"What do you mean?"

"The deal stands."

Even Jamie jumped up at that news. "Excuse me?" he sputtered.

"I'm not backing out of the deal."

Tessa felt sweat break out all over her body.

"They're criminals and psychos!" Jamie yelled.

Eric stared him down. "They're a tool for expanding our business. Nothing more, nothing less."

Tessa shook her head frantically. "We don't want to expand."

"Since when?"

"Since Jamie and I talked about it and agreed we don't want to expand. You're supposed to involve us, Eric."

"You've both been involved from the start. I haven't kept one damn thing secret, unlike the two of you."

She swallowed hard. "I'm sorry. I'm really sorry. I just didn't want you and Jamie to fight. I thought if I got the deal back on track, it wouldn't matter."

He bowed his head and stuck both hands in his pockets.

"I'm sorry," she said again.

"I'm honestly disturbed by the magnitude of this. You betrayed me. And embarrassed me. What else are you lying about?"

"Nothing!" she said quickly. "Nothing. And Jamie didn't want to lie at all. He wanted to tell you what happened, but I was afraid."

"And there's nothing else you need to tell me?"

"No. Nothing. Please don't be mad, Eric. And please don't call Roland Kendall about the deal. If nothing else, we need to wait and see what Luke finds out. We can't trust these people."

"It seems we can't trust anyone," he said quietly.

"I'm sorry. I swear I won't—"

"I already called Roland Kendall."

His simple, quiet words hit her with the force of a train.

Eric cocked his head. "Is there something you want to tell me? Something you left out of your confession?"

The walls were moving again, sliding closer to her, pushing the air from the room. Tessa pressed a hand to her chest. Jamie looked from Eric to her and back again. "What is it?"

"Tessa? Do you want to tell him or should I?"

She shook her head, shame rolling over her for lying to his face.

"Tessa made a new deal with Kendall. She told him that if he signed the contract, there'd be no charge for the first six months of supply."

"What?" Jamie gasped.

She tried to back up a step, but the table was in the way. She ended up sitting down on it, hard. "I just wanted to help."

"Help, how?" Jamie asked. "Where the hell was that money going to come from?"

"From me." Both her brothers stared at her like she'd grown another head. "I was going to pay for it."

Eric's hands rose from his sides before falling down again. "Tessa... Why?"

"I needed to do my part. For the family."

"Your part? You do your part every day. We run this business together. You don't just go off making your own plans and deals, Tessa!"

"You do."

Eric's head jerked back as if she'd slapped him. "You know that's not fair. And it doesn't change the fact that you're still lying to me. *Nothing* changes that."

Tessa couldn't move, she couldn't breathe; she just stared at Eric and wondered how she'd made such a mess of things. "I'm sorry," she whispered so quietly even she could barely hear it. "I just wanted to make it better."

A sharp knock drew everyone's eyes to the door. Luke stood there, sunglasses on and face hard as granite. "Is everything okay here?"

"Everything's fine," Eric snapped. "Do you have news?"

"Not yet."

"All right. I'm done here. Jamie, I'll see you tomorrow."

Luke stepped inside so that Eric could leave, and Tessa just watched him go, her muscles too dull to work. Jamie moved for the door, too.

"I've got to get back to the bar, sis. We'll talk more later, all right?"

She let him go, because what could she do? The harder she tried to hold, the weaker she got. She blinked and found herself staring up at Luke. "What are you doing here?"

"I came to talk. And to…" He gestured and Tessa realized for the first time that he was holding a bouquet of yellow tulips. "I'm sorry."

"You should've warned me."

"I'm sorry, but there was no way to hide the information from Eric, even if I'd warned you."

Tessa's mind buzzed with all the ways he was wrong. All the ways she could have prepared for this and made things better, but she didn't have the heart to argue with him.

"I overheard part of your conversation," Luke said. "You didn't tell me that you were planning on footing the bill for part of the contract."

She shrugged.

"Do you want to talk about it?"

"No."

"Why not? You're obviously upset. Talk to me."

"Why would I? I don't trust you."

That seemed to end his conciliatory attitude, and Tessa was grateful. She didn't want him apologizing and playing nice. She was hurt and angry and overwhelmed. She wanted to yell and scream.

"You don't trust *me?*" he said.

"No, I don't. You lied to me."

He smiled, but the twist of his lips was bitter. "You have got to be kidding me."

Tessa's anger turned to self-righteous clarity. She could see now what Jamie had been trying to tell her. She'd been looking so hard at Luke she hadn't been able to see the people around him. "You and Simone—"

"Oh, Jesus Christ, you're bringing that up again?"

"Why does everyone think you must be the father? Why, Luke? It doesn't make any sense!"

He was good at hiding his emotions. He had to be with what he did every day. But for one split second, Tessa saw guilt flash over his face. "You bastard," she growled. "You did sleep with her."

"No! We never had sex. Not once."

"You never had *sex?* Oh, my God, you've been parsing your words every time we talked about this, haven't you?"

"No," he said, adding nothing more.

Tessa wanted to hit him. She wanted to slap him and scream at him and tell him what an asshole he was.

"We never had sex," he said again.

"Fine, Mr. Detective, if you want to get legal about it, that's fine. Did you ever kiss her?" When Luke's gaze fell to the ground, Tessa heart sank right along with it.

"It was nothing. Just one night."

"Oh, God," Tessa breathed.

"Look, I'd just moved here. We'd both had too much to drink. A few of the guys saw us leaving the bar together. But we didn't… We never… It was a mistake, and luckily we both realized it before it was too late."

"Get the hell out, Luke. Get out!"

"No. I'm not going to let you paint me as the bad

guy just because Simone and I made out two years ago. I never lied to you about that."

"You did!" she screamed. Her anger exploded, amplified by the press of heartbroken tears in her throat. She pushed him. Hard.

"Calm down," Luke said, raising his hands.

"You're a goddamn liar!"

"I told you we'd never had sex. I told you it wasn't like that between us. And it's not. I didn't lie. If you don't trust me, it's got nothing to do with me, Tessa. It's because you know you're lying all the time and you assume other people are, too."

She stepped back, startled by the way his words froze all her roiling emotions. She felt as if time had stopped. "What?"

"You heard me. You lie to people you love."

"How dare you," she pushed past clenched teeth. "You don't know anything about me."

"That's not true. I know you well enough to like you despite all that. You're sweet and smart. You're not trying to be cruel. You think you're lying to protect them."

"I am."

"No. You're just trying to control them, Tessa."

Her anger surged again, and she jerked her hand toward the door. "Get out."

Luke took a deep breath and his shoulders slumped. "Look, I'm sorry. I shouldn't have said that. Not now while you're fighting with your brothers."

"Not *now?* You shouldn't have said it because it's not true!"

He met her gaze straight on, not looking the least bit regretful. "I can tell you have trouble opening up, Tessa. That's understandable, but—"

"Me? I have trouble opening up? You're the one who won't talk about your past! When have you ever opened up to anyone?"

"Don't go there," he said roughly.

"Oh, we're not allowed to talk about your problems?"

"You've got it backward. It's still *your* problem. I know how to open up to people. I've been in love. I've been married. You've never even had a boyfriend, so don't tell me I don't know how to open up."

"That's cruel!"

"Cruel to point out the choice you've made to hold yourself back? I've made myself vulnerable. I've been hurt, and I'm willing to be hurt again. Are you?"

Something powerful pushed at her throat. She thought it was a sob, but when she opened her mouth, she yelled, "No!" No, she wasn't willing to be hurt again, ever. "I've had enough pain. I'm done with it."

"Tessa, how are you going to—"

"I'm done with it! So get out. Leave!"

"Come on. Don't do this. Just…" He gestured toward her, the flowers rising from his hand like an olive branch. She wanted to take it. She wanted to fall into him and let him hold her up. He would. She could see it in his eyes. But there weren't enough strong arms in the world to keep hurt away. She knew that to the very depths of her soul.

"Your brothers aren't going to leave you, Tessa," he said softly.

She drew in a breath sharp enough to stab her heart. "What?"

"They're not going to leave you, even if you stop holding on so tight."

"I know that," she snarled.

"I don't think you do, darling. I really don't."

Tessa squeezed her hands to fists, curling her fingers tighter and tighter. "Don't think you know me. Don't think you can point at my childhood and tell me where I went wrong. I've known you for *two weeks*. Two weeks of sex and not much else. And it's over, do you understand? This is over."

"Yeah," he muttered. "That's fine." He smacked the flowers against his other hand. "I'm no good at this, anyway, am I? I learned that the hard way."

Tessa waved her hand toward the door. She needed him to go. Now. She needed him to go before she broke down and threw herself into him. She didn't need him. She'd never needed anyone but her brothers and she couldn't start needing someone else now. She had to concentrate on making things right with her family. "Goodbye," she said, but Luke didn't say a word. He just turned and walked out, closing the door softly behind him.

And Tessa was alone in her big house again.

HE SHOULD NEVER have pushed her so hard. Not today. He should've backed off and given her a chance to work things out with Eric. But hell, he was just kidding himself with that. She didn't have room for him in her life today, and she wouldn't have room tomorrow.

And maybe he didn't have room for her. After all, instead of working through his feelings over her, he was shoving them aside as he pushed through the station doors, joining the other cops who sat at their desks, ignoring the real world.

His partner included.

He set the flowers on her desk. "They didn't work."

"Oh," she said, leaning back in surprise. "Are you sure?"

"I'm sure. In fact, she ended it altogether."

Simone cringed. "Ouch." She picked up the tulips and touched one of the blooms. "She really didn't like these?"

"She wasn't in the mood for romantic gestures."

When Simone looked up, her eyes snapped from dreamy to alarmed. "Oops."

Luke glanced behind him and saw two other detectives watching with hard eyes. Simone set the flowers down on her desk with a smack. After everything that had happened, Luke could only laugh. "Tomorrow let's go wander around a bridal shop, give them something interesting to talk about."

The flowers hit him in the face.

"Good aim."

"Thanks. Now are you ready to work, or did you want to mope a little beforehand? I'm sympathetic to moping right now, so knock yourself out."

"Nah, I've got a bottle of whiskey waiting for me when I get home. I'll be fine until then. What's up?"

Simone nudged her computer mouse and gestured toward the monitor. "I've been checking out that charity golf tournament Graham Kendall pitched to Tessa."

"And it's all totally legit, right?"

She smirked. "This is his second year organizing the tournament. He's bragging that last year they raised $465,000 from the sponsors. Everything seemed to go off without a hitch. But I checked the online report of the charity who was supposed to have benefited."

"And?"

"And they took in exactly three thousand dollars from the Kendall Group last year."

"Whoa."

"And Graham switched charities this year. The first organization never filed a complaint, but I'd bet they weren't happy."

"I think we'd better give them a call tomorrow."

"Yeah," Simone groused. "Tomorrow. We won't hear from the D.A. until tomorrow. We can't call the charity until tomorrow. I want something to do *tonight*."

"Believe me, I know." They both sat sullenly staring at their own desks. Luke occasionally flipped open a file, but his heart wasn't in it. The breakup was finally sinking its claws into his chest. Strange, how quickly he'd gotten used to the idea of seeing her every night. He didn't want to spend the night alone, even though he'd spent virtually every night alone for years.

Shit. He stole a look at Simone before dropping

his eyes again. "Simone, do you think I have trouble opening up to people?"

"Me? If you're seriously asking *me* that question, I'm doubting your decision to become a detective."

"Everyone has trouble opening up, right?"

Simone sighed. "I don't know. Maybe it's just us. I'm gonna go check on those fingerprints one last time, and then I'm going home. If everyone else can wait to catch the bad guys until tomorrow, I guess I can, too."

Luke paged through the printouts she'd tossed on his desk, but he wasn't a numbers guy. Whatever Simone had managed to glean from the charity reports, Luke would go with that for now. But he could still work tonight. He had two dozen Denver reports to reexamine with an eye toward the Kendalls. Luke would definitely need some coffee.

He rose stiffly to his feet, his body a mass of aching tension, but when he got to the kitchen, he dumped out the coffee and started from scratch. At this time of night, any leftover coffee would likely be pure poison. He grabbed a Styrofoam cup and reached for the sugar, only to find an empty box. "Crap." Opening the cupboards revealed nothing more than ancient leftovers of snacks and taco sauce packets, so Luke left the coffee to brew and walked farther down the hallway to search out the supply closet. They couldn't be completely out of sugar. There would've been a rebellion.

He reached for the closet door just as he registered a rush of hushed voices sneaking past the corner. There was nothing back there but an office they occasionally used for polygraph tests.

Luke froze with his hand on the doorknob of the supply closet and tried to focus his hearing on the conversation. When he got nothing, he eased his head past the corner in time to see Simone spinning around and stalking back toward him. Her head was down, her hands balled to fists. And behind her, watching her walk away, was their boss, Sergeant Pallin. In the moment before he spotted Luke, his face revealed every emotion in clear lines. Frustration, heartache, longing.

It was the truth, laid out right in front of Luke, and his stomach dropped to his feet.

He must have made some noise, because Simone and Pallin looked up at the same time. Luke registered the shock on both their faces before he retreated and walked back to his desk, the scent of brewing coffee taunting him as he passed.

Their boss was the father of the baby. Luke knew it as surely as he knew his own name. Simone had slept with their boss—their married boss—and that was why she couldn't tell anyone.

He watched from the corner of his eye as she approached her desk, and he knew immediately that her strategy was to fake her way through this. She'd pretend Luke hadn't seen, or that if he had, he hadn't connected the dots. She tucked all her files into one drawer and grabbed her purse. "I'm out of here. I'll see you tomorrow."

"Simone—"

"Good night."

She turned away, and Luke just sat there in shock, staring at her back as she grew smaller. But the moment Simone disappeared around the corner, he surged to his feet. No way was he letting this lie for another day. He hurried after her and caught up before she reached her car.

"Simone, I'm not blind."

"I don't know what you're talking about." She stepped around him and continued on.

"It's him. I know it is. Don't deny it."

"Luke, please. Just…please." Her voice thickened with tears.

"I'm sorry. I can't unsee it. I'm not judging you, okay? Don't think that."

Simone drew a deep breath and came to a sudden halt. "You should," she whispered. "Why wouldn't you?"

"Because we're friends, that's why. Come on. Talk to me."

"No." She shook her head, and Luke dropped the hand he'd started to reach out. But then she put her palm to her belly and took another breath. "Not out here."

She tilted her head toward the car before she got into the driver's seat. Luke joined her and closed the passenger door very carefully so as not to spook her. "Do you want to get something to—"

"He's the father," she said quickly. "Please don't tell anyone, ever. If his wife finds out…"

"What happened?"

"The usual thing."

"I know, but...Simone..."

"He was separated," she blurted. She wrapped her hands around the steering wheel and squeezed. "I know that sounds clichéd. He told me he left his wife. He told me he didn't love her anymore. But it was true. He'd moved out. They were getting divorced."

"Okay," he said, though even to his ears, his voice sounded stiff.

"Regardless, it was a mistake. He's my boss. He was still married. And in the end... She was the one who'd kicked him out, and when she asked him to move back in, he went. He went."

"Did he know you were pregnant?"

"No. Even I didn't know. We just... We thought it was over. I won't pretend I wasn't hurt, but I told myself that I deserved it. I screwed around with a married man. I'd fallen for my boss. Jesus, Simone, how stupid can you be?"

Suddenly he could see it so clearly. How alone she'd been. How utterly isolated. She couldn't tell anyone, not even Luke.

"He wants to be married to her, Luke. And if she finds out, he won't be. It's just that simple."

"So he gets off scot-free?"

She raised her hands, holding them up for long seconds. Finally, she let them drop. "It's my decision, isn't it? I could've gotten rid of it. I could've put it up for adoption. It's my choice."

Luke shook his head in disbelief. "Won't he even help?"

"You think his wife won't notice five hundred dollars a month in child support?"

"Jesus!" Luke slammed his fist onto the dash. "He can't just leave you like that."

"That's the way it has to be. No one can find out. Not just because of him, but because of me. I don't want to be that woman. The one who slept with her boss. The one who was made a fool of by a married man."

"No one will—"

"Seriously, Luke? I'm a black woman. And a female cop. Half the guys on the force probably think I spread my legs to get where I am."

"That's not true."

Simone's dry expression radiated scorn.

Luke cursed and scrubbed his face in an attempt to dislodge some sort of rational thought, but his shock was wearing down and exposing fury beneath. And frustration.

"Promise me you won't tell anyone."

"Of course I won't tell anyone! In fact…I'm completely unattached now. Just tell people I'm the father. Okay? Then they'll stop asking. The talk will die down. No one will care."

Her tears had dried, thank God. And she actually smiled when she punched him in the shoulder.

"Ow! I could have you arrested for that, you know."

"You're an idiot. But a sweet one. Thanks, but you're not really unattached."

"Oh, I am."

She shook her head. "I've got to go with my gut here. You're not unattached. And even if you were, you won't be forever. You can't be dragging a fake baby mama around behind you. It tends to scare the nice women away."

"I scare those away all by myself."

"No. Maybe you do have trouble opening up, but you're just a man, after all."

"Yeah."

"But I saw you with her. You were ready." She reached to give him an awkward hug, and when he hugged her back, his hand accidentally touched her belly. It was surprisingly hard and something shifted beneath the surface.

"Oh, shit!" he yelped, jerking back.

"What's wrong?"

"It, uh, moved."

"Feels like an alien, doesn't it? I swear to God, I have nightmares that it's going to burst out of my stomach like a monster. But I think it's pretty harmless."

He laughed, but kept a suspicious eye on her belly. He could *see* it moving.

"Don't look so freaked out. Here…"

She reached for his hand and started to pull it toward her stomach, but Luke jerked back. "Gah!" he cried out.

Simone laughed, then she laughed harder, choking on her own breath as tears ran down her face.

"Sorry," Luke muttered, holding his hands close to his body so she couldn't grab him again.

"I thought you'd been reading baby books," she gasped out.

"Yeah, well, I've never actually been around a pregnant woman before. It's strange."

"It's strange for me, too. I didn't exactly grow up in a nursery. I promise you the idea of having a whole other person inside of me is damn weird. And when my stomach moves like that... Yeah. *Alien* flashbacks, big-time."

"Well, just keep that over there."

She laughed until she cried again, and Luke felt a hell of a lot better when he got out of the car. Still, when he got back to his desk, he spotted Pallin closing up his office, and Luke's fury returned like a lightning strike.

Sergeant Pallin walked out without looking in Luke's direction, but Luke followed his every step. The man was going home to his wife. To his kids. To his cozy house in the Boulder foothills. And Simone was going home alone to her small apartment.

Luke believed in justice. Hell, cops knew better than most that justice was a fickle bitch, but he still needed it. He worked toward it every day. How the hell was he supposed to sit here for fifty hours a week and stare at that bastard without punching him in the face?

But Simone was right. If it got out, it would hurt her, too.

Damn it.

He was a man, and a cop, and it was his job to make things better, but lately... Shit, lately he couldn't seem to help anyone, not even himself.

CHAPTER TWENTY-SIX

TESSA DIDN'T SLEEP at all. She couldn't.

At first, she'd lain in bed and chased plots through her scattered brain, trying to find a way to make things right with Eric. She planned a hundred different schemes and discarded them all as the hours marched past.

Then she'd gotten melancholy. Weepy. She'd thought about all that her brothers had done for her. All they'd sacrificed. And of course, she'd thought about her parents. Her big, good-natured dad and his booming laugh. Her soft, smiling mom and the way she'd said "I love you" twenty times a day.

Three in the morning had found her sitting in the middle of her second-floor hallway, riffling through boxes of pictures she'd pulled from the closet.

The dust that coated the boxes told her how long it had been since she'd opened them. She didn't like to look backward. There was no point to it. Plus…it hurt. It hurt so badly that the moment she'd opened the first box and caught sight of a picture of her mom, she'd begun to cry.

But she'd sorted through the pictures, letting herself feel how much she missed them. They hadn't been perfect. Her dad had worked too much and missed dinner more often than not. Her mom had yelled when she got stressed and snuck cigarettes on the porch when she thought no one was watching.

But they'd loved each other, and they'd loved their kids, and that was more than some people ever got.

That was what she'd always told herself when she'd felt like wallowing in self-pity. Look at all the people who'd never known their fathers. Look at all the kids being raised in foster care. Her family had been great for so many years, so how could she feel sorry for herself?

But it wasn't so hard to pity herself, apparently. She looked at her parents' faces and felt the sharp grief of loss, hardly dulled since that first year without them. She looked at Eric's face and missed his carefree, easy smile. He hadn't smiled like that since then. Not once. And Jamie...she knew he was changed, though she couldn't put her finger on it. He was angrier, certainly. As likely to start a fight as to finish it.

Luke was right. She was afraid they'd leave. She was afraid they'd be swept away on a sudden wave and never come back again. But maybe she'd been trying to prevent that catastrophe in the wrong way.

At five o'clock, she got in the shower and stayed there until the hot water inched toward cool. By the time she dried her hair and pulled on a sweater and jeans it was after six. Eric left for his jog by seven every morning. She hoped he wouldn't mind her interfering with his exercise.

His lights were on by the time she walked over, so she knocked and held her breath.

Eric frowned furiously at her when he opened the door. She felt her heart drop, but then he pulled her inside and glared into the darkness as if to warn criminals off. "What are you doing out this early? It's still dark."

"All the muggers are in bed now. It's all right."

Eric started to stuff his hands in his pockets, but when he realized he was wearing sweats, he crossed his arms and cleared his throat.

"Um…" Tessa couldn't think how to start. "Do I smell coffee?"

"Oh, sure. Of course. Just…have a seat."

Perfect. They'd been reduced to the role of awkward acquaintances. She slumped into a chair and waited for Eric to bring her a cup of coffee as if she were a guest.

He delivered her cup and then perched on the chair opposite her as they both sipped and avoided each other's eyes. When she couldn't take it anymore, she set down the coffee. "I'm sorry. I shouldn't have lied to you."

"It's all right."

"No, it's not."

He shrugged, still avoiding her eyes.

"I just… Ever since Mom and Dad died, I've wanted to make things easy for you."

"For me? I'm fine."

"I know," she said automatically. But then she shook her head. "Eric, you took on a family when you were supposed to be out partying and living your own life."

"Come on, Tessa. Lots of guys get married at that age. It was no big deal."

"Of course it was a big deal! Why do you say things like that? You gave up everything—"

"I gave up an apartment and a few weekends."

"Eric…" She set down her cup and rubbed her eyes, trying to hold tears at bay. "I lied because I was afraid."

"Afraid of what?"

"You and Jamie fight all the time. If you keep fighting like this…"

He raised his eyebrows in question.

"It's okay that you're in charge, Eric. You've been doing this longer than either of us. But you can't be in charge *and* constantly fight with him. He'll leave. Or he'll fight you until you leave."

"Nobody's leaving—"

"And if Jamie doesn't step up and become responsible, he's going to keep pissing you off. And maybe…"

"Maybe what?"

"Maybe you'll finally realize everything you've given up for us. Maybe you'll decide you're done." Her voice wanted to break on a sob, but she held it back by sheer will.

"Tessa!" Eric scolded as if she'd said something inappropriate.

"I'm afraid," she said. "I've always been afraid, so I

lie to you about little things to make sure you're happy. But now I'm lying to you about big things, too."

"I'm not going anywhere. How can you think that?"

"And what about Jamie?"

Eric shook his head. "What about him?"

"You treat him like a little brother!"

"He *is* my little brother."

"I know, but not at work. He's an adult. So am I. We don't need you to take care of everything."

"Ah. But then why would you keep me around?"

"Don't joke. I'm serious! I don't want to lose you." The tears finally broke free then, raining down her face, flooding her throat.

"Jesus, Tessa." She felt him drop onto the couch beside her. His arms went around her and she dove into his chest to sob against him. "I'm not going anywhere. Ever. I love my life. It's not a burden."

"You work too much. You're stressed. You won't let anyone help you. Instead, you just work harder."

"Tessa, come on. I work hard for you guys."

"That's what I mean! You'd be free without us, Eric. And the terrible thing is…" She drew in a deep breath. "I don't want you to be free."

His arms tightened so brutally that it almost hurt, but Tessa didn't try to squirm away. "I'm sorry," she whispered.

"For God's sake, Tessa, I don't want to be free. Who would I be without you and Jamie? I'll admit, I gave up a few things to take care of you two, but you've forgotten something. Mom and I were on our own until

I was eight. I know what it was like not to have you. You have no idea how thankful I was to be part of a family."

"But I heard you," she whispered, clenching her eyes shut as hard as she could.

His hold eased a bit. "What?"

When she shook her head, he leaned back to look at her. "What'd you say, Tessa?"

She hadn't meant to bring it up. In fact, she'd told herself she'd never mention it. But now the memory was there, and it writhed inside her, clawing its way free. "I heard you, a few months after they died.… You were talking to a friend."

His face was only puzzled. He didn't remember.

Tessa took a deep breath. "I couldn't sleep. I came downstairs, and you were on the patio, having a beer with a friend. I don't know who. The whole house was dark, and I remember thinking how bright the moon was out there, hanging over your head."

"Tessa—"

"And then you said, 'Of course I wish there was someone else, but there's not. I'm all they've got, and it doesn't matter how much I might want to walk away.'"

She saw recognition in his eyes first, then horror dawned with hard brightness. "Tessa—"

"I understand. Of course I do."

"I can't believe you heard that. I'm so sorry. My God…"

"It's okay."

"No, it's not. I shouldn't have said it. I was just

talking. Just getting out my frustrations. I was a twenty-four-year-old kid and I was scared to death. That's all."

"I know. I know that, but…I just…"

"I'm not going anywhere, damn it. Not even when you want me to."

She squeezed his hand.

"No matter how much Jamie pisses me off. No matter how many guys you date…though I still don't want to know about that."

She couldn't believe she managed to laugh, but she did.

"And, Tessa…Mom and Dad didn't leave, either. They were taken away."

"I know," she rasped, and she did. But it felt the same in her heart. That fear that anyone could disappear at any moment.

"I should never have sent you to that therapist at the school. She was a quack."

Tessa slapped his chest and managed to laugh again. "I'm sane enough. Saner than you."

"Yeah, I can't disagree with that."

She let herself rest against his chest for a moment, just feeling the solid strength that had always been there for her. She suddenly remembered the time he'd taken her to the park when she was five, and she'd fallen off the top of the slide. He'd held her then, too, but his heart had thundered against her ear as if it were trying to escape his chest. He'd been terrified, she realized now, but his voice had been all soothing calm as he'd tried to comfort her.

"Is there anything else I want to know about right now?" Eric asked. "Anything you haven't told me?"

"Hmm. Well, I didn't really take a summer art class in eighth grade. Jamie had to retake a semester of math, so I went with him to summer school for two hours every day so you wouldn't know."

"Are you kidding me?"

"No. But it all worked out. He graduated and I did really well in trigonometry when I finally took it."

He huffed and nudged her away. "Good God, don't tell me anything else. I don't want to know. But no more lies. No cover-ups."

"Fine. Jamie's gotten really difficult about it, anyway."

Eric rolled his eyes. "Maybe he has grown up."

Tessa's smile faded and she held Eric's gaze. "He has. And if I'm going to stop covering up, you've got to start being more open."

He leaned forward and looked down at his clasped hands. "I'm not really going forward with the Kendall deal."

"What about expansion?"

"We'll talk about it. All of us. All right?"

Relief seemed to scramble her insides and turn her muscles to jelly. "Thank you." She kissed his cheek and gave him one last hug. "I'll let you get to your run. I need to take a nap before work. But tonight's a Rockies game. What do you say we have a baseball night at the brewery? We haven't done that in a while. We could hang out. Watch the game. Play pool."

"I thought maybe you'd need some time to make up with Luke."

She forced her face to stay calm and neutral. "Nah. That's over."

"Really? Just like that?"

"You said it yourself. I can't trust him."

Eric frowned, but he shrugged one shoulder before standing up to stretch. "Whatever you say. Just don't date anyone else, all right?"

"Oh, sure. No problem."

Actually, she thought as she walked out into the pale morning, maybe it wouldn't be a problem. Luke had been right. She'd never made room for anyone else in her life. She'd only dated for fun and sex. And now…who could possibly be sexier than Luke? She knew from experience that it would be a challenge finding anyone else who could so thoroughly satisfy her. They'd had chemistry, if nothing else.

Her shoes crunched against the frost as she crossed a small park and came out on her street. She hadn't noticed the cold on her walk over, but exhaustion was creeping through her now, and she shivered as she moved toward home. The memory of her warm bed pulsed like a beacon as she got closer to her house. Her pillow still smelled like Luke, and torturous as that was, this morning she'd hold it close and sleep with his scent against her.

But tomorrow she'd change the sheets and move on.

CHAPTER TWENTY-SEVEN

A FULL WEEK of investigating. Of long nights and sleep-deprived days spent building a solid case against Graham Kendall. And of course, it had come to this.

"It's official," Luke said. "He's on the run."

"I can't pretend to be surprised," Simone said.

"Wanna take a guess where he showed up?"

Simone rocked back in her chair, tapping her fingers against her chin. "Taiwan, maybe. Or Saudi Arabia."

"You're good. He flew to Taiwan."

"Well, there aren't many nonextradition countries that offer the lifestyle he's used to. Still, he'll run out of money soon, won't he?"

Luke shrugged. "A year or two at the rate he spends it. But I can't tell whether Daddy will send funds or not. He's pissed now, but he's gotten Graham out of sticky situations before."

Once they'd started pulling at the house of cards Graham had built, things had tumbled fairly quickly. He had a gambling problem, as they'd suspected. There was also evidence that he was pretty fond of cocaine. And Adderall.

He'd been running a theft ring in order to sell people's identities and credit card numbers for cash. Luke knew from experience that they'd never track those connections down. It was a crime that spread itself in spiderwebs over the globe. The middleman was probably in Eastern Europe. The final consumers in Asia and Russia and Africa.

But all that mysterious, untaxed income that Graham was bringing in? Oh, that was easier to track. The IRS charges alone would likely send him to prison for a decade or two. Then there was the charity tournament. They were only starting to sort through that mess.

Just like the devil, Roland Kendall appeared when summoned, stepping out of Sergeant Pallin's office along with two attorneys, the division commander and the D.A. Nobody looked happy.

"He pulled some powerful strings to get his son out of trouble in Denver. That's why Graham moved his little operation to Boulder," Luke murmured. "I can't believe his dad won't help him in Taiwan."

"Yeah, but now that Roland knows it wasn't just a one-time deal…"

"We'll see." It was surprisingly easy to let it go. He and Simone had done their jobs. For now, Graham Kendall was untouchable in Taiwan, but he wouldn't be robbing any more Boulder businesses from there. In the end, he'd serve his time. Eventually.

Unlike some people, who didn't pay any consequences for their actions. Luke glared at Sergeant Pallin as he walked his guests out.

"Have you talked to Tessa yet?" Simone asked.

He turned his glare on her, but she only glanced innocently up from her monitor. "You know I haven't."

"You should call her."

"No." No. It was just that simple. He'd traveled from guilt to sorrow to resignation in the past few days. Now he was stuck at fury. If he wasn't open enough, then Tessa Donovan was a sealed vault. He'd made one mistake—one—and she'd tossed him aside like garbage.

He'd reached his lifetime limit of being treated like a disposable commodity. If Tessa thought he wasn't good enough, if she thought he wasn't honest and open and worthy, then that was the end of it.

Or that was what he kept telling himself, anyway. It worked pretty well during the daytime.

"All right." Simone sighed. "I'm heading home. I have to admit that I can't keep up with you anymore."

Luke threw her a surprised look.

"I start desk duty in a week."

He didn't smile, because Simone's face was hard with resentment, but he was damned relieved. "I'll try not to have any fun out there without you."

"You'd better not."

She left with shoulders slumped in defeat and a decidedly pregnant sway to her step. Halfway to the door, she met Pallin on his way back in, and Luke watched her gaze fall to the floor. Pallin stared straight ahead. He didn't see the way her eyes rose to touch him as he walked away.

Luke's anger solidified into a hot, burning sphere beneath his sternum. Not all of it was caused by Pallin, but his rage was thrilled to find a ready target.

He should go. Get out of here and go to the gun range to try to lose his anger in shredded targets. But then it occurred to him that Tessa would love going to the gun range, and the hot ball in his chest burned brighter.

Telling himself not to, he rose and walked to Pallin's office. Pallin was just settling into his chair when Luke stepped in and closed the door.

"Asher. What can I do for you?"

"I'm not concerned about what you can do for me, Sergeant."

"I'm sorry. I don't know what you mean." He didn't. Not at that moment when he said the words, but Pallin's face grew tight with suspicion as the seconds passed.

"You're just going to leave her like this, huh?"

Pallin's face lost all color in the time it took Luke to blink. "I don't know what you're talking about."

"Yes, you do. Don't fuck with me. She needs child support. Hell, she needs all kinds of support, but apparently you're not up for that."

Pallin swallowed hard and glanced past Luke to the room beyond. "You're not going to tell anyone, are you?"

"You're an asshole," Luke snarled.

His boss's shoulders dropped. "I didn't want this. I thought my marriage was over. I swear to God. And by the time we found out about this…"

Luke put his fingertips on the man's desk and leaned forward. "She. Doesn't. Deserve. This."

"I know. I know that! If I could, I'd… Look, I'm going to give her as much as I can, as often as I can.

I swear. And I wish…" His eyes teared up, and he rubbed them hard with his hand. "Please don't tell anyone."

Luke nodded and straightened, staring down his nose at this man he'd once liked. "You can't stay here."

"What?"

"You can't stay here and be her boss and her ex-lover and the father of her child."

"But—"

"Maybe you're not getting this. I won't allow you to stay here. Is that clear enough?"

Now some color returned to his cheeks. "I can't just leave. This is my career. And what the hell am I supposed to tell my wife?"

"You just planned to stay here and treat Simone as nothing more than another employee?"

"I…I don't have a choice!"

"There are plenty of other police departments around here. Denver, Aurora, Fort Collins. And smaller cities where they'd be glad to have you. You'll start looking now, and when you find a position, you'll tell your wife it's an opportunity you can't pass up. And then you'll get the hell out of here and never come back."

"Or what?"

Luke smiled. "Or you'll leave here under very different terms. Sergeant."

The fire in his chest faded as he walked out of the building, but unfortunately it left ash behind. He didn't even feel a spark of hope when his phone rang.

It wasn't Tessa. More than a week had passed and she wasn't going to call.

Just as he expected, when he flipped open his phone, it wasn't her. What he didn't expect was an L.A. area code. "Hello?"

"Luke? Hi. It's Eve."

He stopped at the curb, too shocked to keep his legs moving. He'd seen her only a short while ago, but somehow it was different hearing her voice on the phone. Like they were alone together. "Oh," he finally said. "Hey. How are you?"

"I'm great. Really great."

"Good. You looked great when I saw you."

"So did you," she answered, before they both stumbled into a silence.

Frowning, he slipped his keys from his pocket and made himself move to his car. "So…"

"I'm sorry," she said. "It's just strange, isn't it?"

"Yeah." He sighed as he got in and shut the car door and closed his eyes. "It is."

"I'm sorry about the other day. At your mom's. It wasn't my intention to surprise you like that."

"I know." With his eyes closed it felt like they were sitting in the car together. Luke opened his eyes and stared straight ahead.

"I should've told you then," she said, the words slow and careful. "I mean, I would have, if I hadn't been so shocked to see you. I'm getting married."

"Congratulations. I figured it out, actually."

Her sigh was filled with relief. "You were always the smart one."

"Not always," he murmured.

"No." He heard the phone click against her earring when she shifted. "No, but that wasn't a normal time for either of us. It was hard. I'm really sorry for... I don't know. Everything?"

Luke closed his eyes again, too damn tired to keep them open. "Me, too."

"I could've handled it a lot better. I was young and stupid."

"We both were. Hell, we were too young to deal with marriage, much less cancer."

"Yeah. Maybe we were. So...you don't hate me anymore?" He thought he heard a catch in her voice and felt an answering tightness in his chest.

Did he hate her? Had he ever hated her? That part of his life felt too far away for him to tell now. "No, I don't hate you. I'm happy for you. I hope he's a good guy."

"He is." She hesitated. "For what it's worth, I think I've learned how to be better at this. I kept too much inside before. I never let you know how lonely I felt, even when you were sitting right next to me. And by the time I told you, it was too late. We couldn't get back from there."

He could've argued with her. He could've told her that she was the one who couldn't get back to him. But what the hell did it matter now? She was right; they'd been young and stupid. They hadn't stood a chance.

"It's nice to hear your voice," she said softly.

"Yeah, you, too." And he meant it. But he suspected it would've been even nicer if he knew he was heading home to Tessa. But tonight, the bottle would have to do.

FRIDAY EVENING WAS ALWAYS the liveliest night at the brewery. They usually had a band, and there was a great one tonight. But even without the music, the air thrummed with happiness as their customers bid farewell to another workweek. Everyone was happy. Even Tessa pretended she was happy as she tapped her toe to the electric fiddle and drew another round for table nine.

But she wasn't happy; she was just restless, and resentful. She *should* be happy. Her shoulders were lighter, her heart less full of worry. Jamie and Eric had called a tentative truce, and Jamie had solemnly apologized for sleeping with a thief, or at least a thief's accomplice. It felt like a wound had been lanced, as if pressure had suddenly been released.

But Luke was ruining everything. Luke and his awful absence, and the hole he'd left in her heart, and the way her body wanted him. Tessa stared down into the glass of ale she'd just pulled, trying to decide if the deep brown liquid was darker than Luke's eyes.

"Tessa?" Jamie said. "You okay?"

"Sure," she answered with a smile, then quickly left to serve the table before he could ask more questions. But five minutes later when she made it back to the bar with a tray full of empties, Jamie's eyes stayed on her.

In defense, she stopped to pull out her phone and tweet that there were empty seats at the bar and Jamie would welcome a few more visitors. Unfortunately, a mob didn't rush through the door to save her before he could pounce.

"So what's going on with Luke?" he asked with suspicious lightness.

"Nothing." She gave him a wink. "Just the way you like it."

"Hey. I don't want you to stop seeing him if it makes you mope around all the time."

"I'm not moping around. I'm happy!"

"Yeah, right. So what'd he do to piss you off so much?"

"Oh. Well…" She stacked dirty glasses and hoped he'd get called away.

"Tessa?"

"He called me out on my supposed issues."

"Oh, no. What an asshole."

She grabbed the crate and slid it off the counter. "Date him yourself if you think he's so great."

When she rushed through the doors to the back, Tessa found that she'd jumped from the frying pan into the fire. The fire of acute and startling embarrassment.

"Oh," she yelped, cringing at the sight of Wallace on his knees before Faron, his hands clasped together as if in prayer. "I'm sorry!"

Wallace looked over at her, but Faron didn't even blink. "You don't get along with my husband. I can't possibly keep seeing you."

"Your husband!" Wallace spat on the floor in disgust, making Tessa jump. "He's not worthy of being called a man. Faron, please. I love you."

Faron jerked her hand from his grasp and spun away to stalk out.

Arms aching from the weight of the glasses, Tessa just stood there, frozen, as Faron slid past her.

Finally, she cleared her throat. "Wallace?"

He grumbled as he pushed to his feet, and she was relieved that he was morphing back into his normal, grumpy self. *"Husband,"* he muttered.

Tessa cleared her throat. "Um. You two have met?"

"Met? I used to date him myself, years ago. A blowhard and a liar, and he's not even close to being worthy of Faron. That woman is a goddess!"

Goddess or not, Wallace didn't exactly seem heartbroken.

"Are you sure you're okay?" she asked. It didn't seem as if a man could recover so quickly from going on his knees to beg for a woman's heart.

"I am," he grumbled as he retreated toward his cave and the tanks within.

"Wallace, are you sure?"

He paused and turned halfway back toward her. She watched his face—what she could see of it—for signs of sorrow. But amazingly, he winked and his beard quirked up as if he were smiling. "She'll be back. No way she can resist me."

"Oh. I…see." Tessa watched him disappear into the tank room, then stood there until her arms began to shake. By the time she moved to put the tray down, Wallace was back to his silent monologue to the tanks, perfectly happy in his cave. She hurried out of there as fast as she could…and right back into Jamie's lair.

"You know," Jamie said as if a moment hadn't passed. "I talked to him yesterday."

Tessa groaned and covered her face, sure that she was losing her mind. "Who?"

"You know who. He called about the case."

"Good. Great. I hope you two had a lovely chat."

"He sounded pretty subdued."

Tears sprang to her eyes in an instant. Was he sad? Did he miss her? God, she missed him so much. The hurt was there. Pulling her toward the ground. An awfully melodramatic feeling for such a short relationship.

"Sis. Come on. Tell me what happened."

She shook her head, but the words still pushed out. "You were right. About Luke."

He stiffened and his face flashed to rage. "What the hell did he do?"

"The reason everybody thinks he fathered Simone's baby..."

"That fucking bastard."

She shrugged. "It's not... I don't know. He didn't sleep with her. But apparently they had a thing a couple of years ago. They had a few too many drinks and made out."

Jamie's chin drew in. "Really?"

"Yeah. But he implied that they'd never—"

"They just...*kissed?*"

Tessa slowly registered that her brother's anger had turned to incredulous disbelief. "What? He said they were just friends."

"They kissed one time a couple of years ago and you're pissed about that?"

Now it was Tessa's turn to stiffen. "I don't know if it was one kiss. Maybe there was groping or—"

"Oh, come on. If there was really something going on, there would've been a hell of a lot more than that after two years of seeing each other every day. Jeez, Tessa."

"Hey! You're the one who told me not to be stupid."

"Yeah? Well, then, don't be stupid."

"Screw you!" she gasped, reaching for the beers Jamie had just pulled.

"Hey—" he started, but they were interrupted by a loud squeal.

"Jamie!" a chorus of girls cried from the doorway. "We saw your tweet!"

"Tessa," he said past his welcoming smile. "What did you post this time?"

"Nothing. I just put out the word that there were empty seats at the bar. The enthusiasm is all you, big brother."

"Well, I was going to tell you to get out of here and go see your boyfriend, but now…"

"It's too busy. And he's not my boyfriend." She tried to heft the tray to her shoulder, but Jamie's hand was locked on the opposite edge of the tray.

"You need to go talk to him. And two tables just left. It's not that busy."

"It's slammed." She tugged again, but he tugged back and slid the tray right out of her grasp.

"I want you to be happy, sis. Not just safe and pro-
tected, but happy, too. And maybe he's not so bad. Go
talk to him, all right? Let him apologize for calling you
out on your issues. Because that's what you're really
pissed about, right?"

She looked uncertainly around the crowded barroom and tried to hang on to her anger.

"I can handle twice this many people. Get out."

She wanted to see Luke. She really did. During the
past few days she'd gotten the feeling that holding her
family together was no longer enough to make her
happy. That maybe it was time to learn to trust. And
if even Jamie thought she was being stubborn...

"Well, fine. If it'll make you happy." She pushed
the tray at him, whipped off her apron and started to
race away. Then she raced back to give him a kiss on
the cheek. "Thank you."

But as she got into her car, she still wasn't sure she
was doing the right thing. She'd broken up with him
in a rage of fury and hurt. How the hell was she supposed to approach him now? Should she just knock
on his door and ask if they could talk? Maybe she
should bring flowers. But that might remind him of
the flowers he'd brought her. She'd rather bring him a
gift that reminded him of something good. Something
that would make him smile.

"Bingo," she breathed, finally feeling more hope
than heartache.

SHE WALKED INTO the White Orchid with a big
smile, but that smile faltered when she found herself

confronted with a group of ten or fifteen people gathered in chairs around a podium in the middle of the store. "Um," she managed.

A woman in the last row turned around. "The class hasn't started yet." She patted the wooden folding chair next to her. "You can sit next to me."

"Oh, I'm not here for a class, just, er..." Tessa gestured vaguely to the other side of the store and made her escape.

A class at White Orchid? She was a little afraid to find out what that was about, so Tessa hurried to the back corner of the store and grabbed the item she'd come for. Thankfully, a girl was waiting behind the cash register. "Oooh, how cute! Are you staying for the class?"

"Oh, I don't think... Um, what exactly—?"

"She's starting!" the girl said in a furious whisper, pointing toward the podium.

Tessa handed over her credit card and kept a close eye on the class.

"I'm Beth, the manager of the White Orchid, and I want to thank you all for coming out to our class on the art of fellatio."

Tessa swallowed too hard and had to cough to clear her throat, though she coughed as quietly as any human being had ever coughed. If there was one thing she didn't want at this moment, it was that classroom's eyes on her.

"This is Cairo," Beth went on. "She's going to help with some of the demonstrations.

It was the gorgeous dark-haired woman from

Tessa's last visit. She bounced and waved to the class, but one hand held a green dildo that bobbed wildly when she gestured. The class tittered with nervous exhilaration.

"Let's start with a definition—" Beth continued.

Tessa grabbed her bag and tiptoed toward the door with her purchase, not breathing again until she'd made it outside. She'd tried not to listen in, feeling horribly self-conscious that she was eavesdropping on these people, but the phrase "and this can include the scrotum" followed her out the door.

She only made it four feet into the parking lot before she burst into hysterical laughter. And for the hundredth time that week she thought, *I have to tell Luke about this*. Only this time, she actually could.

CHAPTER TWENTY-EIGHT

LUKE STARED OVER the edge of the crystal tumbler, wondering vaguely if he was drunk yet. He didn't feel drunk. And he'd only downed two fingers of Scotch, but surely he must be drunk. Instead of watching the view of the half-naked blonde writhing in front of him, he kept looking at the glass in his hand.

The crystal had been a wedding present from someone in Eve's family. She'd left him the tumblers when she'd moved out, probably figuring he'd need something to drink hard liquor from every night. He'd put them to good use for a few weeks, but his binge had been cut short by the knife he'd taken to the gut. They didn't allow liquor in the hospital, and even he hadn't been stupid enough to mix it with his painkillers when he'd returned home.

But tonight, he was fully invested in revisiting his previous taste for a good single-malt whiskey.

He hadn't lied to Tessa. Not really. Yes, he'd purposefully left out a crucial bit of information about Simone, but that was only because it didn't matter. How could Tessa not see that? The fact that he felt guilty about it only made him more resentful.

A glance back at the television told him he hadn't

missed much during his daydreaming. The naked girl was still writhing. He still couldn't care less. Clearly, somebody even more pitiful than him had invented soft-core porn.

He wanted to reach for the remote, but the bottle was closer, so he reached for that instead. But as his fingers curled around the cold glass, someone knocked on the door. Luke's eyes slid to the screen. The blonde was finally done with her slightly offscreen gyrations. The movie cut to a kitchen scene that seemed unrelated to the previous story, if it could be called that. The guy's body was suspiciously buff for an average plumber.

"You've got to be kidding me," Luke muttered. Couldn't they come up with any new plotlines for these movies?

Setting the drink down, Luke grabbed the remote to hit the off button. Whoever was at the door, that person deserved a thank-you for the interruption.

But when he opened his door, Luke changed his mind about the thank-you. Instead, he scowled. Then scowled harder at the way his stupid heart leaped at the sight of her.

"Hi," Tessa said, her happy smile dimming a bit at the edges.

He didn't respond, telling himself he was too pissed to say a word to her, but really his throat was stiff and unwilling to let words escape.

"Um. Are you busy?" She craned her neck to look behind him, and Luke was so relieved he'd turned off the TV that he relaxed his guard and let her slip inside.

"You're not saying anything," she said. Her eyes fell on the glass and the bottle next to it.

"What do you want, Tessa?"

"Um, I wanted to talk. And I brought…" She thrust a little white bag in his direction. "It's not flowers, but…"

He took the bag automatically but didn't open it. They stood there staring at each other.

"Actually…" She took the bag back. "This was a stupid idea."

Worried she was about to leave, he snatched the bag back and wrapped his fist tightly into the paper. "What was a stupid idea?"

"I just… I wanted to talk. I don't want you to think I don't take this seriously."

"Tessa, I don't know what the hell you're talking about."

"I'm sorry I got so mad!" she said on a rush. "I'm sorry I pushed you. I was just… I was already upset and then you said that about Simone. I didn't want to listen. But I want to listen now."

"I appreciate that. I do." The thrill of seeing her had faded to only a sharp pain instead of a lightning strike of shock, and now he could feel his anger again. Even though she squirmed, he didn't give her an inch. Maybe he was just done with apologies from exes today.

"I'm really sorry," she repeated. "I said things I shouldn't have said. I was scared. And I was a complete wreck, but that's no excuse."

Shit, she did look sorry. Her green eyes fairly glowed with regret. Pissed as he was, he felt his resolve softening as if he were butter in a hot pan. "I'm sorry, too. About Simone. I should've told you the whole story."

"What is the whole story?"

Luke looked up at the ceiling. He wanted to tell her it was none of her business, but it was. A little. And what the hell did he have to lose? "I was on the rebound. That's all. Feeling a little wounded. We'd been working together a month, and we got along so well. We had a few drinks and I was walking her home, and I thought it would be a great idea. It wasn't. We went to her place, but thank God Simone was sober enough to stop."

"But *you* wanted to? You would've…"

His jaw tightened. "Look, I'm a man. I was drunk. I mistook friendship for something else. But I swear to God, she's been like a sister to me since then." Luke looked up at the ceiling again, resentful of the suspicion in her eyes. "Listen, Tessa…I understand why you were upset that day. I know how important your brothers are to you. But that doesn't change the fact that you don't trust me."

"What?" she croaked, her bright eyes dimming.

"Tessa, come on. You can't trust me. You can't invest in a relationship, and—"

"That's not true! You haven't even given me a chance to explain. I was afraid. I was trying to hold on to every single thing in my life with a death grip, just like you said."

"Of course you were. I don't begrudge you that, but—"

"But I'm working on it. I told Eric everything. More than everything." Her eyes welled with tears. "And I'm trying to figure out how to trust and—"

"Tessa." Christ, he couldn't stand the way her face crumpled when he snapped her name.

"You were right! And I'm sorry, Luke. *Please.*"

A couple of days ago, he would've given anything to have her here. *Anything.* But on the heels of his conversation with his ex, Luke knew it wasn't going to be easy. He couldn't just pull Tessa into his arms and forget everything. "You were right, too. I've got my own problems. But that's the thing, Tessa. Our problems won't fit together easily."

"I don't know what you mean. It's not that I don't trust *you.* Like you said, I can't trust anyone, but I see that now."

He squeezed the bag harder in his hand, crumpling the paper until it tore under his fingers. He tilted his head toward the couch. Tessa edged quickly around it and sat down as if she were permanently laying claim to that spot.

Luke sat with more care, afraid if he moved too quickly, he'd forget not to reach for her. He'd forget that he shouldn't tuck his face against her neck and breathe her in. If he tasted her scent, he'd be lost. Hell, he'd be so lost that he wouldn't even care. So Luke sat on the edge of the couch and clutched the paper bag like a shield.

"I can't pretend that I'm an open book," he said. "But I'm not stupid. I'll fall in love again. I'll have relationships, and those won't be real if I don't open up. But I can't do it with someone like…"

"Someone like *me?*"

"No."

"I don't—"

"My ex-wife," he interrupted. "She's a good person. But we didn't trust each other, not enough to be honest. It was more like a chess match than a marriage. We circled each other like adversaries. But we were so young. I didn't see that."

"I know I haven't been the most honest person in the world, but—"

"It's not that simple. You don't understand…."

"Then make me understand!" she shouted. *"Please."*

He made the mistake of looking at her eyes, liquid with sorrow. She was pulling him in, so he shook his head and looked away. "I was devastated by the divorce. Blindsided. And I hadn't once thought of falling in love again, and how that might happen. But everything about you made me think about it. Made me want it. Still…."

"What?"

"Tessa, I can't spend all my time wondering what you're really thinking. What you're really feeling. What you're keeping from me because you're afraid I won't like it. And shit, I can't do that to you, either. I thought my wife and I had a good, normal marriage. I never realized that she wasn't happy, because she didn't tell me and I didn't pay attention. At all. I lived in my own head, in my job. I loved her. But I didn't know how to be in a relationship. Next time, I'll pay attention, but I can't live with the constant fear that I'll come home one day and find a note...."

He dared a look at Tessa and saw tears running down her face. His heart shook at the sight. "Please don't cry."

"I don't know how to..." Her voice broke on a sob, but she swallowed it back and took a deep breath. "I don't know how to prove to you that I get it, but I do. You were right. I want to control things because... because I never want to be left again. You can't imagine..."

"I know." His hand rose of its own accord, wanting to touch her, offer comfort. He forced it back to the bag, and he squeezed the paper to stop his shaking.

"But I was lying more and more," she said, her voice tight with tears. "And suddenly I'm not really keeping them close at all, am I? It's not really love anymore if they don't know me. How could it be?"

"They love you no matter what."

She nodded. "You're right. So I have to let go of them, and live my own life. Without being terrified. And I want part of that life to be you, Luke. If I promise not to lie to you and you promise not to lie to me... can we just try?"

The ice in his glass shifted, drawing his eye, and he desperately wished he'd downed another shot. Everything inside him wanted to say yes. Yes, of course they could try. Yes, she'd brought him back to life and he couldn't walk away from that.

Christ. He swallowed hard, then swallowed again, trying to clear the lump from his throat. How could he walk away from her? Was he really so weak that he couldn't go after the best thing that had ever happened to him? Everything about her made him happy.

He shook his head, twisting his hands so hard that the bag finally gave way with a weak rip. When he saw what was inside, he couldn't stop his bark of disoriented laughter, but that laughter was thick with pain. "Tessa." He groaned.

When she drew in a breath, it trembled in her throat. He didn't dare look at her, and in the end, that was his downfall. His inattention gave her the chance to sneak up on him. She slid onto his lap and put her arms around his neck, and as soon she touched him, he knew he didn't have a chance.

"I'll take care of your heart, Luke. I swear I will."

He breathed her in, and just as he'd feared, her scent settled inside him, filling up every space in his chest.

"Please believe me. It'll be a relief, being honest. It'll be so much easier than trying to make everything perfect all the time."

He dropped the bag and put his arms around her, and his whole body gave up the fight. It felt good and right with her. It always did.

She wasn't his ex, and he wasn't that man anymore. Tessa made him laugh, she made him happy. He'd never dare to take her for granted.

He closed his eyes and kissed her temple, letting the relief wash over him. She was what he wanted. Pushing her away had felt like the most bitter kind of cure, but maybe it had only been fear, pure and simple. How could he know for sure?

He was gone now. Lost in the weight and warmth of her body curling into him. "Don't cry," he whispered when he felt her breath break against his neck. "Please don't cry."

"I'm sorry," she answered. "I'm sorry I told you to leave. I was scared."

"I know." Boy, did he. He was terrified, right at this moment, but he took that as a sign of what he should do, instead of what he shouldn't. "My wife," he started, and just starting the story hurt. "She got sick. And I thought that was a solution. A way for us to stop arguing and avoiding each other. I thought we'd battle cancer together and we'd get closer and everything would be great. Honestly, I even told myself it would be good for us. How fucked up is that?"

Tessa petted his shoulder and didn't say a word.

"I started coming home early. I insisted on accompanying her to chemo and radiation. I researched wigs and healthy diets and supplements that might help. I thought I was being the perfect husband. And she thought I was more dedicated to the illness than I'd ever been to her."

He heard Tessa swallow hard.

"In my mind, we finally had a great marriage. I was finally a *good* husband. I didn't realize that wasn't what she was feeling at all. She was facing death, and she was realizing that even if she only had a few months to live, she didn't want to spend those months with me."

He felt her sharp gasp. Her fingers curled into his arm, and even though it hurt, he didn't stop her. "She said that?" Tessa whispered.

"Not in those words. But that was what she meant. We were only a few weeks from her final scans. A few weeks from finding out if she was in remission, but the prognosis didn't matter to her. She'd realized that she didn't love me anymore. Said that, at first, she was thankful that I stuck by her side. But as I became more and more invested in her illness, it just showed her that cancer was the only thing keeping us together. We'd been too young and hadn't really known each other when we got married. She wanted something more for herself than a life spent living out a mistake."

"I'm so sorry."

"I was in a daze afterward. Walking around like a zombie. Maybe that was what got me stabbed in the first place. But then… Then I almost died, and I saw what she saw. I saw my life laid out in clear choices, but the thing was, I was alone…. I laid in that bed and I felt my life closing up and all I wanted was her."

He felt the hot seep of Tessa's tears through his shirt, but his eyes were dry as bone.

"So I know how terrifying it is to be left, Tessa. To feel like that alone could kill you just with the pain of it. You don't ever have to hide that from me."

"How could she do that to you?" Tessa cried.

He'd wondered the same thing back then. But now he could see it. "Well, she was right, wasn't she? That was her truth, and she had as much of a right to it as I had to mine. Because we *weren't* happy together.

At some point I would've met someone else or she would've walked out or one of us would've cheated. We weren't happy, so she wanted to move on and be happy, and I wanted her to come back and be happy. But neither of us was wrong."

She lifted her head and kissed him, her lips tasting of tears. "I'm so sorry," she said again.

"I've never told anyone that, because I'd rather people think I left my sick wife than to have them know the truth. That she'd torn me open and left me there without a backward glance."

Nodding, she curved her hand along his jawline. "Thank you for telling me."

"I want to be honest this time."

She gave him a shaky smile. "This time?"

"Yeah. This time. Do you think you can forgive me? About Simone?"

"Everything else you told me was true? You really don't have those kinds of feelings for her?"

"I really don't. Cross my heart."

"And...you're sure you want to try this?"

His laugh was slightly pained. "Yeah. I want to try pretty damn badly. Apparently falling slowly is a scientific impossibility. Falling means that you're not in control, doesn't it? I should've considered that."

Tessa put her knees on either side of his legs and straddled him, reminding Luke that he'd never had any defense against her. "Excuse me," she said before pulling up the hem of her shirt to mop off her wet face. "Sorry," she said, her voice muffled by the fabric.

"No problem," Luke answered, watching the muscles of her stomach shift as she moved. Telling her the truth had lifted a pall from his soul. He felt new and weightless. He felt *good*. And touching her stomach seemed like the best idea in the world. He laid his palm to her naked waist just as she dropped the shirt.

"Oh." She sighed. "I thought we were having a serious talk."

"We were." He slid his hand to her back and snuck his other hand beneath her shirt, as well.

Tessa closed her eyes. Her body stretched, arching into his hands. "You have no idea how good that feels," she whispered.

"I think I've got a pretty good idea." But he didn't take it further. He didn't try to undress her. He just drew her close and held her, feeling the warmth of her skin sink into his hands. "I couldn't stop thinking about you, Tessa. No matter how hard I tried."

She melted into him, her stomach against his. Her mouth sighing against his neck. "I know. I thought I'd never touch you again."

That now seemed like the most ridiculous thing he'd ever heard. That he'd never touch her. That he'd never taste her. How could he have ever summoned the will to imagine that? He was a goddamn fool.

"I need you," she breathed, and Luke thought his heart would give up right then. As a matter of fact, it did. He was in love with her. He knew it right in that moment. Stupid or not, he was gone.

They stayed like that for ten minutes, letting things settle between them. He could've stayed that way forever, he thought, but then Tessa snuggled closer and he had an even better idea.

"Come on," he said. "Come to bed with me."

"The bed, huh? This must mean something special." She got up and stretched, then grinned down at him. "You know what's even more special?"

He raised his eyebrows in question and Tessa reached for the floor to pick up the gift he'd dropped. Luke groaned.

"Fancy lingerie!" she cried.

"Those are Batman underwear."

"I know, but it's not just the logo. There's a Batman utility belt and everything. And…" She leaned forward to whisper. "They're supertight boxer briefs. Rawr."

"No."

She ignored him and stepped over the barrier of his knees.

"I'm not putting those on!" he called out as she sauntered toward the bedroom.

"Yes, you are."

"No, I'm not." But fuck it. He totally knew he was. Because it would make her laugh, and nothing made him happier than Tessa laughing. Except Tessa screaming his name, and that would follow soon enough, ridiculous underwear or not.

He'd tell her he loved her later. It was too soon. Too new. For now, he'd just have to show her. With Batman underwear. And anything else she ever wanted.

CHAPTER TWENTY-NINE

Two months later

THE FAMILIAR SOUND of a clip being ejected from a handgun woke Tessa from a deep sleep. She cracked one eye open, got smacked in the face by a ridiculous amount of sunlight and quickly closed her eye again.

The window was open. She could hear a melody of birdsong from the backyard, and a breeze had cooled the room to a pleasant chill. But her bed was sooo cozy....

The floor creaked near her door and Tessa opened both eyes wide to see Luke sneaking by. "Where do you think you're going?"

"Hey, you. I'm sorry I woke you."

"What time is it?"

"Almost ten."

"You've been gone five hours?" His phone had rung in the early-morning darkness, but Tessa had been back asleep before he'd even left the bed. She snuggled farther into her pillow. "Is it a big murder case?"

"Actually...it might be. We'll have to see what the medical examiner says."

"Poor you. Come here."

Luke smiled. "No, I've got to shower and change. I grabbed a few things from my place."

"You should move your stuff over here," she mumbled. He didn't answer, so she forced her eyes back open again to find him shifting uncomfortably. "What?"

"How much stuff?" he asked.

Oh. She probably shouldn't have said that, not without thinking it through. But strangely, it didn't even scare her. "Come here," she repeated.

He sat on the edge of the bed, eyes narrowed to study her face. Tessa closed her eyes and rolled to her side, letting the blanket fall open just a little. She felt so warm. Her skin hot and naked and beautiful. When the cold air touched her, her nipples drew painfully tight. She looked at Luke again, and he was no longer studying her face. His hand disappeared beneath the sheets and curved around her hip.

"Mmm," she purred, feeling how the warmth of his hand disappeared into the searing heat of her sleepy skin.

"I've got to shower," he murmured, but his hand slid up her waist and over her ribs. "Your brothers will be here in an hour." He cupped her breast and she turned to her back and arched into him.

"Tessa…"

This *could* be her real life if she wanted. This kind of heat. This connection. Up until now, her relationships had all been happy threads, trailing through a life she kept separate. But this kind of connection was an anchor. It was strength. "I love you," she whispered, reaching up to pull him down to her.

"I love you, too." His hand kept exploring her body as he leaned down to kiss her. She never got tired of hearing it. She wanted to hear it every morning. Every night.

"As much as you want," she said.

"Hmm?" His hand touched lower, smoothing down the hair of her sex, cupping her heat.

"As much stuff as you want. I don't like the way you have to leave here in the mornings."

His fingers slid down, and Tessa parted her knees so he could feel how wet she was. She could tell by his sigh that he loved it.

"You want me here?" he asked.

She didn't know if he meant in her house or inside her body, but the answer was yes, either way.

Luke tugged her around until her feet hung off the bed and her sex was open to him. He unfastened his pants and Tessa watched past her lashes as his thick cock sprang free. She bit her lip and wrapped her legs around his hips.

When he reached for the bedside table, he pulled the drawer too hard and everything crashed out. "Shit," he muttered, reaching blindly down to grab a pack of condoms. But his eyes stayed on her. Always on her.

Finally, he was pushing inside her, sliding deep and true.

Tessa couldn't hold back a loud cry as she arched into him. She needed him so much that she felt empty with it. He filled her up, over and over. His eyes watched her hand slide down her belly.

She cried his name as she touched her own body, rubbing pressure into her clit. Pressure that built with ever slide of his shaft. Pressure that felt so good it made her sob.

"Tessa," he breathed. "Tessa…"

Her body broke open within seconds, too full of pleasure to contain it. Luke followed right after, thrusting brutally into her as her hips spasmed against him.

He collapsed, laying his face tight to her shoulder, breathing ice across her breast. She curled her hand into his hair and kissed his temple. "Stay with me," she said, not a breath of hesitation in her voice. "Stay with me, because I'm not afraid anymore."

When she felt him nod, she grinned at the ceiling. This wasn't so hard. Not with Luke. "Are you any good with your hands, Detective?"

He lifted up to frown at her. "Pardon me?"

"If you're going to move in, I thought maybe we could refinish the floors. Fix a few things. Move some stuff out…"

"Sure. Anything you want. But what about your brothers?"

"I'll talk to them. But not today."

"Thank God," Luke muttered.

Today was their first Sunday together as one big happy family. Or one big wary family of men who didn't trust one another. They were easing into it with a Sunday lunch instead of dinner, because there was a baseball game at one that everyone wanted to watch.

"Speaking of which…" he said with a sigh. "I really don't want to get caught in the shower again, so if you'll excuse me…"

"So polite," she murmured, curling back under the covers as he left her. "My brothers would really like that."

He choked in horror before the bathroom door closed behind him.

Tessa needed to hit the shower herself. The chicken she was serving for lunch was marinating and ready to be put in the oven, but she still needed to throw together a salad, not that the men would care. All they cared about was meat, and she was already anticipating the complaints about the chicken not being cooked over an open fire, but she wasn't an idiot. No way was she going to let three big men argue over who was grilling what and which one didn't know his ass from a barbecue fork.

The next time she opened her eyes it was because Luke's hand connected with her ass with a smack. "Get up. It's ten-thirty."

"Fine," she groaned, lurching from the bed. Luke was already dressed in jeans and a T-shirt.

"Is my hair dry enough?" he asked. "I was trying to hurry, but I don't want them thinking I showered over here."

"You look fine. Better clean up the condom wrappers, though."

"Shit!" He jumped toward the bed as she wandered to the shower, smiling at his nervousness.

"I thought you didn't want me lying anymore," she drawled.

"These aren't lies. These are helpful illusions. For your brothers' sake."

"Right."

He'd calmed down a little by eleven-thirty when Jamie knocked, but Luke still watched with wary eyes as she went to answer the door. At least her brothers had finally learned their lesson about coming in uninvited.

"I brought the beer," Jamie said, not looking the least bit happy.

"It's not even noon."

"Oh, we're going to need it." Despite that he'd pressed her to make up with Luke, Jamie still refused to budge on his opinion that a divorced cop he'd once partied with could possibly be good enough for Tessa.

"Come on. It'll be fun."

Jamie flashed a patently fake smile and twirled a finger over his head. "Sure. Good times."

Eric was only slightly more accommodating when he arrived, but all the men seemed to relax when Tessa piled their plates high with chicken. Or maybe the beer was kicking in. Either way, the men couldn't maintain their tension in the face of meat, beer and baseball talk. Despite her triumph, Tessa felt her eyes glazing over.

"Hey," she interrupted. "Did everybody get the

new pictures of Simone and the baby? I emailed them yesterday."

"Uh, sure," Eric said.

Jamie squirmed. "Cute kid."

"She's adorable!"

"Tessa," Eric said carefully. "They kind of all look the same at that age."

"Yeah," Jamie agreed. "Squishy."

"Anna doesn't look squishy! She's beautiful, isn't she, Luke?"

Luke nodded, but his eyes slid away.

"Oh, you're all ridiculous," she huffed, throwing down her napkin. "Just for that, you guys get to clean up."

"Aw, come on," Luke said. "You know I think she's beautiful."

"You won't even hold her!"

"She's too small!" he shouted.

Tessa rolled her eyes and stomped off to the family room to turn on the game. But over the sound of the endless pregame chatter, she heard Luke and her brothers talking. Ten minutes later, when laughter broke out in the kitchen, she couldn't help sneaking back in to a steal a peek.

Eric and Luke were washing dishes, and Luke was laughing so hard about something that he had to wipe tears from his eyes with the dish towel. Though Tessa suspected they were talking about her, she still smiled.

But when she caught movement out of the corner of her eye, her smile faded. Jamie was in the backyard, sitting on a bench near the fence. The bench faced the small stone they'd put there thirteen years before. Their parents' names were carved into the stone.

He must have heard her as she walked down the path toward him, but he didn't look up.

"Hey, Jamie. Are you avoiding the dishes?"

"Nah. Just thinking."

She bumped her hip against his shoulder. "About what?"

"Nothing you want to talk about on a Sunday." She'd made a rule long before that they couldn't talk about the brewery on Sundays, but she didn't like the tension in his shoulders.

"Come on," she urged. "Spill it."

"Eric pissed me off, that's all. He thinks I'm irresponsible. Nothing new."

"So why are you out here?"

"Because I can't do this anymore. Things are going to have to change. I can't keep going like this."

"You have to give him time, Jamie. After your little slipup with Monica—"

"It wasn't a slipup," he snapped.

"Fine. Call it whatever you want. The point is, you screwed up."

His laugh was so bitter that it sent a bolt of alarm through Tessa's chest.

"Give it time," she insisted. "You can't just—"

"Don't worry. I'll figure it out. It's been like this for years. I can deal for a few more months. What do you say we go inside and make your boyfriend uncomfortable."

She wanted to press him. Ask him what he meant about plans and changes. But it was Sunday, after all. So when he stood, she dropped the subject and gave him a little sisterly shove. "Leave Luke alone."

"In your dreams."

As they wound their way through the overgrown garden, Tessa hooked her arm through his. "His nickname isn't Babe Magnet, you know."

"I heard it with my own two ears."

"Nope. You got it wrong. In L.A. they called him Bullet Magnet after he was shot."

He arched an eyebrow. "Is that supposed to make me feel better?"

"He's a good guy, Jamie. I love him."

That chased all the amusement from Jamie's face. In fact, he paled a little. "I'll kill him if he hurts you."

Tessa decided not to broach the subject of Luke moving in. Instead, she just murmured, "I know," and gave him another affectionate shove.

Luke was waiting for her when she came through the patio door. The national anthem floated in from the family room. Jamie left them alone with only a quick glare at Luke. As soon as he disappeared around the corner, Tessa took the opportunity to snuggle into Luke's arms and steal a kiss. "This is nice," she whispered.

"Yeah, it is."

"I meant *this*. You here with my brothers."

"Eric's being nice," he said. "But I admit, I didn't expect Jamie to be pissed for quite so long."

"Well, I won't ask for any details, but I suspect he

might have seen a little too much of your dating life in college."

"Uh. Yeah, don't ask for any details."

She kissed him again before drawing away. "Fair enough. Lucky for me, he didn't see any of my dating life. You'll never learn a thing."

"I've been assured you were untouched and innocent before I came along. What more do I need to know?"

"Nothing. Just don't open any of the closets when you move in. There could be a skeleton avalanche."

He pulled her close again. "You sure you really want me here?"

Tessa closed her eyes and put her cheek to his chest. She listened to his heartbeat. She listened to the sound of her brothers in the next room cheering over the first play.

This was her life now. And all she'd had to give up was fear and a few years of sorrow. And in return, she got Luke Asher and everything he meant to her. Instead of breaking up, her family was getting bigger.

"I'm sure," she whispered, hoping his shirt absorbed her tears. "For once, I'm really sure."

* * * * *

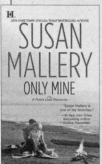
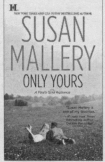
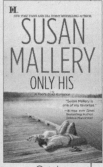

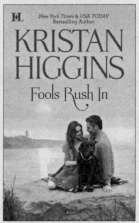

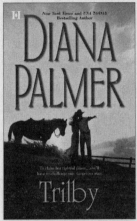

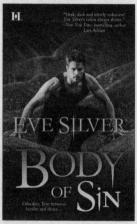

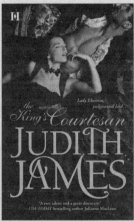

REQUEST YOUR
FREE BOOKS!

2 FREE NOVELS
FROM THE ROMANCE COLLECTION
PLUS 2 FREE GIFTS!

YES! Please send me 2 FREE novels from the Romance Collection and my 2 FREE gifts (gifts are worth about $10). After receiving them, if I don't wish to receive any more books, I can return the shipping statement marked "cancel." If I don't cancel, I will receive 4 brand-new novels every month and be billed just $5.99 per book in the U.S. or $6.49 per book in Canada. That's a saving of at least 25% off the cover price. It's quite a bargain! Shipping and handling is just 50¢ per book in the U.S. and 75¢ per book in Canada.* I understand that accepting the 2 free books and gifts places me under no obligation to buy anything. I can always return a shipment and cancel at any time. Even if I never buy another book, the two free books and gifts are mine to keep forever.

194/394 MDN FELQ

Name   (PLEASE PRINT)

Address   Apt. #

City   State/Prov.   Zip/Postal Code

Signature (if under 18, a parent or guardian must sign)

Mail to the **Reader Service**:
IN U.S.A.: P.O. Box 1867, Buffalo, NY 14240-1867
IN CANADA: P.O. Box 609, Fort Erie, Ontario L2A 5X3

Not valid for current subscribers to the Romance Collection
or the Romance/Suspense Collection.

Want to try two free books from another line?
Call 1-800-873-8635 or visit www.ReaderService.com.

* Terms and prices subject to change without notice. Prices do not include applicable taxes. Sales tax applicable in N.Y. Canadian residents will be charged applicable taxes. Offer not valid in Quebec. This offer is limited to one order per household. All orders subject to credit approval. Credit or debit balances in a customer's account(s) may be offset by any other outstanding balance owed by or to the customer. Please allow 4 to 6 weeks for delivery. Offer available while quantities last.

Your Privacy—The Reader Service is committed to protecting your privacy. Our Privacy Policy is available online at www.ReaderService.com or upon request from the Reader Service.

We make a portion of our mailing list available to reputable third parties that offer products we believe may interest you. If you prefer that we not exchange your name with third parties, or if you wish to clarify or modify your communication preferences, please visit us at www.ReaderService.com/consumerchoice or write to us at Reader Service Preference Service, P.O. Box 9062, Buffalo, NY 14269. Include your complete name and address.

VICTORIA DAHL

77462	CRAZY FOR LOVE	___ $7.99 U.S.	___ $9.99 CAN.
77434	LEAD ME ON	___ $7.99 U.S.	___ $9.99 CAN.
77390	START ME UP	___ $7.99 U.S.	___ $8.99 CAN.
77356	TALK ME DOWN	___ $6.99 U.S.	___ $6.99 CAN.

(limited quantities available)

TOTAL AMOUNT	$ _____
POSTAGE & HANDLING	$ _____
($1.00 FOR 1 BOOK, 50¢ for each additional)	
APPLICABLE TAXES*	$ _____
TOTAL PAYABLE	$ _____

(check or money order—please do not send cash)

To order, complete this form and send it, along with a check or money order for the total above, payable to HQN Books, to: **In the U.S.:** 3010 Walden Avenue, P.O. Box 9077, Buffalo, NY 14269-9077; **In Canada:** P.O. Box 636, Fort Erie, Ontario, L2A 5X3.

Name: _____
Address: _____ City: _____
State/Prov.: _____ Zip/Postal Code: _____
Account Number (if applicable): _____

075 CSAS

*New York residents remit applicable sales taxes.
*Canadian residents remit applicable GST and provincial taxes.

HQN™   HARLEQUIN®
www.Harlequin.com

PHVD0911BL